Catch

and

Keep

Also by Erin Hahn

ADULT NOVELS

Built to Last

Friends Don't Fall in Love

YOUNG ADULT NOVELS

You'd Be Mine

More Than Maybe

Never Saw You Coming

Even If It Breaks Your Heart

Catch
and
Keep

A NOVEL

Erin Hahn

ST. MARTIN'S GRIFFIN
NEW YORK

First published in the United States by St. Martin's Griffin, an imprint of St. Martin's Publishing Group

CATCH AND KEEP. Copyright © 2024 by Erin Hahn. All rights reserved. Printed in the United States of America. For information, address St. Martin's Publishing Group, 120 Broadway, New York, NY 10271.

www.stmartins.com

Design by Meryl Sussman Levavi

The Library of Congress Cataloging-in-Publication Data is available upon request.

ISBN 978-1-250-82713-5 (trade paperback)
ISBN 978-1-250-82714-2 (ebook)

Our books may be purchased in bulk for promotional, educational, or business use. Please contact your local bookseller or the Macmillan Corporate and Premium Sales Department at 1-800-221-7945, extension 5442, or by email at MacmillanSpecialMarkets@macmillan.com.

First Edition: 2024

10 9 8 7 6 5 4 3 2 1

This one's for all the lake girls. The ones with weeds in their hair. The ones with leeches on their toes. The ones with sunburns from where their goggles rubbed the lotion off while they were pencil diving off the end of a rickety dock. The ones who jumped off rope swings and sang karaoke in waterfront bars with their whole family watching. The ones who drove boats before cars, got up early to fish for dinner, and still catch lightning bugs. The ones who shared first kisses behind the fish house, can spot a bald eagle's nest, and fall asleep to frog songs.

I hope you find a piece of yourself in this book.

Also, this one's for Mike Hahn. Sorry I lied and told you I liked fishing, but in my defense, I caught you, so . . .

Muskellunge, also known as musky or muskie, are considered a cool-water species and known as the "fish of ten thousand casts" as they are very wary and elusive to recreational anglers. They are considered excellent-tasting fish with a flaky white flesh. Muskellunge can reach burst speeds of thirty miles per hour and can live as long as thirty years in their natural environment.

These fish possess a large snout full of canine-type teeth and needle-type teeth and are a sight feeder hunting mostly during daylight. Muskellunge are a stealthy ambush predator hunting near submerged weeds and logs.

—Muskellunge Report Overview,
U.S. Fish and Wildlife Service

Catch
and
Keep

Girls Just Want to Have Fun

Summer 2004

"Happy birthday, sunshine! Give it to me straight. Is thirteen freaking magical? You're totally a teenager now."

I sink back against the far wall of the boathouse, my sun-freckled legs sprawled carelessly in front of me, and groan into my flip phone. "Shelb. *God.* Today was a complete disaster. Thirteen sucks butt. Stay twelve forever."

"What?" my best friend's voice chirps through the speaker. "No way! What happened? What about Operation Get Aiden to French Me?" I can practically feel Shelby's indignation all the way from the set of the kids' show she works on in La La Land LA.

"It was a complete bust. He has a girlfriend back home he just happened to forget to mention the last two weeks he's been flirting with me on vacation."

"Yeesh. What a capital-L loser."

"Yeah, I guess."

"Well, it's still early, right?" Shelby starts murmuring and I can tell she's subtracting the time difference between LA and Wisconsin. Math has never been her strong suit. Singing, acting, looking gorgeous, and crying on cue maybe, but not numbers. "Find another cute boy to be your first kiss."

"Right. You make it sound so easy. Not all of us are surrounded by cute showbiz boys all day, every day, you know."

"True, but they're like my brothers. My very annoying brothers, even."

"I don't know, Cameron got pretty cute last season—"

"Anyway!" she cuts me off and I smirk to myself. "I think my mom is calling me back to the set. I better go."

"Yeah, yeah, okay. Thanks for calling, Shelb."

"Happy birthday, babe! I'll talk to you soon!"

I end the call and tuck my phone into my pocket. Well, technically, it's not even mine. It's on loan. I asked for my own cell phone for my birthday and my mom laughed in my face. Oh-for-two on the birthday wishes, now that I think about it.

The woods beyond the boat livery lean-to are calm, the giant pines casting deep shadows in the late-afternoon sun. There's an occasional pop from tree limbs as squirrels chase each other up and down the branches, along with the muffled rustle of birds lifting to take flight. For a minute I consider hiding here, behind the stacked canoes, for the rest of the night. I've been looking forward to my thirteenth birthday for months and now I just want it to be over. I'm ready for tomorrow. It will be a regular old Sunday and the rest of my family and especially that jerkface Aiden and his family will be on their way south and out of my hair. But just as I'm wondering if anyone will care if I curl up to sleep in one of the old wooden canoes, the familiar rumble of Fost's fifteen-horsepower outboard motor hits my ears.

Perhaps all isn't lost.

I crawl out from my place and jog down the shoreline toward the docks, dodging nets and dangling stringers full of today's catch.

"FOST!" I yell, still three docks away from where he's puttering with his boat lights.

"*Fost!* Wait for me!"

I make it in time to hear Fost's fond chuckle skitter over the sound of his motor. "There's the birthday girl. Where'd you get to?"

"Had a phone call. Got room for me?" I'm not trying to hide my pleading look, but it's not necessary. Fost never turns me away.

He shoos me off with a liver-spotted hand. "You'll need to chase down a jacket. I'll wait."

I reverse motion and skip back toward the cute red-and-white double-wide trailer my parents have rented at Cole's Landing Resort for more years than I've been alive. They're sitting in the screened-in porch with the neighbors. *Cocktail hour*, they call it. By the softness in my mother's face, I'd guess she's two amaretto stone sours in. *Perfect*.

The screen door slams shut behind me and I reach for my life jacket hanging on a hook just inside. "Gonna go out fishing—"

"—with Mr. Foster," my dad finishes for me. "We heard you, princess."

"The entire resort heard you," my older brother teases from his place on the floor picking through his tackle box. Liam is eighteen and thinks he knows everything. He used to go out with Fost on his boat. All my brothers did, but then they grew up and started caring more about meeting girls at the lodge instead of chasing musky. Their loss, I say. As much as I wanted to kiss Dumb Aiden on my birthday, no smelly boy who can't even grow armpit hair will ever replace fishing.

"Not too late, Maren," my mother reminds me. "We still have your cake and presents and we've got an early start tomorrow."

Tomorrow my mom and dad are leaving with two of my older brothers, Brett and Kyle, because they have to return to work, but Liam is staying and so am I. He has a job as a dock-boy-slash-bartender with his best friend, Josiah, whose parents own the whole dang resort. I convinced them all to let me stay with Liam so I can fish. I'm so close to my first giant musky, I can taste it.

"Okay, Mom," I agree, careful to keep the exasperation out of my tone. My parents have been on me about my snark all summer and I don't want to risk them making me leave with them tomorrow. "I gotta run. Burning daylight."

I dash out the screen door without another glance and sprint for the water, gear in tow.

"Where's the fire, Jig?" Josiah Cole yells after me.

Normally I'd stick around to answer as it has recently come to my attention that Joe is pretty cute and it annoys the heck out of Liam when I talk to him. Not to mention, the nickname *Jig* is kind of insulting because jigs are small and no one catches a big musky on a jig. Spinnerbait, bucktail, jerkbait . . . but no. He calls me *Jig*. Always has. Tonight, though, I'm too busy to argue, even if he does have big muscles and the bluest eyes I've ever seen in my life.

I nearly skid right over the edge of the dock before righting myself and passing my pole and tackle to Fost. Mom says Mr. Foster was old when she was a kid, which makes him nearly ancient now. He has a tuft of pure-white hair that he covers in a faded blue Cubs hat and gnarled joints in his hands that somehow don't keep him from tying on lures. Though he lets me use my tiny fingers when we're in a hurry.

"All right there, birthday girl?"

"Tonight's the night, Fost. I can feel it." Maybe two of my birthday wishes were a bust, but there're still a few hours of light left and I'm feeling lucky.

After all, the fish are waiting.

ONE

This Woman's Work

Maren

Twenty years later

HALLMARK IS A LYING BITCH.

According to all those Hallmark movies, the best friend always has a simple, perfect life. Doting husband she met in college, two-point-five kids, white picket fence, thriving career that she rushes off to after hanging up the phone with her chaotic main character bestie, slugging back some fresh-squeezed orange juice without spilling a drop on her pressed white linen pantsuit before kissing the cheeks of her family . . .

And a dog, I guess. At least I got that part right. I do have a dog. And I also have two chaotic main character besties, though both have found the loves of their lives on top of their thriving careers in television and in Nashville, respectively. They're downright domestic these days.

So Hallmark got it wrong, clearly, because nowhere in their many, many iterations of romance does the put-together best friend unravel in the midst of a very public proposal from her boyfriend of a year after he steals her work promotion out from under her. Nowhere in those movies does the best friend have a humiliating panic attack, where she vomits spectacularly all over her (presumably ex-) boyfriend's bended knee in the middle of a state park in front of both of their families, sprint away three miles down back-country trails, sneak into her car (therefore leaving the presumably ex-boyfriend stranded), speed home, pack her embarrassingly meager belongings and her confused dog, and drive all day and into the night to a shack in the Northwoods her late fishing partner left her in his will.

Thanks, Hallmark.

It's twilight, but the Northwoods are extra dense this time of year, so I dig around for my eyeglasses and slip them on to better spot deer. I adjust uncomfortably on the bench seat of my old beat-up Bronco and crack my neck side to side, grimacing at the loud pops. I've been driving for seven long hours. My butt is half asleep, my brain is fuzzy, and Rogers, my two-year-old wirehaired pointer, is carsick.

"That's what you get for sitting sideways," I say to him, unsympathetic. "I've tried to tell you, but no. You insist on staring out the window mile after mile." I've already stopped three times to allow him to yack up his breakfast, and the last time there wasn't anything to puke.

"You and me, kid," I mutter with a rub behind his soft ears. "A couple of pukers today. Not our finest moments, honestly."

My phone vibrates with another notification. At the first rest stop I had texted my best friends Shelby and Lorelai something along the lines of **SHANE PROPOSED. I VOMITED. PEACED OUT TO WISCONSIN. TALK TO YOU SOON.** So it's probably one of them following up. Or maybe it's my mom. She was at the ill-fated proposal, along with the rest of my family, including my three older brothers and their families. I doubt she'd be surprised by my running to Wisconsin, though. Everyone knows this is my place. I suppose it could be Shane. Though I would think after twelve months of "falling in love" with me, he would know me well enough to realize how I would react to a surprise public proposal. That said, he didn't know me well enough to figure out how pissed off and hurt I'd be when he applied for my promotion and got it, after a decade of my working my way up the ladder . . .

So I guess it could be *him*, Mr. Doesn't Read the Relationship.

Regardless, I don't check.

"I know this all seems very rash and unlike me," I say to my dog, who gives a whiny sigh in response. "Patient, people-pleasing Maren. Happy if you're happy and all that. But that's just like my work persona, you know? Shane should have seen underneath it all and understood that the real me, the everyday me, is more complex."

I turn onto another tree-lined road, familiar in a way that makes my heart catch a little in my chest. Almost there. Almost home. "And heck if I know *why* he thought after our conversation two nights ago, when I was clearly upset and told him I needed some space and wanted to take a break, he would move forward with a public proposal.

"Actually . . ." I say, jabbing at the air-conditioning and turning it off. We're close enough that I want the fresh air. I want to inhale the sharp bite of pine and rich soil into my lungs and clear my head. "Actually, I do know why he chose to do it publicly. He thought he could manipulate me into saying yes. He knew I wasn't feeling it after the job thing, and he heard me ask for space and thought the way to get what he wanted was to put me on the spot in front of all those people. He thought I wouldn't be able to say no, and guess what?!"

Rogers opens one eye and his tail thumps against the bench.

"Yeah. I said no. The look on his face . . ." I trail off, the smile dying on my lips and my breath hitching. The look on his face was shocked, and that hurt more than anything else. He was shocked that I dared to turn him down.

And I almost didn't. Again. The number of times I let him manipulate me into agreeing to things I didn't actually want to do . . . Going on the all-inclusive luxury cruise to Jamaica that was zero percent my style, wearing those deathtrap high heels out to elegant restaurants with tiny offerings I couldn't pronounce, reading thick political biographies because it made me look smarter, eating keto during the holidays so I didn't gain weight, doing Dry July when all I wanted was a beer and to spend a weekend fishing off the shore . . .

The thing about Shane is that the gaslighting snuck up on me under the guise of "improvements" that I didn't ask for. Instead of learning who I was, he focused on making me who he wanted me to be, and I went along with it.

I roll down the windows. I don't feel like talking or thinking anymore. Instead, I crank up the old radio and let the music lead me home.

♩♩♩

Two days later, I'm not exactly regretting my decision to drop everything and run away to my shack in the Northwoods, but I'm not *not* regretting it, either. My choice may have been a skosh rash. But I've spent the last forty-eight hours deep cleaning decades of grime and rodent feces from the tiny, questionably livable apartment behind the bait shop I've inherited and to give up now would be a waste. I haven't even gotten out on the flowage yet to fish. Heck, I haven't even left this place except to run to town for coffee and a few grocery staples, followed by McDonald's when I realized there wasn't a clean surface to prepare food on the first night.

But there is an outlet to charge my cell phone, though service is negligible, and an old boombox radio, and lots and lots of opportunities to second-guess every decision I've made since I graduated high school. So I have that going for me.

I've managed to clear out the clutter and trash and wipe down and disinfect every surface in the last two days, as well as scare off three mice and adopt the fourth on the sun porch after Rogers and I both failed to intimidate it into leaving. I've named it Lady Gaga because, like its namesake, bitch is fearless. The fridge is stocked and the stove seems safe enough, though ancient. Fost wasn't a messy guy, per se, but he was definitely a hermit. His wife died of cancer before I knew him and they were never able to have children of their own. His life was his bait shop, his old aluminum Lund fishing boat, and the flowage. *And me*, I think with a pang of grief. Regardless, he didn't much care about keeping a tidy house. The shop was marginally better, but two years of dust and total neglect took a toll.

Still, I might be able to make something of it all. I've nearly convinced myself to make my leave of absence with the Michigan Forestry service permanent and spend the next few months here, turning this into something Fost and I could both be proud of. I'm not completely ignorant of home repair, after all. I grew up with three older brothers who all went into various trades and one of my best friends stars in a reality TV home-renovation program. Not only that, I spent a summer fixing up my cute little rental back in Michigan with my landlord's permission and a hefty discount. I might not be ready for anything that requires a building permit, but I do all right with surface-level fixes. The structure at Fost's place is sound. I just need to make it look viable again, and then, maybe in the spring, I'll sell it and move on. Real estate goes for a premium up here. Vacation homes and resorts pepper every shoreline. It would be a solid investment of my leftover YouTube nest egg from back in my college Musky Maren fishing channel days.

It would also be a nice long break from Michigan and Shane and my family and the mess I left behind. I called Shane back from town the first night and made the break official (in case regurgitating my lunch all over his Merrells wasn't clear enough). Since we didn't actually live together (I couldn't leave Rogers, and Shane thought my place was too small for our combined belongings), and we weren't engaged and therefore had no wedding plans to dismantle, it really was as easy as walking away. The year we spent together, making love, playing at love, planning for our future, was just that: a year. And now it was over.

I'm not as sad as I think I should be. My mom, whom I called after Shane, believes I'm in denial. She figures I'll have a delayed reaction, and then the regrets will come. Maybe. Or maybe Lorelai was right when she said, "I don't know, babe. Maybe you weren't as into it as you wanted to be."

When I stop being indignant at the man's goddang nerve of a public proposal, perhaps I'll be able to see through to the depth of my feelings.

Regardless of who's right, I am digging into this project with gusto. What happens next is future Maren's problem.

Rogers whines at the door to be let out, but from the barely suppressed energy vibrating off him, he needs something more than the paltry bathroom walks I've allowed him so far. Pointers are fantastic working dogs. They love hunting, swimming, running, and have all the endurance in the world. I could strap his leash to my bike and ride fifteen miles with Rogers alongside of me and he wouldn't so much as pant.

But after two restless nights followed by two long days of manual labor, I'm not feeling much like a bike ride. Instead, I grab Rogers's inflatable dummy and a Gatorade and head out back toward the water.

Fost's cabin/bait shop sits on a grassy-turned-sandy point that juts out into Bryant Lake roughly thirty meters or so. It's not a vast property, but the location cannot be beat. It's private and cozy while still offering a view that stretches for miles in every direction. Boats will pass through on occasion, but there's a wider passage on the other side of the island that most prefer. It's dinnertime, though, and September. Families are back to work and school and the evening fishermen won't be venturing out for another hour or two.

Which is all to say I feel comfortable standing at the end of Fost's rickety wooden dock and tossing the dummy out over the depths for Rogers.

Again and again, I throw and Rogers retrieves, paddling back and dropping the sopping-wet toy at my feet before I throw it again and he jumps right off the dock after it. At least the water tires him out more quickly than the land. The resistance seems to slow him down the tiniest bit and eventually he flops down at my feet, tongue lolling and chest rising and falling happily.

I take my cue from him and sit down, removing my shoes

and socks and dangling my toes in the water. It's not cold yet, but it's not exactly warm, either. After a sharp inhale, I begin to relax, and the cool water feels good on my tired, aching feet. I sit back on my hands and stare out over the lake. The water is smooth as glass, reflecting the early evening sun. Above us, puffy cotton-candy clouds break up the blue and a couple of loons coo back and forth. I let my eyelids fall closed and take in several deep breaths, pulling the clean pine-scented air into my lungs and imagining it filtering into my bloodstream and clearing all the recent bullshit out of my system. A shriek echoes in the silence, but it doesn't sound scared, so I don't even open my eyes at first. It's more like a laugh. I feel Rogers perk up next to me, but he doesn't move, so I figure I'm right about the laughing.

It's confirmed a minute later when I hear a man's growl followed by even more childish shrieking. Peeling my eyelids open and squinting at the disorienting brightness, I search the shoreline and locate the source. A tall and very attractive blond man, built big, is chasing after two smaller blond kids. One, possibly a boy, looks to be about eight or nine, if my many nieces and nephews are anything to go by, and the other is younger. Maybe four or five? The man's long, tanned arms are raised like he's some kind of bear or monster and the old-est slips behind a tree, cackling, hurriedly beginning to climb the low-lying limbs. The younger one tucks herself behind her brother, less sure. He reaches behind himself and tugs her along with him on a small limb reaching out almost horizon-tally toward the shoreline.

"Maren?" I hear my name called from somewhere behind me and it shakes me out of my nosy musing. I recognize the deep, booming voice of my oldest brother, Liam, though it takes me a beat to realize he's actually *here*, and not in Michigan where he lives with his wife, Jessica, and their two kids. I scramble to my feet just as Rogers takes off like a rocket in the direction of his call.

"Liam?"

TWO

All I Really Want

Maren

I BLINK AT THE IMAGE OF MY BROTHER STANDING IN FRONT OF ME, duffel bag in hand and shit-eating grin on his lips. Liam is still tall, though he's gone softer over the years since he spends more time behind a desk than out in the field. He used to work as a line technician but these days he's a district manager for an electric company.

His hair is still a darker shade of mine, though every time I see him, it's slightly more speckled with silver at the temples, and despite being hidden behind expensive sunglasses.

"Hey, kid," he says, dropping his bag to the ground with a thud.

I frown at his calling me a kid. Though, I suppose to him, what else could I possibly be? "What are you doing here?"

"Thought I'd better check in on you after the barf-posal heard 'round the world."

I stifle my groan at his corny teasing. "Tell me the truth—you thought of that at home and spent the entire drive laughing to yourself in anticipation of the delivery."

"Nah. I didn't come up with it until I hit the bridge."

I wrap my arms around his waist, and he hugs me back, tightly, squeezing the air from my chest. "This is from Mom and Dad, too," he murmurs to the top of my head, releasing me before squeezing again, "and this is from Jess and the kids."

"Please tell me that means they aren't all coming."

"Relax." He steps back and takes off his sunglasses, eyes twinkling in amusement. "I convinced them to stay back. It's just me. You're welcome."

I roll my eyes at his presumed sacrifice. "Yeah, and I'm sure the impromptu trip up north without your lovably loud family had nothing to do with your decision."

He shrugs affably and the movement is so familiar, I feel a pang in my chest. Despite our age difference, Liam and I have always been close. It must have something to do with being the oldest and youngest sibling. We didn't have to compete with each other growing up. "Wait till you have teenagers someday. You'll understand then."

I take his arm, leading him back up the small hill toward Fost's place while Rogers bounds excitedly around our heels.

"How long are you here? I don't know if I have a place for you to sleep. Or food for you to eat. Or, well, anything, actually. Things are a bit sparse at the moment . . ."

"Easy. Don't hurt your brain, kid. I know I surprised you. I called Joe and they're letting me stay at the resort."

"Oh," I say, feeling both relieved and jealous. I wouldn't mind staying at the resort. But then, this isn't a vacation for me. "Well, in that case, I can show you around, and after, maybe you want to head over there to settle in?"

"Actually, I was hoping to take you out for dinner. I know you're busy, but I really am here to check in with you, and you did break up with your boyfriend when he tried to propose to you three days ago. Not only that, you left town without warning. Your house, your job, your family and friends . . ."

"People break up every day, Liam. Every minute, even, someone is breaking up somewhere. And my landlord found a subleaser already, and I told my job I was taking a leave of absence. Considering Dickhead Shane is my new boss, he couldn't really complain about the timing."

"Okay, but you have to admit, it was a little rash, even for you."

I stop short and peer up at him. "What's that supposed to mean, 'even for me'?"

His amusement doesn't slip for even a second and I bite back the irritation clawing up my throat.

"I just mean," he starts in a patronizing tone I know he uses on his kids, "you dropped all of your responsibilities because some guy had the nerve to propose marriage. A guy, I might add, who you dated for a year, so clearly you didn't dislike him."

"First of all, I already explained how I didn't drop anything. Everything is still very much being handled, even if it's not by me. I arranged for that. I'm not irresponsible, I'm in transition. And second of all, are you telling me that I should have said yes to Shane *just* because we dated for a year? Even if everything inside of me knew it would have been the wrong decision? I thought you hated Shane."

"I didn't hate Shane, I just didn't think he was good enough for you."

"So you think I should have settled?"

"No, but is it too much of a stretch for you to act a little more like an adult?!"

"Says the man who insists on calling me *kid* even though I'm in my thirties!"

"Hello, camp, is it okay if we enter under a flag of peace?"

Liam and I both spin around to take in the little family I'd been watching earlier standing barely twenty feet away. I hadn't even noticed their approach, though Rogers is happily greeting them, tail beating, tongue lolling.

"Hey, man," my brother is saying, crossing the distance with his long strides and swallowing the blond man in a back-thumping hug. "Good to see you. Tell me this isn't Anders. Dude, you've grown at least half a foot since last summer."

Please tell *me* that's not Josiah Cole. Oh my gosh, was I checking out my brother's best friend?

"Hey, Jig," Joe says. His wide, bright smile splits his tanned features, and he holds up his arms for a hug. Which would be a totally normal thing for siblings to do. I hugged Liam not ten minutes ago. But also, I stopped thinking of Joe Cole as an annoying big-brother type right around the time I caught him swimming bare-assed with his girlfriend on my way back from fishing the summer before my junior year of high school.

I step closer, curling in so my breasts don't rub against him like they clearly want to, and return his hug before quickly stepping back and dropping my arms. "Hey, Joe. What a surprise!"

Joe lets out a deep chuckle and the low vibrations of it wash over me, head to bare toes. He bends over Rogers, who's still demanding his own greeting, and I can't help but take the opportunity to study him. He's solidly built, like someone who used to be an athlete and is still active. His golden hair is longer and wavy around his ears and the nape of his neck, and his eyes are covered by sunglasses. He's dressed in a denim button-down with the sleeves cuffed, revealing nice, tanned forearms, and a pair of heavy-duty work pants. The older child, Anders, I believe Liam said, grins at me, revealing a mouthful of new grown-up teeth and sparkling blue eyes. I notice his nails are carefully painted with a bright pink glitter and I dig the shade.

"I love your dog," Anders says to me, beaming, scrubbing at Rogers's wiry coat. My dog has never looked so loved. Stuffed to the gills under the ministrations of this blond family.

"He loves you, too, I'm afraid. There will be no getting rid of Rogers now. He's adopted you."

Anders reaches out a hand toward his younger sister, perched on a tree branch, still several feet away. "Luce, come here and pet Rogers."

The little girl shakes her head quickly back and forth from the limb. At first glance, she seems shy, but something about the way her eyes dart to the side and stay there, as if she's avoiding my gaze, sticks out to me.

"That's okay," I assure her gently. "Maybe another time." She shakes her head again, even more quickly, and I don't push.

"So, Jig," my oldest brother's best friend says, his voice softening. "How've you been?"

"Your name is Jig?" Anders asks.

I snort. "Only to these two. Liam is my big brother, and he and your dad—Wow . . ." I exchange a look with Joe, feeling my cheeks heat at the intent focus of his attention. "That's weird to think about—annoying Joe's a dad. Anyway," I turn back to the kid, "that's what these two used to call me."

"Her real name is Maren, but she was a fishing nut as a kid, so we called her Jig." To me, he explains, "Anders here is almost as big a fishing nut as you were." He tugs the child closer to him. "And that's my daughter Lucy."

"So you and Kiley really did get married and make beautiful babies . . . I believe I predicted that."

He distractedly ruffles at his hair and makes a face. "Well, you were mostly right. I'm guessing Liam never told you Kiley and I are no longer married."

I wince. "He might've mentioned that, actually. Sorry."

"Mom lives in Florida now," Anders adds matter-of-factly.

"Ah," I say, a little taken aback by his forthright response. "I'm . . . so sorry," I repeat, dumbly.

"It's fine," he replies, assuring me with little-kid confidence. "She couldn't handle it."

"Oh," I say, and wait for clarification, but none comes, so I press on. "Well, I should probably get back to work."

"Are you staying at the resort with Liam?"

"Uh, no. Actually"—I turn to my brother—"he surprised me just before you walked up."

"Right. We might've heard some of that."

"Get this, man. Her boyfriend of a year calls up the entire family to come and witness this epic proposal. We all take the day off work and hike up this mountain—"

"It was barely a hill and maybe Joe doesn't want to hear this story right now . . ." I hedge, eyeing the tree limb where Joe's daughter Lucy is still standing.

"—and he gets down on one knee in front of everyone and Maren barely lets him get the words out before she's puking and running back down the mountain."

"Hill. Not a mountain. Hill."

"Before the rest of us even make it back down the mountain, she's packed up her apartment and gets the heck out of Dodge—"

"Yes. Well. That's about the gist of it, anyway," I cut my brother off. "You heard the rest. I'm here to work on Fost's place. He left me the bait shop and the attached apartment."

Joe's eyes first widen and then narrow. "Last I saw, the place was a decrepit dump."

"Yes, well," I repeat, forcing my tone to sound cheerful. "Now it's just as decrepit but much cleaner."

"Does the shop even have locks?" Joe asks. Ah. *There's* the big-brother type I remember. Maybe I should call the other two up and we can have a party while they all give me disapproving looks about the length of my shorts and fart on my pillow at bedtime.

"Does any place up here?" I ask, pointedly rolling my eyes, because honestly, no one locks their doors around these parts, but also I'm not an idiot. I'm a grown woman who has lived alone for over a decade.

He crosses his arms. "That wasn't an answer."

I cross mine, straightening, so I'm every bit of my five foot seven *and a half.* "Okay, Mr. Army Guy, stand down," I tell him, and he rocks back in amused surprise, before crowding forward just as fast, straight into my space, his chest inches from mine and his gaze towering over me.

"It was the Marines, and you still haven't answered my question."

"Yes!" I tell him, feeling the furthest thing from tender now that nagging Joe is back and way too close on top of that. I'm also very aware of the way my nipples are practically tingling at his nearness. "*Of course* I have a lock and use it. Not that anyone knows I'm here nor even cares."

Anders's eyes, which have been volleying back and forth between his father and me, widen with curiosity and he interrupts, "We know you're here! You and Rogers should come over for dinner tomorrow."

"Oh," I say, feeling flustered, both at my body's reaction to Joe's continued proximity and the suddenness of the invite. "That's okay. Thank you, but I'm pretty swamped with the cleanup I'm doing."

"She's in way over her head, if you ask me," Liam says.

"No one asked you and also you didn't even see inside."

"Jig will come?" Lucy speaks up from the tree, and her dad and I both start at her small voice.

"One day," I hedge, trying to remove myself from any kind of promise. "I'm sure if Liam is there . . ."

"Dad is making lasagna and garlic bread," Anders continues.

Guh. Of course he is, and I have one of the seventeen turkey-and-American-cheese Lunchables lining my mini fridge to look forward to. "Another time, really. I am up to my eyeballs in faux wood paneling and will be for a few days, I expect."

"Another time," Joe blessedly agrees. He uses a firm dad tone that cuts off any further argument. I'm not sure if it's for my sake or his, but I decide it's for the best. I'm on a mission, and anyway, my life is a capital-M mess right now. I'm definitely not in a good spot to be having cozy dinners with a single dad and his cute kids. And my brother. Can't forget that idiot.

Regardless of how the mere *suggestion* of bubbling, cheesy lasagna and perfectly toasted garlic bread makes my mouth water.

And further, *regardless* of how I feel like the invite would really annoy Joe, and making that guy squirm has been a favorite pastime of mine since 2000. It's the sworn duty of pesky little sisters of best friends everywhere.

Alas, capital-M mess. Besides, I'm thirty-three, not thirteen. I pucker my lips together and make a kissing noise to call Rogers to attention. He comes, albeit reluctantly, and stands at my side like I've trained him.

"It was good to meet you, Anders and Lucy. Good to see you, Joe. Liam, I'm assuming you'll go with them from here?"

"I'll catch up with you," he tells Joe. "I want to see inside this place for myself."

Ugh.

Joe catches my eye and smirks, his expression knowing. Which makes sense. If anyone knows my brother as well as me, it's him. They've been friends for over thirty years, at least. "See you around, Jig. You know where to find me if you need help."

"Sure," I say, knowing I never ever will. "Let's go, Rogers."

♪♪♪

Liam spins in a slow circle, taking in my mess, and lets out a low whistle between his teeth.

"You're fucked."

"Am not."

"Maren, this is too much. Even for you, all in your feelings or whatever the kids say . . . I'm being straight with you. Go back home, go back to work, and figure this out. This isn't the time to be playing *Eat Pray Love* with your responsibilities."

"That's not what I'm doing. This is a fresh start for me and I'm taking it."

"And then what?"

"And then what, what?" I ask, rubbing at my temples where an ache is beginning to build. "I thought you were coming here to be supportive. Isn't that what you did for Joe?"

"That's another thing, kid," my brother says, as if I'd just reminded him. "I saw you checking Joe out. Don't even go there."

"What?!" I exclaim, my entire body flushing. "Are you joking? I was not!"

"You were, and not only are you completely on the rebound and, frankly, kind of immature, Joe just went through a nasty divorce where he spun out and doesn't need another kid to take care of."

"Are you *out of your mind*?" I ask, seeing red. "Do you have any idea how insulting that is not only to me, but to your best friend? What is the matter with you? Is this your version of checking in on someone?"

Liam instantly looks contrite. "Fuck. I'm sorry, Mare. You're right. I'm . . . I don't know what came over me. That was wrong of me to say. I'm tired and this place is a dump and I—I worry about you, okay?"

He seems sincere. He *is* sincere. That doesn't take the sting out of his words, but I'm too exhausted to fight anymore anyway, and besides, I knew my family wouldn't understand my coming here.

"Okay. I'm sorry for yelling. I'm pretty tired, too. And this has been a lot and this place is a shithole, I know that. But it's my shithole now. And you have to let me make my own mistakes, Liam. I'm a grown woman."

"Hardly."

"Good night, big brother." I know he said he wanted to

take me out to dinner, but I'm not up to it. He pauses, indecision clear on his face, but he eventually relents.

"Sure, sure. Okay. I'm leaving." He presses a kiss to the top of my head. "I'll call you in the morning. I'm only here for the weekend, but I want to help as much as I can until I leave."

I close the door behind him and turn the deadbolt (thank you very much) and sink to the floor.

"Well," I say into the empty, echoing space, "hell."

THREE

Under Pressure

Joe

THE SUN IS JUST MAKING AN APPEARANCE AS I STEP OUT ONTO MY back patio, steaming cup of coffee in one hand and protein shake in the other. The early morning breeze cools the sweat, making my running shorts and T-shirt cling uncomfortably to my skin. I put both drinks down on the railing with a click before stretching my calves, glorying in the burn. I hate running on the treadmill. It's never as good as running the trails through the woods, but with school being back in session, it's either the treadmill in the basement while my kids sleep or leaving them vulnerable and alone in the dark just so I can run outside.

Which is to say it's not really an option at all.

My mom offered to come over in the mornings to sit with the kids but sitting would turn into coffee and making pancakes and asking me probing questions about my nonexistent social life and no thanks. It's enough that my parents live next door with a clear view of my drive and every time I come and go. I appreciate their help, and I'm not too proud to admit I couldn't do this without them, but they're still my *parents*.

I gulp back the protein drink with a grimace because I'll never get used to the chalky flavor. With that out of the way, I grab my coffee and lean against the railing looking out over my backyard.

This part I don't mind. The back view. From the front, you can see the resort, the lake, the never-ending litany of things needing my attention with regards to being in charge of a thriving family business. I took over four years ago after I was honorably discharged from the Marines. My parents have run things for over thirty years and, while they still want a say in the important decisions, they're less interested in the day-to-day.

It seemed ideal at the time. My wife, Kiley, had just given birth to Lucy, and we needed the stability. Besides, I'd always wanted to raise my family at the lake. I wanted my children to grow up the same way I had—safe, surrounded by family, and with the outdoors at their fingertips.

Kiley had other plans. I could raise our children on the moon if I wanted, but she was out. She said it was my turn to stay behind. She'd been doing everything alone for over a de-cade, following me from base to base while I "sowed my oats in the Marines." Though, in my defense, I wasn't doing much of anything besides just trying to stay alive in the Marines, so "sowing" is an exaggeration. I was blindsided. I'd stupidly thought she was happy building our family all that time. That was on me. I was so busy feeling lucky, I didn't even clue in to how the woman I'd loved since I was eighteen was suffocating.

But she'd made it known in a really big, earth-shattering way, and that was that. There was more to it, of course. A lot more, but whatever it was was done now, and because of that, in the mornings, before the day presses in on me, I prefer my backyard. A small one-acre clearing surrounded by dense pines and wildlife. Some days, I'm even greeted by a herd of deer passing through. It's quiet and all mine.

So I stand there, at peace, sipping black coffee and staring at nothing, until I hear the sliding door open behind me.

"Hey, Dad."

Anders. I immediately turn and offer him my arm. He comes out—barefoot, sleepy-eyed, wearing his pink *Encanto* pajamas—and curls into my side. Truthfully, Kiley wasn't on board with his "girly" clothes, glittery nails, or anything else. She thought Anders should be a "tough guy" like his dad.

I'd seen enough tough-guy shit to last a lifetime, though, and honestly, if pink makes him happy, I'll buy him every shade of pink in the world. And seeing as Kiley is in Florida living it up with her new husband and I have full custody, she doesn't get to have an opinion.

"Did I miss her?" my son whispers, peering attentively at the edges of the forest.

Her being the mama doe we've been watching since last spring, along with her growing baby.

"Not yet," I answer softly. But as the words leave my mouth, he gives a sharp inhale, and there she is, slipping into the opening between two massive Norway pines. Anders reaches for my hand and squeezes. I squeeze back. In another life, I would have been eyeing up that doe for fall hunting. Setting up trail cams and planting a feed pile.

But my kid has a soft heart. Too soft for this world, probably, but that's fine. I'll protect him until he's ready to face it on his own.

"The baby's big."

"He is. He'll come back with a starter rack next year."

"And then he can look after his mom?"

I swallow and ruffle Anders's hair at the nape. My boy is soft, but he's noble. "Yup."

"Is Uncle Liam coming over today?"

"He should be here when you get off the school bus," I tell him. "You'll have to show him your crayfish collection."

"Doesn't Uncle Liam hate crayfish, though?"

I share a conspiratorial grin with my kid. "Yup."

Truth be told, my best friend offered to stay with me and help with the kids this morning, but I turned him down. Firstly, because we have a pretty strict morning routine and I don't need him in the way. And secondly, because his pitying looks annoy the shit out of me. I am in a very different place than I was two years ago. I don't need him to get me out of bed anymore.

Oh, and thirdly, and perhaps most importantly, because he's supposed to be here to help his little sister, not me.

Or should I say his not-so-little sister. Hell, Maren grew up hot, didn't she?

But she's entirely out of bounds because she's Liam's sister, and he would murder me for even noticing how she looks. Obviously. I give myself half a second to remember the way Maren's shiny ponytail swung and swept along the soft-looking slope of her tanned bare shoulders in the late-afternoon sun and then scrub it from my brain. *Jig.* She's just Jig.

And I'm a horny single dad with way too much on my plate and less than nothing to offer. Plus, didn't Liam say she just broke up with a guy?

Doesn't matter. Unavailable.

Anders and I watch a minute longer as the mom and baby meander across the corner of our yard, nibbling on grasses, before heading to the hidden spot we found this summer where they like to bed down.

"It's cold," I tell him. "And you aren't wearing shoes. How about we head inside, and I wake up Lucy while you pour yourself some cereal?"

♪♪♪

Lucy is not a morning person. Something she got from her mom. I've always preferred to be awake before sunrise, ready to face whatever comes my way. Not Luce. She likes her sleep and is slow to start her day. My mom bought her one of those sunrise alarm clocks when she started at the special preschool in town a few weeks back, and it helps some, but I have a feeling we'll have a long road ahead of us when this one hits middle school.

The sunrise clock is full-on awake, with gentle music and birdsong, and I perch on the side of her tiny toddler bed and brush Lucy's forehead the way she likes. After Lucy was diagnosed with autism spectrum disorder, we started working with an occupational therapist right away. They told us some children with ASD disliked touch, while others made connections through it. Same with speech, sound, reflexive movement . . . Just like the rest of the human population, people with autism were unique in how they manifested their sensory habits. If they liked something, they let you know. If they didn't, they also let you know. The important thing was to let them reveal themselves to you and to give them a safe space to do so.

That's about where Kiley lost it. She didn't like someone telling her she didn't know her own kid. She didn't want to let Lucy tell us what she needed from us, and she really didn't want Anders expressing himself in any way but purely masculine. She wanted "normal," whatever that even means. So she left and found her version of normal somewhere else.

Turns out, Lucy loves gentle, repetitive touches. Massaging her arms and hands, rubbing her back, smoothing her forehead. She doesn't love speaking, though she *can* speak just fine—it just took her longer to find her voice. She likes some noises, but zippers and loud machinery like power tools, Jet Skis, and blenders set her off.

"Good morning, Luce." I speak in a low, soothing tone to ease her awake. "Time to get ready for school."

Lucy blinks, staring at the ceiling above her.

"School?" she asks eventually.

"Yeah, kid. School." I pick up the clock and show her its glowing screen and point out the numbers the way the therapist told me to do. "Time for Lucy to get up."

"Anders up?"

"Anders is eating cereal. Do you want cereal, too?"

Lucy sits up and I stifle a grin at the way her fine blond hair sticks straight up in the back. "Cereal?"

I put down the clock. "First, potty," I say, before pointing to the clothes we laid out the night before. "Then clothes, then breakfast."

I learned this method the hard way in those first days of preschool when I realized that once Lucy left her room in the morning, it was nearly impossible to get her back there. We have to stick to a routine. A strict one. Which, honestly, works for me, especially after a decade and a half in the Marines. They love that shit. But it was a little trickier to get my free-spirited older kid on board.

Thankfully, he'll do anything for his baby sister.

"First, potty," she repeats to herself and shuffles toward

the en suite bathroom. She takes care of business and I try to give her privacy while still remaining close enough to help her out. She washes her hands and comes to stand in front of me, though her eyes, as usual, are looking over my shoulder. "Clothes, please."

She removes her pajamas piece by piece and replaces them with fresh clothes at a snail's pace, but she does it all independently. One might think it would be faster with my help, but we learned that the hard way, too, when she pitched a two-hour-long fit after I tried to speed things up. Once she's dressed in her leggings with an elastic waistband, a plain graphic tee with the tags cut out, and a cardigan with no buttons, I pass her a pair of special socks with no seams and she slips them on before stepping into her tiny Croc Mary Janes.

I'm feeling pretty good about this, since it only took us twenty minutes altogether and we're early enough for her to watch an episode of *Bluey* while she eats her cereal, which means I can maybe jump in the shower. I'm just turning her tablet on when she accidentally upsets her bowl, pouring almond milk all down her front.

"Uh-oh!" she shouts.

"Oh no, Dad," Anders says.

"Uh-oh!" Lucy says again. "Uh-oh. Uh-oh. Uh-oh," she repeats over and over and over. She will do this until it's cleaned up, so I toss a roll of paper towels to Anders, who starts the mop-up, and I lift a sopping Lucy and carry her in front of me back to her bedroom. "Uh-oh, uh-oh, uh-oh," she says.

We peel off her wet clothes and I scramble in her drawers looking for something new. She starts to scream because her "tummy is sticky," and, hiding my sigh, I carry her to the bathroom, running warm water and plopping her in the tub.

"Dad! The bus!" Anders yells from the other room.

"Is it here?" I yell back.

"Yeah!"

"Can you make it?"

I hear the screen door open and Anders yell out, presumably to the bus, "I'm coming!" before he directs his yelling at me. "Gotta go, Dad!"

I don't have time to check on him—see what he's wearing, make sure he brushed his teeth, combed his hair . . . I only have enough time to shout back, "Hot lunch, okay, bud?"

"Okay, Dad, bye!"

The screen door slams, and he's gone. A moment later my smartwatch buzzes and I see a text from my mom.

Mom: Anders made it to the bus.

I sigh, relief battling it out with annoyance that I even needed the confirmation battling it out with guilt that Anders once again ran after the bus on his own.

"Uh-oh," Lucy whispers, splashing in the tub. She picks up two rubber ducky bath toys and squirts them at her chest. "Uh-oh." She giggles to herself and starts speaking to her ducks using an Australian accent and lines I recognize as being directly from the cartoon she loves watching.

I slump against the vanity cabinet, raising my knee and hooking my arm around it and letting my head fall back and my eyes close. I did three tours in Afghanistan. *Three*. Fought terrorists. Faced down a whole hell of a lot of scary dudes who wanted nothing more than to end me.

But I'll be honest. Those motherfuckers had nothing on my four-year-old.

FOUR

Into the Ocean

Joe

FORTY-FIVE MINUTES, A NEW SET OF TAGLESS, SEAMLESS, ZIPPERLESS clothes, and a cherry-frosted Pop-Tart later, I walk Lucy into her special preschool. My girl's not much for dramatic farewells, so she runs in ahead of me and plops down in front of her favorite toy: a spinning globe.

I pass Lucy's backpack and lunch over the counter to her teacher, an endlessly patient woman in her early fifties who wears a modified gardening belt filled with communication tools and goodies to help her attend to her small classroom full of autistic kids. She takes one look at me, still in my running clothes, and her silver eyebrows rise with good-humored curiosity. I grimace.

"I got cocky," I tell her, and she releases a tinkling laugh that carries out over her students.

"It happens to the best of us, Mr. Cole. We'll see you this afternoon."

🪝🪝🪝

After a quick shower and change of clothes, I scramble four eggs and gulp down a second cup of microwaved coffee that is somehow both scalding and lukewarm before I head out the door and hop on my ATV. I usually walk to and from the resort, but I'm already behind. I was supposed to meet my dad down by the villas at nine thirty and it's close to ten. When I roar up, he's sitting on the tailgate of his and my mom's golf cart, scrolling through his phone and sipping from a cardboard cup of coffee from the lodge.

"Sorry I'm late."

He waves me off. "Figured when we saw Anders sprinting out the door without you that something happened with Luce."

"Last-minute spill and wardrobe change."

My dad nods as if to say, *Like I said.*

"You know you have help if you ask. Your mother doesn't want to push, but we're next door. You don't have to do everything on your own."

I bite back a grunt and repeat my usual response. "Kiley did."

My dad shakes his head and smiles sadly at me. "Those were different circumstances. You were overseas. And she didn't, anyway. She dropped Anders off every morning when she was working. It takes a village, Josiah," he finishes quietly, using my full name.

I don't argue. We've had this conversation many times. They think I'm being proud, and I am. But this feels like the least I can do after abandoning Kiley with two small kids. If I'd been around more, maybe the idea of a child with sensory disabilities wouldn't have been so daunting for her. Maybe she'd still be here, dividing and conquering.

It feels like cheating somehow to accept help from my parents more than I already do, village or no.

"So what are we looking at here, Dad?" I ask, changing the subject.

He fills me in on his consultation with the contractor who's doing the bathroom renovations on villas one, two, and three this winter. Every winter, we try to tackle one update or another. Last year was new docks for the cabins. The year before that was air-conditioning for the entire resort, minus the trailer park we absorbed into our fold decades before. People have been coming to Cole's Landing Resort for decades with their families, and so we try to embrace the nostalgia and not get too swept up in modernizing the cabins and villas, but some fixes just make life easier. I've been working on convincing my parents to have Wi-Fi installed in the units. They are reluctant, of course, because they feel like being up north and away from it all should include a break from the internet and social media. And that is something our guests have appreciated in the past. But social media is here to stay, and as someone with an autistic preschooler, I see the benefits of a tablet and some age-appropriate learning cartoons.

Just saying.

"Did you see the Laughlin girl is back, fixing up old Foster's shop?"

"Maren," I remind him, figuring he wouldn't remember her by her nickname.

"Didn't you boys call her Jig?"

I stand corrected. Sharp as a tack, my dad. "Yeah, we did. And yeah, the kids and I ran into her and Liam arguing near the point last night. He followed her up here and I booked him in number five. Maren said she got here a few days ago and has been staying at Fost's while she cleans it up."

My dad's nose wrinkles, making his thick, white mustache scrunch up. "I don't know about that," he says, echoing my exact thoughts. "I remember her always running after you big kids and heading out on Fost's boat every morning and night to catch musky. She was cute. Did pageants, right? And had a YouTube channel?"

Like I said, sharp as a tack. "She did, but that was fifteen years ago. I'd caution you on saying anything to her about it now. She's a grown woman with a mind of her own."

"She's stubborn," he says, and I don't miss the implication that it's something we have in common.

"Very," I say back, implying *I know*.

"Your mother will want to have her over for dinner."

"Good luck with that," I tell him. "Anders already invited her to our place tonight with Liam and she turned us down. If she can turn Anders and Lucy down . . ."

"Anders did?"

"He tried."

"Guess I'll have to send you to ask her, then."

I shift my feet, meeting his gaze. "Dad, lose the fucking twinkle."

"What?" my dad asks, his mustache twitching. "She's not as cute as she used to be?"

"Considering she's my best friend's little sister and like five years younger than us, I didn't exactly think she was cute. Annoying, maybe."

"But now she's a grown woman with a mind of her own. You said so yourself. So is she cute now?"

Actually, she's beautiful, I think. *Long, wavy auburn hair,*

choppy bangs over hazel eyes, trim figure with gorgeous curves.
Freckles and a summer tan.

And I'm scrubbing her from my brain again.

The truth is, Maren'd always been naturally pretty, even when she was annoying and too young for anyone to notice. Liam was constantly complaining about her YouTube channel and how popular it was, particularly with men. After all, it was basically a hot girl fishing, with the added bonus that she knew what she was talking about. She didn't need someone else to bait her hook or remove the fish from her line. She had endorsements because she knew her shit when it came to lures and hardware.

Not that I watched. Well, not that often anyway. It's just that she filmed her show up here at the resort the summers she was in college, and at the time, I was on the other side of the world, sleeping in the sand and dodging IEDs. I liked the reminder of home and what I was fighting for.

But I would die before telling Liam or anyone else that. It wasn't weird. I didn't jack off to it or anything. Maren wasn't being sexy. She was this girl who looked like she grew up next door to you. She was everyone's little sister. Practically.

I work really hard at not letting myself think about the fact that she is at least thirty-three now and that Liam will be leaving in two days. Or the fact that I haven't had sex in over three years because dating as a single parent with full custody of your two kids while living next door to your parents is hard.

"And . . . I lost you," my dad says with an amused grin. "I'll take that as a confirmation."

"Confirmation of what?"

My dad's grin grows into a full-blown smile. "That yes, Maren Laughlin grew up cute. Never mind," he says, rounding his golf cart and sliding in behind the wheel. "Invite her to our place for dinner. This coming Saturday. Your mom will be beside herself with excitement."

"She'll say no," I warn him.

"I don't think she will," he says with another fucking eye twinkle. "But if you can't get her to say yes, I'll do it myself."

Jesus. That's the last thing I need. My dad accosting the poor woman and guilting her into showing. Not to mention he would probably try to *put in a good word* for me and make things even more awkward than they already are after I overheard her and Liam fighting last night.

I used to be smooth, years ago, but now I think I might be broken. Like I peaked too soon? That would figure.

"I'll ask her."

"Today."

I huff out an exasperated breath. "I have shit to do. It's getting colder every day and I still need to winterize."

"It's September, kid. You have plenty of time. Take the ATV and report back by this afternoon so your mom can figure out what she wants to make and plan a trip to town."

With that, he takes off and I'm left standing there, staring after him.

⌡⌡⌡

I pull up to Fost's—or rather Maren's now, I guess—bait shop literal minutes later. In fact, it was so close to the resort, I'd looked into purchasing it after Fost died. We have a modest bait counter at the lodge that is available to guests, but I was open to expanding. I'd heard ownership had transferred hands when he'd died, but I'd never followed up on the lead to find out who it'd gone to.

I hear Rogers barking the second I cut the engine, and before I can knock, the front door of the bait shop opens and Maren stands in the doorway, arms crossed and a suspicious expression on her face.

"I come in peace," I offer, hands raised in front of me. I try for charming, but I'm rusty and it's pretty clear by her stony expression that I don't pull it off.

"The locks work fine, Joe, and you can see Rogers is plenty enough warning for unwanted guests."

I want to laugh at her tone and the defensive set of her slim shoulders, but I swallow the urge. "Right. Not here about that, but I'm glad to hear it."

"Well, my brother ran to town for a work call, but he should be back in an hour or so. Want me to have him stop by?"

"Not here about Liam, either, though he could have made his call from the lodge. There's Wi-Fi there."

Maren's eyebrows scrunch together cutely. Sexily? *Both*, I decide. "Then what?"

"My parents want to have you over for dinner. Saturday night."

"Your parents?" she asks, dubious.

"I swear."

"Are they also making lasagna and garlic bread?"

"If you want to make a request, I'm sure it can be arranged."

"Nah," she says with a grin, leaning against the doorjamb. "How'd they know I was even here?"

"Small resort," I hedge. "So I can tell them you'll come?"

She sighs, but it's relaxed. "I suppose I can manage to suffer through a delicious home-cooked meal and your parents' cozy company for a whole night."

"Along with two kids and their exhausted dad?"

Maren pretends to hesitate. "Whoa, whoa, whoa, now you're throwing two cute kids into the mix?"

I try not to feel proud that she thinks my kids are cute, but hell, they *are* pretty cute. "I know, it's a lot. That said, I'm warning you now, my dad had a twinkle in his eyes."

She smiles and I feel it like a sunny punch to my gut. "Oh no. Not a twinkle."

Without thinking, I take another step toward her. "Full-on twinkle and probably a knowing look. He's a meddler."

"I shall do my best to endure. Though I'll remind you, I recently broke up with my boyfriend by throwing up on his shoes after he had the nerve to propose. I'm not exactly what any parent wants for their son."

I wince and let out a low whistle between my teeth. "You're a fucking heartbreaker, Jig."

She lifts a too-casual shoulder and drops it lightly. "He's probably already over it, honestly."

If he's over it after half a week, he never deserved her. "Well, shit."

"Yeah," she agrees. "So yes to the dinner, yes to the company, and I can survive the twinkling as long as he doesn't fall in love with me."

I take the easy brush-off for what it is. She's up here and she wants space. I've been there. In fact, I'm still there. Deeply there.

"I don't think that will be an issue, but I'll pass it along."

"Thanks, Joe. I need to get back inside. I poured some paint just before you pulled up and I don't want it to turn tacky before I get it on the walls."

For half a beat, I consider offering my assistance. I don't mind painting, and I find I don't really want to leave. Despite the conversation, or maybe because of it. She's not looking for anything right now and I *can't* look for anything right now. It's kind of perfect.

Instead, I say, "See you Saturday, Jig. Bring your dog," and, with a salute, I start the ATV and roll away.

FIVE

Doll Parts

Maren

THERE WERE TWO REASONS WHY I STOPPED MAKING VIDEOS FOR MY Musky Maren YouTube channel. The first was because I was offered a legitimate entry-level job after graduation with Michigan's Forest Resources Division that paid less but felt like real validation and that was important to me. This was the more digestible reason I called upon whenever I met followers who recognized me from those days, which happened a lot, especially working at a state park.

The lesser-known (read: no one knows aside from Shelby and Lorelai—and presumably Cameron and Craig) but more accurate and far darker reason I quit was because of a man named Bryce Callahan.

I knew Bryce lived in northern Wisconsin, but never his actual town. After all, Wisconsin is a big state and I wasn't a local. I grew up in Michigan and always stayed at an obscure family resort miles outside of civilization whenever I filmed my videos. Therefore, I first met him at a meet-and-greet during a Great Lakes outdoors show that I'd done. Unfortunately, things got uncomfortable real fast. It was clear the guy was delusional, and his favorite delusions revolved around me and had been building for a while. He started to show up at any in-person gig I was a part of. He'd wait in line, ask to take a selfie with me, and brought me gifts. Then he began emailing me through my website. I never responded, but that didn't prevent him from sending me unhinged messages about how much he loved me, wanted to marry me, and spent his nights jacking off to photos of me.

And, listen. It isn't uncommon for strangers to fixate on someone they met on the internet. I know what I look like. I competed in and won pageants for over a decade. I'm not an idiot and I've heard it all. But I was in college when this went down. I didn't have a security detail and I lived in a dorm room, hours from my closest relative. My early roommates were nice enough, but they didn't see the attention as anything to worry about. They either wanted me to share the wealth or they didn't like the way their boyfriends looked at me. By my junior year, I moved off campus into my own studio apartment.

Through it all, Bryce persisted. I started having panic attacks before meet-and-greets, worrying he would be there. I kept up with the channel because the money was good and I enjoyed what I did and the respect I started to get within the fishing community, but the trade-off was being vulnerable to men like Bryce. I should have filed a complaint with the police. Gotten a restraining order. Advocated for myself. But I didn't. I didn't think anyone would care. It scared the shit out of me, but it wasn't like he threatened my life. Sure, he made gross comments, but so did every boyfriend I'd ever had, and he *thought* he was my boyfriend in his own fucked-up head.

So I didn't do or say anything until I got my job offer after graduation. It was my chance for a clean break, so I deleted my channel, went dark on all my social media accounts, and moved to another state. Since then, I've kept minimal social media and the ones I have are set to private. I have two very famous best friends who live their lives well in the spotlight, but it's been over ten years since I've heard anything from Bryce or anyone else, so I've relaxed.

Turns out, I shouldn't have.

Five days. Five measly days I've been back. Two days since my brother had hit the road finally. I was at the hardware store in town, needing some assistance with drywall, and sure as shit there he was at the counter. He looked very nearly the same but was carrying more weight around the middle and less thatched brown hair on his head.

"Maren?"

Weirdly, for as much time as this man has spent living rent free in my brain, haunting my dreams, and causing me all sorts of anxiety over the years, I didn't recognize him at first. I wish I had. Hell, do I wish I had. I wouldn't have said a word, just run straight out the doors.

But I couldn't place him at first and I'm a naturally friendly person, so I say, "I'm sorry, do I know you?" Before the last words leave my lips, I remember. I remember who he is and a whisper ekes past my lips, "Bryce?"

The way his mouth spreads into a hopeful grin. "You remember me?"

I feel like a robot as I nod, my heart racing and my palms sweating. My brain short-circuits.

"It's so amazing to see you—wow. Musky Maren. In my store. I was just thinking about you"—*oh god*—"and then you appeared. Like out of a daydream. This is insane." Yeah. Insane. "I'm sorry, I'm rambling. You caught me off guard. Did you need something? Anything? A tool, a husband? Ha. Just kidding. Unless you're not married. Are you married?"

I immediately cover my ring finger and step away from the counter. "S-sorry. I'm . . . I forgot what I was . . . My husband! Yes." I plaster a tremulous smile across my lips. "I have a husband. He'll be right back. I'm such a dunce." I hit my forehead lightly and keep walking backward toward the door. "I always forget—bye! See you! Bye!"

I hit the door with a jangle of the bells and spin, practically sprinting to my car and climbing up into the seat where Rogers is on high alert. I shakily reach for my dog, burying my hands in his coarse fur, and he turns his head, giving me small, warm licks along my wrists.

"Shhh, shhhh," I whisper to him, as if he's the one freaking out. "Calm down. Just breathe." Rogers keeps up with his kisses and I tilt my forehead to his, soaking in his comfort. "It's all good."

Eventually, I pull myself together and turn on my car, glancing ahead of me one last time before reversing. And when I do, I see Bryce is still standing behind the counter, his gaze intent, watching me. I'm paralyzed but don't want him to see, so instead I force my body to move and wave before pulling out and driving straight back to my cabin in the woods.

♪♪♪

I know my fears are irrational, but it still takes three more days before I stop jumping at every creak and shift in this old cabin. I park my old Bronco in the empty storage shed that used to be a garage but needed to be cleared out. I invite Rogers to sleep in my bed next to me. I'm ruining him. He's crate-trained and has been perfectly okay with his little house in the corner of my bedroom, until now. Now, he's discovered what it's like to sleep spread out on a soft mattress with a down comforter, pressed against me, and he'll never want to go back. RIP my personal space, I guess.

But I can't find it within myself to care. Even when I tell myself it's been over ten years and Bryce is probably married and has moved on and has three kids and a two-story house he built himself. Even when I'm like "Stop being so conceited, he was never obsessed with you, you're just paranoid." Even when I remember no one even knows I'm here or where I'm staying or how to find me. Even when I remind myself that I lied to Bryce and told him I had a husband.

For the tiniest portion of a split second, I second-guess myself turning down Shane, because if I hadn't, I would've had a real fiancé in Michigan and would have been safe from weird guys who fixated on my fishing videos from 2010.

But that goes away as soon as I remember the way Shane told me he didn't think I was serious about the promotion and thought I wouldn't care that he interviewed for it behind my back, because he would provide for me anyway, and after we were married, I'd be busy starting on our family.

"After all, Maren, you're going to be thirty-four by the end of the year."

I don't return to town. When I need to buy more paint, I head south toward Chippewa Falls, which is a ninety-minute drive, and pack a long list with everything I can possibly think of, including paint, more cleaning supplies, more trash bags. I even hit up Walmart and purchase new towels, bathroom products, kitchen utensils and dishes, a new microwave that won't short-circuit, rugs, and curtains. All in an attempt to make my little home cozier, or even just livable, for the coming months before I dive into the big project: the bait shop.

It's not terrible, as long as I plan ahead.

By the time Saturday rolls around and I'm supposed to go to the Coles' house, I'm seriously ready for a real home-cooked meal. Unlike my besties, I actually love to cook and don't suck at it. Back in Michigan, my kitchen was fully stocked, and I loved hosting my friends and coworkers for dinner parties or holidays. Fost's kitchen is more utilitarian, as in it's perfect for a single guy who liked to reheat but definitely not set up for anything that requires basic prep.

So I'm really looking forward to eating something not out of a can.

And I'll admit, I'm lonely. Now that the shock of my breakup is past, and my brother finally got out of my hair, I realize I don't really want to hole up by myself to lick my wounds for an indeterminate amount of time. I miss interacting with strangers, the way I did for my job as a park ranger every day. And I miss being in a relationship.

I don't miss Shane, but I kind of miss *having* a Shane.

By the time five o'clock rolls around, I'm ready. I've made an effort to look nice, blow-drying my hair and applying makeup. I put on a pair of cuffed olive-green boyfriend-cut jeans and a thin, fitted black turtleneck sweater. I even slip on a pair of black loafers and put thin gold hoops in my ears, which would honestly feel like overkill for a family dinner at the resort, except I've been in holey leggings and paint-spattered tees all week. I've needed this.

It's not a long walk to the resort property from my place, but I don't know how late I'll be, and I don't want to have to come back in the dark. It's not like we have streetlights up here in the woods, and anyway, I've had enough late-night encounters involving bears digging through the trash to know I'd better bring the Bronco. I load up Rogers and a bottle of red wine I picked up in Chippewa Falls in lieu of baking something to share. If I remember, Donna is a wine drinker. I wish I had something for Lucy and Anders, but I figure Rogers is enough.

Turns out I was right on that account.

"Rogers!" Anders calls from the porch of the familiar giant A-frame, and my dog answers with a happy bark.

The little boy is followed by his dad holding his sister on his hip and his grandma and grandpa. I'm startled by the emotion clogging my throat at the sight of them.

I don't know what's wrong with me, but I think this means I made the right choice coming over here tonight.

♪♪♪

"So I know you're wrapped up in Fost's mess, but have you gotten out on the water yet?" Simon Cole asks after practically licking his plate clean of his wife Donna's peach pie à la mode. I hide my smile as Donna wordlessly dishes him out another piece.

"Not yet," I admit. "To be honest, I might've underestimated how bad Fost let things get toward the end. It's taken me all week just to make it clean enough that I'm no longer thinking I'd be better off in a tent. I don't know how he managed it. If I'd known, I would have intervened."

Joe shifts his position at the table, his arm around his daughter's chair while she watches something on a tablet, her ears covered in soundproof headphones. "Don't beat yourself up over it. He hadn't been living there for years."

I raise my eyes to his, surprised. "He wasn't?"

Donna shakes her head. "No, hon. He was living at the resort. In cabin fourteen."

I blink. Cabin fourteen was nice. Like, really nice. The Coles had a massive resort with twenty cabins, six villas, a full-service lodge, and multiple trailer parks. Cabins one through ten were original to the resort. Super basic, cozy, and nostalgic. One or two bedrooms, tiny kitchenette, tiny bathroom with a stall shower, and a cute picnic table out front for outside dining. They provided zero extras like air-conditioning, television, microwaves. But about ten years ago, the Coles had built ten more cabins, all along the water, and rented them for a premium. They had modern amenities and as far as I knew, they always had a waiting list to rent.

"How'd he manage that?"

Simon chuckled low and sipped the rest of his beer. "He didn't, but we owed him. That man brought us a lot of business over the years with his guided tours and bait shop. It was the least we could do."

"Somehow I can't see Fost accepting that very easily."

"Which is why I went over with decades of figures that proved our point and convinced him to take me out weekly and show me his best spots," Joe says. "Told him I would barter the cabin rental for his priceless wisdom."

"Smart," I tell him with a smile. "But you know there's no way he showed you his best spots."

Joe grins in return, his tone good-natured. "I suspected. Why share his secrets with me when he was saving them for his favorite girl?"

I ignore the pang in my heart at his words. I miss my old

friend more than I can say. "I'm guessing your 'decades of figures' were bullshi—baloney as well?"

Joe shrugs.

"Well," I say, settling back in my seat, lifting my glass of wine, and putting it to my lips. "That explains the condition of things, then. I was wondering how he lived there, but I guess he didn't."

"He didn't. He tried to visit often enough to check on things and keep it clean, but toward the end, he didn't have the energy."

"If we'd known he was leaving it to you, we would have kept better tabs on things, Mare," Donna says, apology clear in her expression.

"Oh, no. That's okay. I didn't know, either, obviously. He wasn't exactly sentimental."

"You know," Simon begins in a singsong tone, and I can't help but notice the eye twinkle Joe warned me about.

"Here we go," Joe says, getting up to clear the table. "Why don't we move to the porch, Dad. I want to be able to keep an eye on Anders while you meddle in Jig's business."

I stand and pick up my plate and reach for the empty water glasses. "That's a good idea. Rogers is well trained, but I don't want him to go after wildlife and get lost in the woods as the sun goes down."

I'm adding dishes to the pile by the sink as Joe automatically fills the dishwasher. "Hear him out, Jig. I don't know what he's planning, but I can guess, knowing him. They love Maggie and Hudson," he says, speaking of my parents, "and they think of you as one of their own."

"Of course I'll listen to him," I say, affronted.

Joe raises an eyebrow.

"What? I'm not rude. I love your parents."

"I know you aren't rude. But you are stubborn and clearly going through something—"

"Right," I cut him off. "Joe. I turned you down for dinner. That's all. I was up to my eyeballs in fixing that shithole"—my voice lowered to a whisper on the cuss—"to make it habitable and you were being patronizing about me, a grown woman, locking the door. It was one conversation. I'm not an unreasonable person as a rule."

Joe's eyes search mine and after a pause, his shoulders slump. "I'm sorry."

"You are?"

"You're right. I won't bring it up again. I might be sensitive to women holding grudges."

I press my lips together, rolling them in. "Kiley?" I ask finally.

He just nods, placing the last dishes and then pouring soap in the dishwasher, starting it up right away. Which, it should be noted, I've never seen a man do ever. Nevertheless, I try not to stare.

He doesn't seem to want to say anything more about his ex and honestly, who am I to pry? I've known Josiah Cole since I was a baby, but I don't really *know* anything about him. Five years' age difference isn't a lot as adults, but growing up, it was a canyon.

"Can I top you off?" Joe asks, raising the wine bottle, and I pass him my glass.

"I'm not unreasonable, but I have a feeling this is gonna go down better with a second glass."

◊◊◊

I was right. We move to the porch, and Simon and Donna make a cozy pair, sitting side by side on the porch swing. Donna's petite form means her feet don't hit the floor, so Simon rocks them back and forth. Seeing them reminds me to call home again. No doubt my mom and dad are worried about me leaving the way I did, even if they did send Liam in their stead.

Anders is tossing a neon tennis ball over and over for Rogers, who shoots out after it with the same amount of enthusiasm time and again. Joe's sitting on the top step of the porch, his back to the railing and his long legs crossed at the ankles across the stair, his beer resting in his lap.

I'm in a double-seater rocker next to Lucy as she plays with my phone. She's letting me rock us gently as she settles against my side, not quite intentionally. Her little brow is furrowed as she concentrates on a game that requires you to pop bubbles on the screen. It's not complicated, but I've always found it soothing after a long day. I figure she probably likes the bright colors and the soft *pop-pop-pop*s emitting from the speakers.

Because of this, I'm forced to hear out Simon's meddling start to finish, Joe shaking his head and smirking into his beer bottle the entire time.

I've been played by the Coles, and all it took was a super-cute four-year-old blond. I said I was reasonable, and I am. I love the Coles as much as my own flesh and blood, but that doesn't mean I'm comfortable with what they are suggesting.

"I can't stay at the resort for free, Simon," I finally respond, my voice soft but firm.

He doesn't even stop his rocking. "It wouldn't be for free. Johnson's staying in Green Bay for the winter to recover from open-heart surgery and Casper's splitting his time with his charter business in the Florida Keys. I need someone to take

out tours until the water freezes over. We have cabin book-
ings through Thanksgiving, and the villas and cabins eleven to
nineteen are booked even further because of snowmobilers.
And that's without me advertising that Musky Maren is back
in town."

The hair on the back of my neck stands up at the old moniker. "If you're booked solid, why would you offer me a cabin?
I don't want to cut into your profits."

"We're booked, but we leave cabin twenty open year-round
for visiting family and close friends. You never know when one
will show up and want to stay."

"And they won't need a place this winter?"

"Not as much as you."

I inwardly cringe, still shaken from my encounter in town.
"What if the lake ices over early?"

"Then you can bartend for us at the lodge. Either way, it's
a trade. Though anything over rent you keep, obviously. And
full gratuity, no matter what."

"I still need to work on Fost's place in my spare time."

"Of course."

"And as soon as it's habitable, I'll move back."

"Suit yourself. We can work that out later."

I swallow past the anxiety crawling up my throat and Lucy
turns to look at my face, reminding me I've stopped strok-
ing her soft, fine hair. I start again. "Because I have so much
to do, I don't think I want to advertise anything about, um,
Musky Maren. I deleted the channel a long time ago. I'll fill in
and help out with what's already in the books, and if someone
calls to schedule a tour, it's obviously fine to let them know
I'm not Johnson or Casper. But I'd rather not market it or
anything."

I can feel Joe's eyes on me, but I'm intent on his parents in the swing. Donna seems to be reading something in my face that likely only moms can see, but Simon doesn't hesitate to agree. "Of course, if that's what you want."

I don't want. Not really. Though I do I miss giving tours. There was a time in my life when I really thought it was all I would do. Live up here, do guided fishing tours by day and raise a small family by night. Simple and sweet.

But life got complicated, and as much as I want to work for the Coles, I don't want to draw the wrong kind of attention.

"It's for the best, I think. I'm on a leave of absence from the park service, but I haven't made it permanent yet." Not that I imagine they'll hold my position forever or even as long as the winter, but I'm not a complete flake. I've put in a lot of years to the parks. My entire career. Just because my promotion went to my ex-boyfriend, which, to be clear, sucked, doesn't mean I couldn't start over at another park someplace new. *God*. I'm thirty-three. Am I seriously considering starting over?

I take my time and rock back and forth with Lucy's warm weight pressing against me. The sun is setting quickly, but it's still mild after the warm early autumn day. The sky takes on a sepia glow and the water beyond the docks sparkles, absorbing the lush colors of twilight and refracting them in a magical way. Bats swoop and swirl in the sky, darting between the extra-tall pines. Frogs sing and fish splash. Anders laughs and Rogers pants and still I rock back and forth.

Eventually, I decide. "Okay," I say softly and swallow hard. "Thank you."

SIX

Waiting for a Girl like You

Joe

IT'S THURSDAY NIGHT, FIVE DAYS AFTER MY DAD WORKED A MIRACLE and somehow convinced Maren to move into cabin twenty and work at the resort. I was skeptical and halfway expected her to change her mind after she lost the weight of my daughter holding her in place and woke to the light of day, but I should have known better than to bet against my dad.

Or maybe Fost's cabin *is* just that bad.

Scratch that—I know Fost's place is that bad. It was that bad five years ago when we moved the old man out. It'll take weeks, maybe even months, to fix up—a fact that I am finding too encouraging even though there's no fucking way I'll examine why. Let's just say I'm glad she'll be safe where my parents can keep an eye on her.

"Six Spotted Cows, Joe. For cabin four. And can we put in for a few pizzas?"

I take down Gus's order without asking for clarification on the toppings. This group of retired firemen come up every year in mid-September, renting half our cabins (the older ones, of course) and parking themselves on my barstools every night after dark. They only ever order two meat-lover's pizzas with extra cheese, though Big Freddy will take a small dish of sardines on the side.

"How're the fish biting?" I ask, passing the first few glasses from the tap.

"Like shit," Gus grouses, but he's smiling huge, revealing a missing incisor, and already pouring his beer down his throat.

"He's full of it." Jack Dawson, another member of their group, climbs onto his own stool and reaches for his glass with a tip of his head. "That little girl took us all over god's green earth, making sure even All Thumbs over here limited out."

"Maren did all right, then?" I ask, being polite, even though I know she did.

"All right? I've never seen so many fish. Felt like we should have paid more! A couple of us wanted to check on her availability later this week. Can she fit in a musky trip?"

I pull the guide schedule notebook out from behind the counter. I've worked pretty hard at updating the resort into the twenty-first century, but the last time we lost power for three days, my dad drew the line at computerized records. "I'll have to confirm with Maren. She's on loan, but muskies are her bread and butter. She might be convinced to carve out time for a tour."

More men show up and they eventually move the group to a couple of tables. I fill orders and keep an ear to the loud conversation happening in the dining area. It's evident Maren won over the group of old guys when a loud cheer erupts as she finally makes it back to the lodge. From the waist down, Maren's swallowed up in navy rain gear, but her jacket's tied around her small waist and she's wearing a fitted white tank top over a sports bra, her hair in a messy topknot.

She steals the fucking air from my lungs.

I watch as she walks over to the group of men, passing out high fives and sweet smiles. The effect would be hilarious if I wasn't so caught up in it myself.

"Who's that?"

I jerk my gaze back to the job literally at hand. As in, I'm filling drinks from the tap and need to focus. Angela Hartley, one of our daytime bartenders, hops behind the bar and fills a plastic cup with a few maraschino cherries and lemonade. Angela only works summers since she teaches high school English the rest of the year.

"Here to pick up your last check?"

"Yes, but Matt's supposed to meet me here. I hate this time of year. I'm basically a single parent. Sorry," she offers belatedly. Matt is Angela's husband. He teaches at the high school, too, and is also the football coach.

"No harm, no foul," I say, waving her off. "And that's Maren Laughlin."

"Oh! Liam's little sister? I remember her. Didn't she have that YouTube channel way back when?"

"She's a park ranger these days, but on a sabbatical. Fost left her the keys to his empire, so Dad recruited her to do guided tours while she fixes things up."

"She looks like a hoot. Those geezers are a tough crowd to win over."

Just then Maren makes her way over and plops on a stool, her hands slapping playfully on the polished bartop. "Bartender, pour me a drink."

I swallow a grin. "Got an ID?"

"In my other rain pants, I'm afraid." She bats her lashes and smirks. "You want to call my mom and ask her my birth-date? I'll warn you, she loves to talk about the episiotomy."

"All right, smart-ass. What'll it be?"

"Leinie's on tap?"

I nod and pour her drink, tilting the glass expertly to mini-mize the foam, before slipping a lemon slice on the rim.

Maren plucks the fruit in her fingers and squeezes it in her beer. Then she takes a long sip, closing her eyes. "That's good."

"Don't they have Leinie's in Michigan?"

"Sure," she admits, wiggling happily in her seat. "But it tastes better in Wisconsin, at a bar with Foreigner playing on the jukebox after a long day catching walleye on the water."

I'll give her that.

"I'm Angela," Angela says, holding her small hand out to Maren. "I knew your brother."

Maren's nose scrunches up as she takes Angela's hand. "Sorry to hear that. Which one?"

"I ran around with Kyle during the summers, but I married Mathew Hartley, who was close with Liam and Joe."

"Woof," Maren says, good-naturedly. "Well, you saved the best for last. I'm Maren."

"Musky Maren, right?"

It's fascinating to watch, the way Maren's face ices over. If you blink, you'd miss it altogether because just as quickly she's back to her naturally warm and open expression. I tuck it away to dissect another time. "That was me. These days you can just call me Mare, though."

The two get along like a house on fire, and after two more

rounds, their stools are practically attached. Matt walks up behind them, his eyes round.

"You didn't wait for me?"

"You can have an annoyed sober wife tapping her toes waiting for your ass to get here or you can have a happily tipsy wife who might let you cop a feel in the bathroom, if you're lucky."

A stool opens next to Angela and Matt sits down and orders a drink. "Just a beer. It's a school night and it looks like I'm driving."

"After a trip to the bathroom, don't forget. Cleaned it this morning, just for you."

Matt smirks, then tips his bottle neck-first at me as Angela introduces him to Maren.

He chokes on his sip. "Little Laughlin?"

"Jesus. Always the little sister," Maren says, owlishly. "You know I've been up here way more than all three of my brothers combined, right?"

"It's not that," Angela offers helpfully. "You were just such a little tomboy running around after Fost. It's hard to imagine that little girl growing up to be . . . well, you know. A knockout."

Maren's face flushes, but she's saved by the fishermen who have finished their pizzas and are heading back to their cabins.

"Hey, darlin'," Gus says, approaching her as if he's her long-lost uncle. "You got another trip in you this week? The fellas want you to take us hunting for musky."

"I think so." She looks to me. "Am I available?"

I lean forward so only she can hear and speak in her ear. "Do you want to be? They're essentially asking for Musky Maren."

Maren blinks at me, slowly. Her tongue darts out to lick

her bottom lip and I watch it before suddenly shifting back-ward. She shakes herself and pushes her half-finished drink toward me.

"I think I'm done. I just realized I haven't had dinner."

"Mare, you available?"

She nods. "Okay."

I look to Gus. "Give me a second to double-check the schedule." Then I turn to Matt. "Cover me a minute?"

I don't wait for his response. I just round the bar, tug Maren off the stool, and lead her back toward the small kitchen.

"I said okay," she tells me, sounding more herself.

"I heard you," I tell her, squeezing her hands in my grip. "But I don't want you to feel like you're put on the spot. You get a weird look on your face whenever Musky Maren comes up. You don't have to tell me why, but if you're gonna work for my parents, I don't want you to feel pressured into anything."

"For you, don't you mean?"

"What?"

"I'm working for *you*, Joe. Your dad might've meddled, and your mom might've played the mother card, but you're the one in charge. I work for you."

I choose to ignore the way those words shoot straight to my groin. "Fine. Sure. Do you want to do the musky tours or not?"

"Yes. But please don't advertise it. I'll do them on a case-by-case basis."

"You got it. But you realize there are going to be a lot of cases that come up at this rate."

Maren nods, and looks down at her hands, still clasped in mine. She pulls them away and I clear my throat. What am I doing?

"Sorry. Force of habit," I joke. "I hold Lucy's hands a lot to get her attention when I'm talking to her."

Maren relaxes. "Yeah. I get it. The kid thing again."

That's not it at all, but I don't know what it actually is, so I let it drop.

"Okay, so I'll sign the firemen in cabin four up for a musky tour and you let me know when you're ready for more."

"Thanks, Joe. I'll stop in tomorrow for details. Close me out? I should get back to Rogers. We both need to eat."

"Drinks are on the house when you're an employee. See you around, kid."

Maren waves her goodbyes to the old guys and Matt and Angela and gives me a small salute before leaving. I return to my place behind the bar.

"Liam know she's here?"

I look at Matt and nod. "He followed her up for a few days, though he stayed here while she was out at Fost's place."

"He know she's working for you?"

"No idea. I don't talk to him every day. He's got a life." And he does. There was a time, during and just after my divorce, that Liam checked in on me nearly every day, but that was years ago.

Matt nods, tipping back his bottle. "She grew up well. She married or anything?"

"She just broke up with her boyfriend," Angela offers. "They worked together and apparently he went behind her back and applied for the promotion she's been working towards for the last decade. Won it out from under her and then had the nerve to propose marriage in a very public way, thinking she would be cool playing the little woman, barefoot in the kitchen."

Yeesh. That's worse than I thought.

"And now she's working for you."

I shrug. "Technically. You know my parents, all up in everyone's business. But she's a hell of a guide and the old guys love her."

"I'll bet they do."

I narrow my eyes, but Angela is the one to snap, "What's that supposed to mean?"

Matt smiles into his beer. "Nothing, dear. I swear. I just meant she's a lot more appealing than Johnson or Casper. Not only her appearance," he clarifies. "She's the whole package and she probably doesn't cuss them out when they talk too loudly on her boat."

"Probably not, though I don't think they'd mind if she did."

"Well, I have a couple of girlfriends from school who've been wanting to hit the water and try for some musky. I never wanted to deal with Johnson or Casper, but Maren is a goddamn delight. Think she'd take us out?" Angela asks me.

"I'll check. But I'm sure it wouldn't be a problem. Just call me back to schedule."

ᒍᒍᒍ

By ten, I'm turning off the lights and locking up the lodge. It's a weeknight and technically the off season, so it's not uncommon for me to get home before midnight, as opposed to the height of the summer when I often close down after two A.M.

The air is unseasonably warm, still, and clear. I slip my hands into the pockets of my hooded sweatshirt and double-check the locks on the outside storage shed. It used to be a padlock,

but I convinced my parents to put a little more advanced security up. Though, to be honest, the only times anyone was
caught breaking in, it was me. Me and Kiley, most often, but
Liam and I snuck out for underage beers a few times as well.

Kiley never loved the resort the way I did. She was always
ready to move on from the Northwoods and go anywhere
else. Which was why she loved my being in the Marines, at
first. It was our ticket out. For the first decade or so of our
marriage, she was cool with it. Loved to travel, didn't mind
base living, had lots of friends and a real estate license . . . She
never seemed to mind when I was shipping out for training
missions or longer. She liked her space. When I was around,
we were together, and when I wasn't, she could do her own
thing. Not that she was unfaithful or anything. At least not
that I knew, and the shit she told me makes me think if she
was, she would have owned up to it. No, she just liked living
as a single woman, focused on her career.

Which was fine until it wasn't. I always wanted kids and I
always hoped to move back to Wisconsin one day and help
my parents with the resort and raise my family here. I'm an
only child, and, practically from birth, they talked about how
it would all come to me one day. Kiley knew, but I don't think
she ever took it seriously. Not that it mattered. I would have
given it up for her. If she told me she couldn't come back, I
would have figured out something else. My parents would
have sold the resort or passed it along to a cousin and moved
on. It wouldn't have been worth my marriage.

But that never came up. We never even made it that far. She
wanted Anders as bad as I did. It was time and we felt ready
for the next step. I was still active duty, but Kiley felt solid in
her career and had a lot of friends on base with kids. She was

confident she could pull it off. And she did for a while. So well, in fact, she wanted to try again and became pregnant with Lucy almost immediately. Almost overnight she went from wanting me to stay in the Marines as long as possible to needing me home. Needing something more—something more that would require a livable income—so I brought us all back to Wisconsin to the resort. My parents were ready to hand over some of the power and wanted to have their grandkids close by. For the first year, it was good. We adjusted, I thought, to living together as a family. Kiley set up her real estate business locally and I kept the kids with me as I slowly took over the day-to-day responsibilities of the resort.

It was pretty clear from early on, however, that Lucy had developmental delays. We were able to confirm by her second birthday that she was autistic and would require intervention and assistance. That's when Kiley decided she was out. She'd adjusted to living in Wisconsin, but the market wasn't as incredible as it was in California. She hated the cold. She didn't want to deal with the resort. Lucy wasn't the reason, but her diagnosis was the last straw in a package of a lot of fucking straws. Within the week, she'd packed her bags and moved out of the state. First to California, then to Florida after she fell in love with her new husband.

If you'd told me twenty years ago that I could be where I am, with all that I've done and everything we'd built, without Kiley, and be okay with that, I wouldn't believe you.

But it turns out it's pretty fucking easy to move on from someone who's capable of leaving their kids.

Kiley had her straw. I found mine.

The lights at the resort are few. Just enough to illuminate a safe path from one end to the other where my house sits. The kids are sleeping at my parents' tonight. Some nights, when I'm bartending, they sleep there; on others, my mom or dad will come to my place and sit up with them to try to keep a schedule for the kids. I pass by the cabins one by one, not really taking them in until I come to cabin twenty.

"Hey, stranger," Maren says from a chair on her small deck. There's a battery-powered lantern on the ground next to her and her feet are perched on the railing. I detour toward her, and she offers the second chair.

"Beer?" she asks.

I should probably get home. I'll be up before sunrise. But I'm feeling wired, so I sit and take the bottle she offers me, cracking it open and settling back in the chair.

"These chairs are shit," I say.

"I mean, I wasn't gonna say anything, but . . . yeah. They're not great."

I shift to get comfortable. "These are young people's chairs."

"Someone needs to inform management. Adirondack or nothing else."

"I'll put a note in the suggestion box."

She snickers. "Do they still have that thing?"

I shake my head. "Nah. Dad got tired of kids spitting their chewing gum in it."

Maren narrows her eyes amusedly in the flickering light. "Wasn't that you who did that?"

I shrug. "Not every time."

We sit in silence after that, and it doesn't feel weird. Just two old friends having a drink.

"Where's Rogers?" I ask her, eventually. Unhurriedly.

"Inside. He goes to bed early. Once it hits nine, he gives me a disapproving look and puts himself to bed."

"That's handy."

"Not exactly. He gets up early, too. He's got a puppy's bladder and an old man's spirit."

"How was he sitting in the cabin all day?"

Maren makes a humming noise in the back of her throat. "He's fine. I worked longer hours at the park service, though I had a neighbor boy come and walk him on the really long days."

"I bet Anders would be happy to come by and walk Rogers or even pick him up and bring him back to my place anytime you need. That kid loves dogs."

"That would be super nice. Thank you. I'll ask him."

"No, thank *you*. This way I don't have to get him a dog yet. I've been putting it off."

"Why? Having a dog up here is surprisingly easy."

"At first it was because of Lucy. Not because she doesn't like dogs, but I was wary of adding anything else to the general chaos that is our house. I guess maybe that's still the reason, though we're settling in, so maybe I should start looking. Anders has been patient."

"He's a good kid," Maren says.

"He is," I agree. "The best." And then the words just keep coming. "I worry about him feeling neglected, though, pretty much all the time. There's only one of me, and even with my parents helping, Lucy gets so much of my attention just by being her. Anders likes to play it cool, but he's angry about Kiley leaving. I tried to shelter them from it, but he heard her complain about having an autistic child. It pisses him off and makes him that much more protective of his sister. There's just a lot to unpack there and not enough minutes in the day to unpack it."

"Oof. I'm sorry, Joe. That sucks."

I sip my beer, bemused at the way all of that somehow spilled out of me at the slightest provocation from Maren. She must have some kind of magic "confide in me" gene at work. Still. I guess I needed to get it off my chest. Which is strange, because Liam tried to get me to talk when he was here, and I shut him down. I suppose the difference is Liam always tries to fix everything before taking off again. I don't need a fixer. A partner, maybe? Or even just someone to say "That sucks," I guess. Because hearing Maren say it really feels nice. "Yeah."

"No. Really. What a shitty situation. I can't begin to relate to parenting an autistic child, but having met both of your kids, I can tell you, they're awesome. Really. You're doing a great job."

"Thanks. Just don't ever come over at seven thirty in the morning when I'm trying to get Lucy dressed and Anders off to the bus. It's a disaster."

"Ha," she says, smirking behind her bottle. "I'll take your word for it."

SEVEN

Alaska

Maren

TWO DAYS LATER, I'M THINKING THIS IS PROBABLY A HUGE MISTAKE. After all, he told me *not* to come over early in the morning. But also, I'm already up, thanks to Rogers McBaby-Bladder, and if we're up, we might as well stop by and offer assistance. And anyway, I made blueberry muffins with a crunchy, sugary topping and I can't eat them all myself.

(That's a lie. I absolutely could and have, just not today.)

Also, I live four minutes away. Joe is practically my big brother and if my actual big brothers lived a four-minute walk down the road and were trying to raise two kids on their own, I would be doing exactly this.

I knock on the front door, but, although there's lots of noise inside, no one comes to answer. So I knock again, feeling stupid. If it was my brother, I'd just walk in, of course. But I don't know how Joe would feel about that, so I wait, one hand gripping Rogers's leash, the other a Tupperware of warm muffins.

Still no answer, though Lucy's crying gets louder. I bite my lip, considering. Worst case, Joe feels like this is a massive intrusion and yells at me. That would suck, but it's worth the risk. I shift the loop from the leash further up my forearm and open the screen door, ducking in. Then I test the front door. It's unlocked, so I knock again and poke only my head in before giving a whisper-shouted, "Hello?"

"Maren!" Anders looks up from where he's sitting at a tall breakfast bar, eating a bowl of marshmallow cereal and watching something on his dad's phone.

"Hey, bud, I brought someone to visit you, but now I wonder if this is a bad time."

"Rogers?!"

"Yeah," I say, putting my auntie hat all the way on and making a snap decision. "I'm gonna leave him tethered on the porch for a second. You're welcome to come visit him, but first let's make sure you're set for school. Then, you can love on Rogers if we have time before the bus arrives. That cool? I'll help. It'll go faster if we work together."

"Deal!" Anders scarfs the last of his cereal, drinking the milk directly from the bowl and placing it in the sink. I plop a muffin on a plate and direct him to sit back down. He blinks up at me. "You baked?"

"I did and it's still warm, so you'll want to eat it now. Do you want butter?"

He nods eagerly, taking an enthusiastic bite from the top and smiling. "This is delicious," he says. Or at least that's what I've managed to translate around his full mouth. I help myself to the fridge, noticing the dazzling artwork covering nearly every square inch. Brilliant coloring, abstract shapes, minute detailing . . . it's clear they were made by a child, but only because of the materials used: crayons, watercolor, and construction paper.

I pass Anders the butter before digging out a knife from the drawer and passing that along as well. "Did you create these?" I ask, gesturing to the artwork.

He shakes his head, taking another bite.

I turn to take in the designs again. "Lucy did these?"

He swallows. "Pretty good, aren't they?"

"More like incredible," I agree. "Do you have a lunch made?"

He shakes his head before picking up the knife and digging into the butter. "Dad usually has me do hot lunch when Luce wakes up on the wrong side of the bed."

I can't help the gooey feeling in my chest at his description of his sister. It's both gracious and accurate. Lucy's crying hasn't completely stopped, but she's calmed to a hiccuping whimper. From the kitchen, I can hear Joe's deep, soothing murmur. Since I don't have a ton of experience with morning meltdowns, I figure I would be most helpful sticking with Anders. I'm not trying to be in the way.

"What kind of sandwich do you like, kid? I'll make your lunch for you while you finish the muffin. What else do you need to do get ready?" Anders shrugs and looks so much like his dad when he was younger, I barely keep from laughing. "Okay. Let's see. Did you brush your teeth? Comb your hair? Is your backpack packed up? Any, um . . . permission slips?"

The kid has mercy on me and grins, peeling the paper wrapper away from his breakfast. "No permission slips or anything to sign. Dad takes care of that before bed. I'll brush my teeth after I'm done eating. And I like SunButter-and-jelly sandwiches."

I get to work, pulling ingredients out and making sure to fill both sides of the bread with a generous amount of SunButter and strawberry jam. I tuck that away and throw in a small lunch-size bag of chips, apple slices, and another muffin to go. "For a snack," I tell him. "That will leave one more for your dad and your sister."

I zip up his lunch container and hold it out, but instead of taking it, Anders surprises me with a hug around my middle that makes me say, "Oof."

"Thanks, Maren."

I don't know if he's talking about the muffins or my dog or just being around to keep him company for breakfast, but I wrap my arms around him, smoothing his blond hair. "You're welcome, kid." I look up and realize it's quiet and we have an audience.

"Maren?"

"Heyyyy," I say to Joe. "I made muffins. And, let myself in. I hope it's okay."

"She made my lunch, Dad. With extra SunButter. I'm gonna go brush my teeth, and then she said I can play with Rogers until the bus comes."

"Only if that's okay with you," I assure Joe. "I didn't mean to intrude . . . much."

Joe raises his eyebrow but it's Lucy who cries out, "Muffin!"

I instantly move toward the island, avoiding Joe's eyes. "Would you like a muffin? I can cut one up . . ."

"I got it," Joe says. His voice is strange, but not mad, or even annoyed, so I decide not to overthink it.

"All right. There's one for you, too," I tell him. "I gave Anders the last in his lunch as a snack."

"Along with extra SunButter, I hear. Thank you," he says. *"Really."*

Joe sets Lucy down on a chair and turns on a cartoon with dogs that for some reason speak with Australian accents, then hands her a muffin, whole, after removing the paper.

Then he fills a cup of water from the tap and plops a heavy-duty straw in the top.

"Learned this one the hard way. She gets so into her show, she doesn't want to lower her eyes to drink from her cup. I'll challenge her at dinnertime or when we're eating without the screens, but I don't have it in me to fight it in the mornings."

I nod my head, thinking I already heard plenty of fights for one morning. I don't blame him one bit for taking the easy out. I don't want to say something I know nothing about, though, so instead I say, "No judgment here. If anything, I feel her pain. When I'm on a tear, bingeing past seasons of *The Great British Baking Show*, I barely remember to breathe during the showstopper round. Drinking would be a disaster. My best friend Shelby bought me a bib two Christmases back. It said, DOES THIS BIB MAKE ME LOOK BALD?"

Joe stops what he's doing, his entire muffin halfway to his mouth, and blinks, and then Anders shouts, "All packed and ready! Can we play with Rogers now?"

Thank god. Get me out of here. I don't even know what I am saying. "Of course! As long as it's okay with your dad."

Joe seems to come back to himself after my awkward word vomit and nods, chewing. He swallows, opening his arms for a hug. "Have a good day at school, bud. Love you."

"Love you, too, Dad!"

I follow Anders out the door and immediately unleash Rogers, who's been taking advantage of a sunbeam warming the porch. I hold out my hand for Anders's backpack and settle on the top step to watch boy and dog play in the dewy grass.

A moment later, the door behind me opens and it's Joe. He passes me a steaming mug of coffee.

"Wasn't sure how you took it, but we only have almond milk anyway."

I take a sip and it's delicious. Rich and warm and all I need. "It's perfect." He hesitates, seeming as though he wants to say something more, but he doesn't. Anders shrieks and Rogers barks and we are quiet, but like the other night, it's not uncomfortable. We wait, side by side, me sitting, him standing; me sipping and Joe watching, before he turns and, with a low, "Thanks for this morning, Maren," goes back inside.

I smile into my coffee and whisper, "You're welcome, Joe."

꩜ ꩜ ꩜

I knew better than to assume Shane wouldn't fight for us. Up to even a few months ago, I swore I was in love with him and he was in love with me. The sex was pretty good, we had lots to talk about, both working as park rangers, and I liked how secure he was. It'd been my experience that men either were intimidated by my face or took one look at me and assumed I was vapid. Shane hadn't been like that. He listened and made me laugh and respected my opinion.

Mostly.

So I figured it was only a matter of time before he made the trip. It's a quiet Tuesday afternoon and we're in the lodge because Shane wasn't familiar enough with the resort to find my cabin. I gave him the address to put in his GPS and then spent the fifteen-minute walk over calming down and reminding myself of the litany of ways we aren't compatible as a couple. Building up my defenses, brick by brick.

Shane is a good-looking man who knows how to use what

the Lord gave him, and I don't need that temptation. I want a clean break.

Turns out it was the right choice.

"Babe, come home. I talked to Evan and Jerry. They said they could only hold on to your job for another week. Tops."

"Aren't you my boss now?" I work to keep the peevishness from my voice and channel my inner-Zen Maren.

He sighs, and I can literally feel the patronization wafting off him. "Mare. Seriously? You need to get over that. We both applied. They chose the best candidate."

He's right, which is even more irritating. "I know that, but . . . in all the times we talked about work and how I was going to apply for the position, you never said a word. Shane, you proofread my résumé. You get how shitty that is, right?"

"I figured you would be surprised."

Surprised? That's a bold take. "I'm not really a fan of surprises," I tell him.

"I noticed," he returns dryly.

Something gross slithers in my stomach and then freezes in my veins. "Hold on a minute—it didn't even cross your mind that I could have won the position, did it?"

"Babe," is all he says, but his eyes are amused, and the entire situation ticks me off.

"Listen, Shane. I'm not upset you applied for the job, and I'm not even upset that you won it over me. I'm angry that you lied to my face about it, *for months*, and I'm hurt that apparently, you didn't ever believe I was good enough. You patronized me and appeased me and because of that, you embarrassed me."

It's like the words don't even hit before he's opening his mouth again. "So we'll find you a new park. I get it, Mare. It would be weird to be your boss and probably unethical besides. We can file for a transfer."

"That would fix the problem of working together, sure, but it wouldn't fix the problem of our relationship. I don't trust you."

Shane presses forward in his chair and leans on the table, making it wobble. A lock of his stupid, shiny hair falls in his face, and I have the insane urge to stalk over to the bar and beg for a pair of scissors so I can chop it off. Which I figure is a bad sign. "Christ, Mare," he says, placating tone still in place. "Don't you think you're being a little overdramatic?" I snap out of my hair-cutting musings and tip my head to the side, narrowing my eyes.

"What part of your actions in the last several months were in any way indicative that I should trust you?"

"I asked you to marry me!" he practically shouts, and I can feel eyes on us from the direction of the bar.

"That doesn't indicate I should trust you, Shane. That tells me you had zero read of the way things were between us."

Shane sinks back in his seat, and I think maybe finally, *finally*, he is hearing me. "So now what, then?"

"I'm sorry. Really. But things have run their course between us. Honestly, this is a good thing. You deserve someone who says yes when you ask them to join their life with yours and I deserve someone who knows never to propose to me in public. We both get a do-over."

"I don't want a do-over," he says. "I've invested nearly a year into us, and you ended it over a measly proposal." He scrubs his hand through his perfect hair. "Forget the proposal, okay? Let's pretend that never happened."

"Even if I could, it wasn't just the proposal. That was the

impetus for me leaving, but I've come to realize there were so many signs prior to that. Why did you apply for that promotion, Shane?"

He blinks, startled at the change of subject. "Because I wanted a job to support us."

I'm already shaking my head. "No, I mean, what are your goals? Long term?"

"To be a politician and eventually work in state government."

I hold out a hand between us, palm up. "Yes. You want the promotion as a step up to your next position. You're climbing the ladder. You want a career in politics."

"That's the best way to implement change—"

I wave him off. "I know. You're absolutely right. But, Shane, I don't want to be a politician's wife. I don't want to wear pearls and do black-tie fundraiser events. I don't want to watch my caloric intake and have regular overpriced haircuts. I like to be outdoors. I like the Northwoods. I am passionate about nature and fishing."

"But you're so good at those fundraisers and events . . ."

I shrug. "Must be the pageants, I guess. But I don't enjoy it, and I definitely don't want to spend the rest of my life doing them."

"So that's it? You're absolutely positive?"

I don't have to think about it, or rather, I've *been* thinking about it. I'm done thinking about it. It wasn't just the job thing or the proposal, though admittedly those were what really solidified my answer. Rather, the longer we were together, the less I loved him, not more.

I stand up, reaching my hand for his, and he takes it, getting to his feet. I lean in, give him one final hug, closing my eyes at the sensation of his strong arms around me one last time, though I note I don't feel like melting into him and wonder if I ever did. That seems like something I should have noticed before now.

"I'm sure. Absolutely positive," I whisper in his ear, and I press my mouth to his cheek in a dry kiss. "Take care of yourself, Shane. Congrats on your promotion and best of luck in all your endeavors."

He holds me tight for a long moment and I think to myself that it's nice, but not nice in the way that means I want to make up, accept his ill-timed proposal, and drive back to Michigan where I can start making babies and decorating his home and hosting cocktail parties.

Not nice like *that*. But usually my breakups are a shit show. So maybe I'm grateful he asked me to marry him. I didn't know the answer until he was on his knee in front of me.

EIGHT

Alone

Maren

WHEN I STARTED DRINKING AFTER SHANE LEFT, DONNA WAS THE bartender. She hooked me up with a classic Wisconsin Bloody Mary that was half vodka, half charcuterie, and just a splash of spicy tomato juice. The bar was practically empty but for the occasional bait, fishing license, or gas fill-up request, so we spread out and Donna let me pick whatever songs I wanted for the jukebox.

"Oh, play something by the Chicks next, will you?" my best friend Lorelai requests. She and Shelby are joining me in my day-drinking via FaceTime. Thankfully, the lodge has decent Wi-Fi. My phone is tilted on its side and leaning up against an empty glass. Lorelai is drinking a glass of high-priced chardonnay that her fiancé Craig poured her before blowing me a scruffy long-distance kiss and going back to work at the record studio he owns.

Donna hops over from behind the bar and clicks a few buttons on the music. "You got it, Mizz Jones. What else?"

"Hm," Shelby says, sipping from her glass of orange juice, with a straw. She's six months pregnant with her and Cameron's first baby, so no alcohol. She was able to take the afternoon off from filming for the reality home-renovation show she and Cameron star on. Honestly, Cameron seemed relieved to have an excuse to ban her. While she was getting settled, he confided that she was on a mission to wallpaper everything. Considering Shelby's role was generally in the realm of carpentry and furniture making, this was alarming on many levels.

"Hm?" I prod, biting into a pickle with a loud crunch.

"I think I feel like some Heart. Do you have any Heart over there, Donna?"

Donna perks up and I can already tell Shelby has won her over. Being the mom of one uber-masculine son, it seems Donna has been missing out on the female bonding. We're giving her a fill of all she's missed this afternoon, between my breakup, Shelby's pregnancy, and Lorelai's wedding planning. The older woman picks a few more selections and then scoots back behind the bar, shimmying to "Alone" by Heart.

"Hey, Donna, you guys still do karaoke?" I ask her around my pickle.

"During summers, sure. It's not on the schedule, but we have some long-timers that spot Joe across the bar and immediately make a request. It's a good moneymaker, so we don't mind. We keep a couple of mics on hand in case."

"Joe is Donna's son," I explain to my best friends. "He was besties with Liam."

"Big brother Liam?" Shelby perks up. She might've had a tiny unrequited crush on my older brother. All of them, even, at one point or another.

"Yep. And back in the day, Joe used to always get requests to sing on karaoke night when he was bartending." I'm feeling oddly flushed, just thinking about it. Back then, teenaged and tanned Josiah Cole mixing drinks and singing to eighties classic rock was my early sexual awakening. "The man could belt like Bon Jovi. Even my thirteen-year-old emo-girl heart would skip when he sang 'I'll Be There for You.'"

"Really, Jig. Bon Jovi, eh?"

I straighten on my stool, caught in Joe's teasing gaze. He smirks and passes me a dog leash, from which Rogers is tethered. "As long as he stays out from behind the bar," he warns, gesturing to my extremely happy dog who immediately plants his butt on the floor next to my stool.

"Rogers!" my best friends shout together. I pull the phone down and bring it close to my boy, whose tail wags hard, whacking against the floor with an echoing *thud, thud, thud.* The two of them cover him in baby talk while I hold the phone at my waist. I reach for my drink and pluck the beef stick from it, taking a bite. My stomach growls, reminding me I didn't have lunch today, since Shane showed up.

"Bloody Marys, Heart, and I'm assuming your best friends . . . Everything okay?" Joe asks in a low voice while Shelby and Lorelai continue to coo.

"My ex came for a visit."

"From Michigan?" His blond brows raise. "That's a long drive for a visit."

"Yeah," I say on a sigh. "He thought maybe if I saw him, I might change my mind about not marrying him."

Joe's lips twitch, amused, and I find it's not nearly as annoying as when Shane did it, probably because even though he's practically my big brother and has known me since I was in diapers, so far Joe hasn't been patronizing about this. Other things, sure—but not this. Believe me, I'd have noticed.

He crosses his arms over his broad chest. "Did you?"

"What do you think?"

He shakes his head, then pulls out the jar of pickles and refreshes my garnishes. "Heart isn't exactly wedding-planning music."

"Nope," I say, immediately going for the pickle.

I raise my phone and place it back on the bar.

"Sorry, ladies. It's been a real cute afternoon, but I need to get back to my hubby," Donna says, waving goodbye to my friends on the screen. She wraps me in a half hug and says, "You'll find someone better, hon."

"I'm not sure I could find anyone better than Rogers," I tease. Donna gives her tinkling laugh, and it warms me inside out. She's not my mom, but she's the next best thing. "Thank you for this afternoon, Donna. It meant a lot to have you here."

"Of course, honey. I'm happy I was able to be here." Donna leaves after another round of cuddles with a spoiled Rogers and I turn back to my friends and Joe.

"So, ladies." Joe presses his hands to the bar, spreading them wide and speaking into the phone as if Lorelai and Shelby were on stools next to me. "What'll it be?"

I watch as my best friends take in the vision of Joe in totality, and I try to imagine him from their perspective. He's not a bearded giant like Cameron Riggs, but he's not a lanky-artist type like Craig, either. Josiah Cole is a man all his own. With thick, wavy blond hair and smooth-shaven cheeks that reveal two dimples. He's wearing a navy Henley that brings out the crystal blue of his eyes, with the sleeves pushed up past his forearms, and a pair of well-fitting jeans. Simple. Masculine. No-nonsense. Handsome in his own understated way.

"Um." Shelby blinks. Lorelai has a calculating look about her as she leans closer to the screen.

Maybe not so understated.

"Joe, tell us what Mare was like as a kid. Shelby knew her from beauty pageants, but I only know her as park ranger material."

If Joe is flummoxed by my famous besties, he doesn't show it. Instead, he pours himself a beer from the tap and shifts, one hip pressed to the bar between us. "Hm. What can I tell you about Jig?"

"First of all, what are you calling her?" Shelby asks, leaning even closer around her belly and glass of OJ.

I speak up, rolling my eyes to my friends. "Jig. As in the fishing lures . . . jigs."

"*That's* what Maren was like as a kid," Joe tells them. "She was the most fishing-obsessed person, male or female, old or young, any of us knew. Aside from maybe Old Man Fost, who took her out on his boat all the time."

"So she was outdoorsy? That's not a stretch."

"Always outside, always chasing after her older brothers, and always covered in dirt because if she wasn't fishing, she was digging for worms."

I shrug. "Nothing walleye love more than a fat and juicy nightcrawler. I stand by that."

"And this is the girl who kicked my ass in pageant after pageant," Shelby mutters into her screen.

"That was all my mom's doing," I tell her. "She was determined to have her girly-girl after three rambunctious asshole boys. And there was nothing more girly-girl than being crowned Little Miss Michigan. It's probably why I went so hard every summer with the fishing. I finally broke free of the endless cycle of pretty dresses, sunless tanning, and hair teased out to here," I say, holding my hand well above my head.

"What about when she got older?" Lorelai asks. "Teen Maren?"

Joe screws up his face, thinking. "That's harder to say. I'm five years older, so by the time she was a teen, I'd graduated and was in the Marines, getting married. Everything I know I got from Liam, and it was mostly grousing about his friends perving on her YouTube channel and stuff."

"That's not true!" I say, cutting him off.

His eyes glitter, challenging me. "How do you know? I'll call him right now and confirm it."

"Oh, please. His friends did not watch my channel."

"We all watched your channel, Jig."

"What?!" I screech, hopping to my feet.

The change is instantaneous, and Joe goes from calm and collected to a bright cherry red. "Well, everyone but me, I mean."

"You said 'we'!"

"You absolutely said 'we,'" Lorelai confirms with a giant cat-that-ate-the-canary grin that practically splits her stunning face.

"I meant *they*," Joe tries.

I move around the bar and step up into his space, looking him in the eye and jabbing my finger in his hard chest. "Tell me you didn't watch my channel."

"I maybe saw it once or twice," he hedges, his face growing redder by the moment.

"Josiah Cole, you big fat liar. You watched my channel?"

"Relax, kid," he eventually scoffs. "It's not like it was a sex tape. I watched a few episodes, okay? It was nice. I missed home. I could watch a girl I knew, safe at home, fishing on my lake, and it felt like there was a good reason to be missing home."

"Oh," I say, feeling my stomach squirm and flip at his explanation. "That's a good reason."

"Yeah, I know," he says, defensively.

"Thank you for telling me. That's really nice, actually."

We're close again. Too close. This time, I know it's my doing. I'm the one who rounded the bar and got in his space and jabbed my fingers at his (very) solid chest.

He's looking at my mouth. Which makes me want to look at his. So I do. And I watch his nice lips wrap around the words, "That's good."

"Good?"

"Really good," says Shelby from the phone.

"Super-duper good," Lorelai says with a smirk.

I clear my throat, feeling unsteady, and travel back around to the other side of the bar just as a couple of guys walk up to order a drink from Joe. That's my cue. I reach for my dog. "I should probably get home. I missed lunch."

I pick up my phone in one hand and Rogers's leash in the other, before waving over my shoulder at Joe.

"Aw, I wasn't done talking to Joe the singing bartender," Lorelai pouts once I've reentered the sunshiny outdoors.

"Joe the exceedingly attractive bartender, you mean," Shelby says. "How come you've never mentioned Joe? No wonder you decided to stay up there and ditch Michigan."

"Oh, hush," I say into my phone, checking my peripheries that I'm alone out here. "You know why I decided to stay and it has nothing to do with Joe. Though, off the record, I agree, he's extremely attractive."

"I said exceedingly," Shelby reminds me. "But I'll allow *extremely* as long as the record shows you're the one who said it."

"He's hot," I admit with a huff. "Obviously. And he's also

a single dad with two kids and a resort to run. And also Liam warned me off him already. Like on the first day, within the first five minutes, so that's that."

"Boo, Liam!" Lorelai and Shelby shout in unison and I work to turn down the volume while laughing at the sour expression on my best friends' faces.

"I know. Total buzzkill. But it's okay. I have a lot on my plate right now and besides, I think we could both use a friend."

Lorelai taps her chin with her pointer finger while tilting her head to the side. "Hm. I wonder if your version of *just friends* will work better than mine and Craig's."

Secretly, way, *way* down deep inside tucked somewhere between my heart and my vagina, I wonder if it will, too.

NINE

Every Little Thing She Does Is Magic

Joe

"DID YOU SEE THE GUY, THOUGH?" LIAM ASKS ME. "PRETTIER than Mare. That shit ain't right."

I snort into the phone speaker and complete my turn into the hardware store in town before putting my truck in park and settling back in my seat. "I didn't. Mom did, though, and according to her, he looked like Rock Hudson."

"Who?"

"An actor. Died . . . Never mind," I tell him. "She also said he was too smooth, and your sister didn't seem all that broken up about it, which she figured meant it was a good thing she showed him the road back to Michigan."

"Yeah. I guess. I just don't know what she was doing dicking around with him for the entire past year."

"I imagine she didn't think she was dicking around." I haven't known Maren super well until recently, but I've never gotten the impression that she was the kind to play around with someone's feelings. "She loved him is my guess."

I can hear Liam's scoff over the speaker. "She doesn't even know what love is; she's a kid."

"Bro. I hate to be the one to tell you, but she's not that much younger than us," I say, glad my best friend can't see the way my face burns. But *fuck*. She's not. "And we both got married barely out of college."

"Yeah, and what did we know? I lucked out, but you got a raw deal with Kiley, man."

Maybe I did, maybe I didn't. I've never been super comfortable with anyone in my circle going on the offense against Kiley. Yeah, things didn't work out, but she's not a bad person. Or even a not-good person. Unfortunately, though, Liam saw me through my worst. He was there when Kiley left. He took the first flight out and stayed for two weeks, holding my shit together and making sure we ate. He, more than anyone, knows how bad it got.

But that was me then, *and* it was over two years ago. "Point is, Maren is old enough to do what she wants with her life, whether that is fall in love with guys that look like Rock Hudson or break up with them in front of their families."

"Did I tell you she puked on his shoes?"

I grin at the image of put-together Maren heaving her guts all over Rock Hudson's shoes. "Yeah, I remember you saying something like that."

"I have to admit, that shit was hilarious."

Even though I agree a thousand percent, it feels unfair to Maren to say so. "Probably not for your sister."

"Nah." A pause, then, "I should call her to check in again."

"You should," I tell him, removing my keys from the ignition and preparing to hang up. "But maybe don't mention the ex or the puking . . . or the job thing," I add.

"What am I supposed to ask her about, then?" Liam asks, sounding aggrieved, and I can't help but smirk at his familiar tone. Liam is really good at two things: showing up when you need him the most and giving you shit when you need it the least.

I try to keep the humor out of my tone when I suggest, "Maybe just text her. Or send her flowers or something. Send it to the lodge, and I'll get them out to her."

"I can do that."

"All right, man. I gotta run. We have a shower leak in cabin four and I need to get the parts."

"Okay. Just . . . well. Thanks for being there for Maren," he says. "I'm glad she has family close."

"Yeah. Happy to do it." I end the call and hop out of my truck, slamming the door closed and crossing the small lot. When I pull open the door, a tinkling bell rings out, announcing my arrival, and I know better than to travel the stalls of a hometown store. Instead, I pause, shifting my weight and inhaling the overwhelming perfume of fertilizer. A moment later, Bryce Callahan makes his way to the front, offering a friendly smile.

I went to school with Bryce, but he was a few years behind me. I never knew him all that well, but he seemed like a nice kid, if a little strange. Not in the way that he had his quirks. Hell, we all did. I just always felt like he was too familiar and he really, really liked to be important. His uncle owned this store and was a fixture in town, but Bryce took over when he came back after college. He's a collector of sorts. For example, his giant display of pictures on the walls with various low-key celebs he's met at different Comic-Cons and things. I was never into fandoms or cosplay myself, but that was mostly because I was too busy overseas trying not to die. I get the appeal, I guess, though I've never really felt comfortable with the whole "take a picture with a celeb just because they're famous" thing. Celebrities are just people whose job put them on the screen or in our ears. Like Maren's friends Shelby and Lorelai . . . I know they're famous. I'm not *that* removed from pop culture. But seeing them on the screen of her phone yesterday, they felt very normal to me. Meddling, nosy, supportive, funny, and very normal. They loved Maren and Maren loved them.

Anyway, all of this is in my mind as I pull out my list and pass it to Bryce, trying to ignore the urge to peruse his fan wall.

"Plumbing issues at the resort?" he asks, his eyes skimming the items from behind thick lenses.

"Small one that I'm trying to keep that way. Do you have everything in stock or do I need to special order?"

Bryce nods once, quick. "Should be on the shelf. I'll check the back for these washers, but I just got in a shipment. Haven't had a chance to put it all out yet. Give me a few and I'll put it together."

Nothing better than a hometown hardware store. The options are limited, but the service can't be beat. There are bigger box-store options, but they're another twenty minutes down the road. I'll make the drive when I don't want the hassle of someone else picking out my things, but this isn't a job with design preference in mind. It's not worth offending Callahan by insisting on picking out my own washers.

I settle my hip against the counter and lose my battle with the pictures, scanning the framed photos behind the checkout. Bryce with some giant Viking-looking dude, dressed in a medieval getup, both standing in front of a curtain in an obvious photo op. Bryce shaking the hand of some kind of alien-looking thing with tentacles coming out of its chin. Bryce dressed as Captain Hook, standing with another man dressed in a higher-quality Captain Hook costume.

My eyes continue their casual appraisal of Callahan's personal Wall of Fame when my gaze snags on a familiar form and unease slithers up my spine.

Maren.

It's not just the picture. Like I told her the other day, I've seen her videos, and it's clear this was taken at the height of her Musky Maren days. It's at least a decade old, if not older. Maren's hair is longer, with blond streaks, and she's got that photogenic beauty-queen smile affixed to her glossy lips. She's sitting behind the table with her logo on it, while Bryce is crowding as close as he can over it, toward her, placing their heads together. Bryce is pink-faced and looks seconds from wetting himself. Maren looks like a doe caught in the high beams.

Which would maybe be okay if it wasn't for the fact that I know her picture wasn't there two weeks ago. Or the month before that. In fact, I've never seen the photo on his wall. I don't know where it's been the last decade and maybe I don't want to know, but I do know it's up there now—when Maren just showed back up in town—and it doesn't feel right.

Does he know she's here? Did she come in here? It would make sense, being it's the only hardware store for miles and she's doing heavy renovations on Fost's place. Did she see the picture? Or did he put it up after seeing her?

Christ, I hope she didn't see it. I can't imagine her feeling comfortable having her picture up on Callahan's weird collection wall.

"All right. We lucked out. The washers were in stock,"

Bryce says, unloading his arms of my requested items onto the countertop and beginning to ring them up.

"Great." After a beat, while he's sliding my items across his scanner, I decide to straight-up ask about the picture. "Hey, man, is that a new photo you've added to your collection? I don't think I've seen that one before."

He doesn't even look back or play dumb about which one I'm asking about. Instead, the fucker gives a shit-eating grin and shakes his head. "Nope. That's one from my personal collection. I've had it at home for years, but I saw her, here," he says meaningfully, waggling his brows, "a few weeks ago, and I wanted to surprise her with it when she comes back."

"You saw her?" I'm trying to play it cool, to keep my voice casual, like I would back when I was interrogating civilians in the service, but my jaw clenches tight around the words.

"Yeah," he says, tossing the last item in the bag. "It's been years, but she looks even better. She's back, man. Musky Maren. I bet she's making more videos. You haven't seen her around the resort? I thought she used to spend time with her family there as a kid . . ."

I don't know how to respond. This guy knows she came here with her family? I wasn't around in the Musky Maren days, but she kept that personal stuff on lockdown. I knew it was my home flowage, but her viewers didn't. Further, the resort is miles outside of town and one of dozens of others. Yeah, we are a successful resort, but it's not like anyone would have access to information on our guests, unless they dug.

This guy had clearly done some digging. Hell, she'd straight-up said she didn't want anyone advertising Musky Maren, using the name, or spreading the word she was in town. She'd made it seem like it was because she might return to work as a park ranger, but what if there was more to it? We'd teased Liam about his little sister being a babe with a YouTube channel and even joked about the guys who were probably slobbering all over her videos, but this being the reality suddenly feels very unfunny.

I decide in that instant to play dumb with Callahan. Whatever is going on, I don't want him to know she's still around or that I know where she is. I am suddenly very, very relieved my dad is such a meddler and convinced her to stay in the cabin at our resort. He unknowingly made her that much safer. Jesus.

I tap my debit on the card reader and wait for it to process and for my receipt to spit out. "Nah, Bryce. Haven't seen her in a long time. You sure you really saw her? Well," I rush on, not letting him speak, "good for you, man." I reach for my bags and turn for the door. "See you around."

And I get the hell out of there.

TEN

Secret Garden

Joe

I NEED TO ASK MAREN ABOUT BRYCE CALLAHAN, BUT I DON'T know how. Another week passes before I find the right moment. During that time I see her almost every day. Either in the mornings when she comes and hangs out with Anders, using Rogers as a transparent excuse to help my son feel cared for while leaving me space to focus on Lucy, or in between guided tours where she charms old cusses with her bright smile and big brain.

So between my kids and the off-season guests always loitering around the lodge, I can't ever seem to find the right time to pull her aside. Part of the problem is that I have a gut feeling bringing up Callahan is gonna suck and Maren seems so happy these days. Genuinely relaxed in a way she wasn't when she first showed up—planning to bury herself in bait shop renovations—and I want her to stay that way. I feel like I owe her that much for all she's managed to do for my kids in such a short time.

The opportunity to get her alone arrives on an unseasonably warm Saturday—the last Saturday in September. It being a weekend, Angela offered to come in and man the bar, and my parents purchased tickets months ago to see "*Encanto* Live" with my kids. I packed the pair up for an entire day, including spare clothes and noise-canceling headphones for Lucy, and dropped them off early this morning. They plan to be back by dinner, but in case it's too much stimulation for Lucy, they have a backup plan to stay at a hotel in Green Bay if they need a quiet place to crash. Anders packed his swimsuit, so I know which version he is secretly hoping for. I make a mental note to take him swimming if it doesn't work out this time.

The kid deserves a break as much as any of us.

At any rate, this is why I'm knocking on cabin twenty at ten A.M., my own bag packed for a day out on the water, hoping I can talk Maren into taking a day off from her renovations.

She answers with a surprised grin and steps out onto the porch, allowing Rogers to dance around our legs and demand his own greeting.

I scrub his head, saying hi for probably longer than is necessary, trying to find the words. I've gone back and forth about this and still haven't come up with a sure answer on whether "Come out on my boat for the day" qualifies as a big-brother-adjacent activity or not. If Liam were here, there would be no question. Or, like, if my kids were around. But only the two of us?

All I know is I want to spend the day on the boat with her. I want to see her relaxed. Like the time on her deck and the mornings on mine. I crave her version of calm. I don't know what that means.

"What can I do for you, Joe?" Straight to the point.

I decide to answer the same way.

"I'm headed out on the MasterCraft. Wanted to know if you'd want to come?"

I know in an instant I have her attention. "The Master-Craft?"

"It's supposed to be nice out, maybe the last really nice day of the year. Angela is tending bar and I have the day ahead of me. No kids, so no pontoon. I feel like cruising. Rogers can come."

"Oh, I wouldn't want him to scratch . . ."

"She's already scratched to hell and over a decade old, but she still purrs like new. Rogers deserves to feel the wind in his hair, too."

She pulls a face, as though considering. Faker. "I was gonna work on the bathroom floor today, but if you really think it's the last nice day . . ."

"Get your suit on. I'll wait."

"Should I pack us some sandwiches? A cooler?"

"Already done. Just a suit and sunscreen if you want to use your own. I think there's some organic, nontoxic baby SPF 360 or something on the boat already, but I'll warn you it's like painting yourself in tar and waiting for the feathers to arrive."

Maren laughs out loud and I feel it all the way down my body. I don't want to even think of how long it's been since I've made someone laugh, let alone a woman. And I really don't want to think about how much I like it.

She leaves me on the porch with Rogers and runs inside to change. Minutes later, she shuffles out in a pair of cut-offs and a loose-fitting long-sleeved white linen top. Her feet are bare except for a pair of flip-flops, but her toes have bright-pink polish that matches the bright-pink swimsuit strings tied around the back of her neck. Her reddish-brown hair is back in a simple ponytail that swings behind her and she's wearing a pair of sunglasses on top of her head. She's somehow also packed a tote bag with a towel and some kind of dog toy for Rogers, thrown over one shoulder, and filled a giant water bottle that rattles with ice cubes.

I've obviously gotten too used to my kids' timeline because this feels miraculously quick.

"I'm ready!"

"Okay. I already filled up the tank this morning. She's parked at the lodge."

We walk down the path toward the lodge, taking in the nice weather. I studiously avoid glancing toward the big bay windows when we get near. Being an owner, I always get some attention at the resort. My parents and I are the ones everyone knows, and while we like it that way, on days like today, when I'm off, I prefer to just be me. Not to mention, I don't even want to think about what Angela will say if she sees me taking my best friend's little sister out for a solo cruise.

The sun is already beating down, though it's not as intense as, say, July. Rogers trots between us, tongue lolling and tail wagging as we make our way down the dock toward the boat. I wasn't kidding about how old my boat is. It was once top of the line, but my parents don't water-ski anymore and it's easier to take Lucy out on the pontoon when we play on the water. I swallow back the usual surge of guilt, thinking about Anders and how he should be comfortable on water skis by now. I just haven't had a chance to take him out and teach him. We'd need someone to drive the boat while someone spots and . . .

"Hello, gorgeous," Maren interrupts my self-flagellation, walking up to the MasterCraft and rubbing a palm against the faded blue fiberglass, affectionately. I hop in, setting the boat to rocking. Maren passes me her tote and water bottle and then dips into an easy squat, picking up a wriggling Rogers. I hold out my arms and take him from her, placing him on his feet between the seats. Before I can hold out a hand to Maren, she hops in behind me like the pro she is.

"Where to?"

"I thought we'd cruise and then park on Evans Lake for a while."

Mare nods. "I like it. There's sure to be traffic today with everyone trying to make the most out of the weather. Evans is tucked away."

I settle in the captain's chair and turn over the engine, backing us out while Maren takes care of the ropes that tether us to the dock. I watch her expertly wind and then stow them so they don't get tangled, before settling on the chair next to me and reaching for her water and taking a sip.

I ease us past the no-wake zone and Maren slips her sunglasses down over her eyes just as I gun the engine. We cruise for a while. Evans Lake is on the other side of the flowage, through and around bogs, islands, bridges, and no-wake zones that delineate the various resorts along our way. Maren eases back in her chair, arm outstretched and dancing in the wind, her ponytail whipping around. Rogers settles easily between us on the floor, along for the ride.

And it's nice. Really, really nice.

I ease up on the engine once we hit Evans Lake and am glad to see we basically have the entire thing to ourselves. We cruise the shoreline and I keep one eye on the depth finder even though I know these waters like the back of my hand. Once I find a spot deep enough where we can float but shallow enough

I can toss an anchor, I cut the engine. I fiddle with the anchor and Maren turns on the radio, finding us some Jimmy Buffett.

Then she cracks open a beer from the cooler and removes her shirt and shorts, stepping out of them with those bare bright-pink polished toes like it's no big deal. Because it's not. We're adults who have known each other our entire lives on a boat on a lake and it's hot outside. This is the exact situation you should take off your clothes in.

Which is why I don't understand why the fuck my face is burning like a kid who just got caught watching porn by his mom. I continue to mess with the anchor far, far longer than is necessary, tugging on the rope and pretending to tighten the knot at the base. I fuck around so long, Maren asks, "You need help?" And starts to head my way.

"No!" I practically shout, before turning it into a self-conscious laugh, clearing my throat. "Sorry. No. No need to walk over here. I got it. There was just . . . something. On the . . . like a weed, or . . . I thought it was a fish."

"A fish?"

"Or something. It was nothing." I step down and move past her, avoiding staring at her curves, of which there are plenty, and also why are they so perfect? I have seen Maren in a bathing suit before. When she was a teenager. I don't remember her having curves then. Definitely no swells or swoops and absolutely zero dips. Now there are all of those in all of the right places.

Holy fuck this was a mistake. Liam will murder me.

"Can you help put this on my back?" Maren asks, holding out a bottle of SPF 35. I notice it's also organic and nontoxic, but when I rub it between my palms, it's smooth and slippery.

Great.

"I'll do you next," she offers.

I swallow and grunt my agreement somewhere in the back of my throat.

She turns, catching her pony up in one hand and twisting it in her fingers. Which makes me think of twisting it in *my* fingers as I sink into her from behind.

I shut my eyes, shaking the thought from my brain. *Liam.* Think of Liam. And her other brothers, Kyle and Brett. Hell, think of Mrs. Laughlin. That helps, and I start to spread the sunscreen over the soft skin of her shoulders, down her spine, along her trim waist and across the dimples in the small of her back. I manage all of this while fighting off the hard-on to end all hard-ons, and even manage to collect myself enough so that when she spins to face me again, smiling gratefully, I pass her the sunscreen and remove my own shirt.

"My turn."

ELEVEN

A Sorta Fairytale

Maren

"MY TURN."

I will not perv on my big brother's best friend. I will not perv on my big brother's best friend. I will not perv on my big brother's best friend . . .

Even though Liam is easily thirteen hours away. Even though I'm almost thirty-four and Joe's thirty-eight so it's childish to classify him as my big brother's anything. Even though he's a hot single dad who used to be in the Marines and runs every morning to maintain his sanity but also has a pretty stellar physique for someone who drinks beer and eats a regular diet of leftover bar food.

Even though I accidentally saw him tangled up with his then-girlfriend-now-ex-wife behind the storage shed the summer I turned fourteen, and while I didn't understand what I was looking at at the time, her soft whimpers imprinted on my brain for eternity and basically became the blueprint for my sexual awakening.

Even though there's . . . *all of that* . . . I still won't perv on Josiah Cole. He deserves better than that. He can't help any of those things and he doesn't need me drooling on him. So I swallow down my lust and ignore the recurring tingle in my nipples and spread the damn sunscreen all over the solid planes of his muscular back, making sure to be thorough and totally platonic about it.

Mostly. I probably do a shitty job hiding the flush in my cheeks and the racing in my heart, but his back is turned and anyway it's pretty hot out.

After sunscreen is applied all around, Joe grabs himself a beer from the cooler and we both move to the front of the boat to spread out on the deck. The lulling sound of the waves slapping against the side of the boat has me closing my eyes and leaning back against the window. I soak in the vitamin D and feel my entire body melt into the cushion. I'm so relaxed, in fact, I have to remind myself to inhale and exhale, but I don't mind because it's literally my only responsibility for the time being.

No one else exists for me here, except of course the man next to me and the dog panting happily between us.

We don't talk, we don't move. We just lie there and float, listening to Jimmy Buffett sing about a pirate looking back at forty, and sipping our warming beers. An hour goes by, and I barely notice. The best part is Joe doesn't, either. Something about seeing him so still, so quiet, so content, makes me feel better than I have in a long time. He's always moving, rushing between his kids and the resort guests and his parents. Everyone demands so much from him, and he doesn't complain. He does it all with a teasing grin and a patient temperament.

He gives and gives and gives and I want him to take for once. Take time and sunshine and beer and Jimmy Buffett. With a start, I realize I want to take care of him. Badly.

Not fix him or change him or anything like that. Just . . .

take care of him. He takes care of everyone else; maybe for the short time I'm here, I can give him some peace in return.

"Mare?"

"Hm?" I ask, not bothering to open my eyes.

"I have to ask you something, but I don't want to make a big deal out of it."

At this, I let my head fall to the side and open one eye, flipping down my sunglasses against the brightness. "Okay?"

"This is going to sound weird, but have you been to the hardware store in town? Callahan's?"

Thoughts of relaxation fly out of my head, and I jerk to sitting.

"Why?"

"Fuck," Joe says softly. "Fuck," he repeats, just as quiet. "That's exactly the response I was hoping you *wouldn't* have."

My brain feels sluggish, but it turns over his words and I sigh. "I'm okay. Why are you asking?"

"Because I saw a picture of you up on Bryce Callahan's weird-ass collection board in his store the other morning and when I asked him about it, he was excited to tell me Musky Maren was back in town."

I drop my head with a whimper, pulling my knees to my chest. "Was it a new picture?"

"Not new. Though he just put it up in the store . . . Said it was in his house before."

"Gross," I whisper.

"Yeah. I get those vibes, too. Is there more to the story I should know?"

"Depends," I say, irritated. Though I don't know who I'm irritated at: Joe, Bryce, myself? "Who else did you tell?"

"No one, and if you're asking me about Liam, still no one.

I swear. Though, Liam did call me the same morning. It was before I went into the store."

I lay my chin on my knees and stare out at the waves. "There's not a lot to tell, really. Bryce became a little . . . *fixated* on me back in the day. He'd show up at my live events and send me emails through my website. He wasn't the only one. You said yourself, lots of guys watched my videos and not all of them cared about catching musky.

"But Bryce . . . well, he would show up at events that he'd have to fly to get to, and he started talking about how he'd . . . get off to my videos. He would ask me out whenever he saw me and I'd see him taking pictures on his phone from the line and it just felt . . . like *more*. You know? More even than the stuff I'd gotten used to from the typical weirdos."

"Did you get a restraining order? Call the police?"

"For what?" I ask, lifting my gaze and narrowing my eyes at Joe. His jaw is clenched, and I can see a tick in the muscle there, but I press on, getting mad myself and feeling the usual sense of helplessness that Bryce Callahan and others instilled in me back then and now. "He never hurt or threatened me. He never followed me to my car or showed up at my house. He never emailed my personal email, and he never called my phone. He showed up at public events. He watched videos I intentionally released online. He sent messages through my official website."

"He knew you came to the resort with your family. I know you didn't put that shit on your videos, Maren."

I inhale sharply at his words and his accusatory tone. "Are you blaming me?"

His eyes widen and he straightens. "No. Absolutely not. I'm sorry," he apologizes instantly. "I'm mad that you went through that. You must have been terrified."

"I was. Which is why I discontinued the account and moved out of state. I accepted the job in Michigan and left Musky Maren behind. I made all my social media private until just a few years ago, and even then, I didn't post anything tying me to her. I closed down my website . . . All of it. Gone."

"Did it help?"

"One hundred percent. Until I went into town a few weeks back and ran into Bryce at the hardware store. He acted like it was Christmas. Asked me if I was married and wanted to know if I'd be around. I told him . . ." I feel my face heat at the memory. "Well, I let him believe maybe I was married, and I ran out of there. I completely freaked out. Clearly there is some residual trauma to work out, but I felt like I handled it. I haven't been back. God," I say with a groan. "I can't believe he put my picture up."

Joe winces. "At least it was an old picture. I pretended I hadn't seen you and didn't know what he was talking about, so there's a good chance he doesn't know you're still here. For all he knows, you left town weeks ago with your, um, husband?"

Out of the corner of my vision, I see his lips twitch. I press my lips together, annoyed at his teasing. But it is kind of funny. "I told you, I panicked."

"Does this fake husband have a name? What's his job? I bet it's something really masculine like a firefighter or a construction worker."

"Are you just naming characters from the Village People?"

"I was actually thinking of male stripper characters."

A stream of giggles erupts past my lips, and I let out a very uncool snort.

"Oh god, Jig, did you just snort?"

I snort again, erupting in more giggles. "Yes!"

"I don't know whether that's cute or disgusting."

"Fuck you!" I cry, smacking his firm bicep. "It's adorable."

"Whatever you have to tell yourself."

And I realize he's done it again. He's taken care of me—made me feel better, safer, somehow.

"Want to swim?" he asks, moving to the anchor.

"Yeah," I tell him. "Let's find a beach and let Rogers run for a while."

"Your wish, my command."

♪♪♪

We spend the rest of the day on the shore, waist-deep in cool lake water, drinking beer and talking like the kind-of old friends we are. I laugh more than I've ever laughed in my entire life and that includes anytime I've been with Shelby and Lorelai. It's as easy as breathing, being with Joe. We swim, we throw the dummy for Rogers, we climb back in the boat and nap. We jump in the water when it gets too hot, and bake on the deck when the clouds cover the sun and it gets too cold in the lake. We eat ham-and-cheese sandwiches for lunch and stop on the way home at a pet-friendly bar with outside seating for dinner after Joe gets a phone call from his parents saying they're keeping the kids later. Everyone treats Joe like a long-lost friend, and we spend too long drinking all the free drinks people buy us, so we end up having to sit on the boat at the dock watching the sun set and drive home with our lights on in the dark after we sober up.

It's the best day I've had in a really, really long time.

Another thing he's given me.

TWELVE

You've Got a Friend

Maren

OF ALL FOST'S THINGS, I'VE LEFT HIS BEDROOM DRESSER TO tackle last because it feels too personal. Especially knowing he moved to cabin fourteen the last few years of his life. In my initial search, I cracked open the drawers and saw they were overflowing with personal items. Fost didn't have any family and this is all technically mine, but part of me wanted to toss the whole thing, leaving its secrets intact.

But that feels disrespectful to someone who meant the world to me.

Instead, I amble over to Fost's place, crunching through leaves, Rogers and a six-pack of Fost's favorite beer in tow, on a sunny Sunday afternoon in early October.

I let us in, cracking open the heavy curtains I'd picked up recently, and opening a few windows as well. It's chilly, but the lingering smell of dust and disuse still covers the walls. I might be sad, but I'm not a masochist.

I put some Carole King on, because Fost told me she sang straight from the soul and he dug that. I crack open a beer, still cold from the lodge, and grimace as the first sip goes down.

Gross.

The second is moderately better.

As Carole croons, I make my way to the bedroom. It's really only the top drawer that's full of personal items. The others contained clothing that was donated to Goodwill ages ago, according to Donna. But the top drawer is where he kept his life.

I take a deep breath and pull it open, spending the next hour sipping disgusting cheap beer and letting Carole King and Fost make me cry. There are gift receipts, ticket stubs, and birthday cards. An address book, overflowing with loose papers stuffed between the bound pages. Photos upon photos upon photos. Some are black-and-white, some are sepia, and some are full color. A few have me in them at various points of my childhood . . . toothless, sunburnt, all legs, and moody. Every stage captured in a neat little stack. I get to the end of the pile and there's a piece of loose-leaf paper, folded in thirds. I recognize his familiar scrawl.

(please add to will and testament)

For Maren Laughlin,
  You brought this old man sunshine in his twilight years. I'll never be able to thank you for that, but maybe this will be the push you've been dreaming of. Be your own boat daddy.
Love,
Fost

I laugh so hard I cry, and then I cry some more.

♩ ♩ ♩

Six years before

I've been gone too long. I never meant for so many years to pass. My parents come back year after year. Most of my brothers and their families as well. I park my car, not even bothering to close the door behind me as I make my way to the shore.

I stand at the end of a too-rickety dock and my lids fall shut as I inhale deep into my lungs, capturing the first full breath I've had in what feels like years. A hot tear slips from under my eyelashes, and I don't stop it. It's joined by more, but I don't care. I don't even know why I'm crying. I'm not sad, exactly. My life is fine. More than, probably. Just . . . something about this place. It makes me feel right. I'm more myself here than anywhere else in the entire world. I should come back. I want to come back. I'm sure I could make something of myself up here, guiding and maybe working for a resort. It wouldn't be a lucrative living, but it'd be a good one.

Or a lonely one.

"Is that my girl?"

I suck in my breath and swipe the tears from my face, spinning, wide-eyed to face the shore.

"Fost?" I'm running toward him, his arms stretched wide to catch me, but I gentle the last few steps because he's not as sturdy as he used to be. I wrap my arms around his thin frame just as he squeezes me to his chest. He smells like sunshine, fish guts, and old man. He smells like home.

"Hey, kid, thought I heard you might be in town. But not until tomorrow?"

"I got off work early," I murmur into his shoulder. "And I couldn't wait one more minute."

"Well, I'm sure glad to see you."

"*Come and sit with me,*" I say, pulling away and reaching for his arm. I lead him back out onto the dock and we sit on a bench at the end.

"*How're the fish biting?*" I ask, and with a glint in his rheumy eyes, he tells me.

♪ ♪ ♪

"*Don't think I haven't noticed how quiet you've been about your life, missy. Not to mention how many years you've stayed away. What gives?*"

"*Ugh.*" I tilt my head to his shoulder, wrapping my arm around his. "*There's nothing to tell. I'm single because men are stupid, I like my job a lot, but it's not here, and I'm enjoying being the favorite aunt as all my brothers take on the challenge of procreating with gusto.*"

"*There're men here who aren't stupid.*"

I shake my head, rolling it against him. "*Sorry, I should have been more specific—men my age are stupid. There are plenty of old geezers around here who have grown out of their stupid phase, but I'm not looking for a boat daddy.*"

Fost snickers. "*Boat daddy?*"

"*Sure. Like a sugar daddy, but with a nice fishing boat instead. Like a Ranger or a Skeeter, with a top-of-the-line trolling motor and GPS that you can mark and lock . . . I'm thinking red glitter.*"

"*Are you interested in the boat or the daddy?*"

I sigh. "*That's the question, isn't it?*"

"*You can come back here, set up shop as a guide.*"

"*Hm,*" I say.

"*Buy your own sparkly fishing boat, even.*"

"*That's the dream, Fost. That's the dream.*"

꒰꒰꒰

I'm not saying Anders is a better fisherman than me, but the potential is there. I wonder if this is how Fost felt, taking me out all those years ago. Not that I was better, because he was a great fisherman, but all that untapped potential, and hell, how I loved to practice. That's something that hasn't faded in all the years away from this place, and though I would go fishing in Michigan, it wasn't the same. This is *my* water. Thirty-plus summers spent studying these depths, marking the bogs as they emerged and submerged year after year. That's not something I could replicate anywhere else in the world. A terrible day on my water was still a thousand percent better than the best day in one of those overcrowded, hotshot lakes.

Anders feels that. He's got the itch so bad it's more like a full-body rash. Night after night, I see him standing on the shore, casting a line, next to his hand-me-down tackle box, self-dug bait, and a rod and pole set up that he'll grow into. I'd watch him reel in something—*anything*—smile at it or maybe himself—before tossing the lucky fish gently back in the shallows with a murmured, "See you next time."

That right there is the difference between a real fisherman and a fair-weather opportunist. The casual catch and release. All Anders wants is to perfect his art, and he's comfortable letting them go and grow until they're big enough to get his name on a wall.

I spotted Anders from the first and picked him as the one I wanted: the perfect fishing partner. Joe laughed when I asked him but agreed easily enough. "I can't imagine there's anything left for him to catch off the dock. He's literally caught everything in the lake three times over."

The weather is starting to turn. Not all the way, but enough that I know we have maybe weeks left. You can fish as long as there isn't ice (and then you can ice fish) but musky go deep, chasing warmth, and the lake might be my happy place, but I don't need to freeze my ass off chasing the littles.

No, thank you. I'll take a cozy fireplace and a romance novel.

But for now, we fish.

"Ease up on your tension, kid. They can sense when you're desperate."

"I'm not desperate," he scoffs, licking his lips and rolling them together with concentration. This is our third time out and I'm determined to land him his first musky. Something so big, the net won't even hold it. So big we both need to pull it into the boat, and even then, we're sore the next morning from the effort.

But I'm starting to lose hope that tonight is it. The sun's already dipping low in the sky. Even if he did hook one, we'd have a struggle getting an eye on it.

"Hey, let's switch things up. Pull in. I'm gonna move us over by Harper's Bridge for some smallies."

"Aw, I don't want bass."

"Sure you do. Better than going in. Plus, even if you got a musky on the line out here, we could lose it to the dark. You don't want to lose your first musky. You'll spend the rest of your life telling people it was *this big*"—I hold my hands out expansively—"and everyone will just roll their eyes like, *Sure, buddy.*"

He looks so disappointed, it makes my heart squeeze. "Look," I say, using my best Ranger Maren voice that always worked on my educational tours when I needed to convince hikers to climb the biggest bitch of a hill on the trail. "I only have a morning group tomorrow. Let's check with your dad, and if he's okay with it, I can meet you right off the bus and we'll get out by four. That will give us plenty of daylight."

He brightens at the prospect of another day. "Okay."

"So smallies, then?"

"Yeah." He grins, already reeling in his line.

♪ ♪ ♪

"Maren?"

"Yeah?"

Anders doesn't look at me, his eyes on the transparent line dancing in the still water. But I sense his attention is fixed on me more than usual. There's an intensity about him that he's not quite old enough or adept enough to bury under pretense. Because of this, I reel my line in, unhurried.

"Dad said he knew you since you were my age?"

"Longer, even, though I'm sure he doesn't remember that far back. It was a really, really long time ago," I exaggerate with a wry grin.

"Does that mean you knew my mom, too?"

I blink. Of all the questions he could ask me, this wasn't anywhere on my radar. I decide to be honest.

"A little. She would come to the resort to hang out with your dad quite a bit when they were teenagers, dating, and you know Uncle Liam is my big brother. He spent time with them, too. I was around, but much younger. Liam didn't like me tagging along, and I was like you—I'd rather go fishing than hang out with big kids doing boring big-kid stuff. Why? What do you want to know?"

"What was she like?"

I tilt my head to the side, remembering back and trying to picture Kiley in my mind as she was then. "She was pretty and sweet and very outgoing. And she was very in love with your dad."

"Did my dad seem to be in love with her?"

"Very. They were kind of gross, honestly. Super in love."

"Until they had kids."

I press my lips together, alarm bells ringing in my brain. How to handle this? "I'm not sure that's exactly it, Anders. Firstly, because the way I hear it, kids make your love multiply, not divide. You're learning about multiplication and division, right?" At his nod, I go on. "Okay, so then you know multiplication means things grow.

"I don't even have kids of my own, but just knowing you and hanging out with you and your sister, or my nieces and nephews, makes my heart swell so full it feels like it could explode. It used to be so tiny. I'm telling you," I say, and hold two fingers really close together to show him. He smiles. "Like minuscule. But then I met you and . . ." I make a fake explosion sound, waving spirit fingers. "So that wasn't it."

Anders's smile fades. "But then what happened?"

I lift my shoulder, letting my arms fall to my sides. "I don't know for sure. You'll have to talk to your dad. I think sometimes, we can love the wrong person. Maybe they are the right person at first, and then time passes, and they become wrong. Your mom and dad were in love, and they were right for each other because they were supposed to make you and Lucy. And they did."

"And that was it?"

I shake my head. "I guess so, bud. Though I wouldn't call that *it*. That's a lot. That's everything, even. You and Lucy are amazing."

"Sometimes I get mad at Lucy," he admits. "But I still love her."

"That's pretty normal. I get mad at my brothers, too. But I still love them, and they love me."

"I get mad at my mom sometimes."

"That's okay, too."

"It is?" he checks, his voice small.

I release a long breath, looking out over the water and praying I don't mess this up. I'm really, *really* not the one he should be talking to about this, but he clearly needs to talk. I think ruefully of all the emotions I dumped at the feet of Fost over the years and figure this is his revenge from the great big lake in the sky.

"You're allowed to have feelings, Anders. We all are. And we can't really control them, anyway. We feel what we feel," I say, internally wincing at how cliché I sound. "Does that make sense?"

"Not really."

I huff out a laugh. "Yeah. You're right. I don't know what I'm talking about. I dumped my last boyfriend by throwing up on him."

Anders snickers. "That's disgusting."

"Super gross," I agree.

"But you think it's okay I'm mad at my mom?"

"Yes. I do. You're hurt and she isn't here. That's fair. But I would call her."

"No thanks."

I don't push it, but I make a mental note to see if maybe Joe should pass on the message to Kiley to call him. After all, it's not Anders's job to be the one to reach out. But just as quickly, I shake off the thought. I'm not involved, and I don't need to be inserting myself into this family. It's one thing for Anders to pour his heart out. He's my fishing partner. It's a whole other thing to start mediating parental duties.

"Okay. That's your choice."

"I think I want to just fish for a while, Maren, okay? I'm done talking about it."

"Of course," I say, picking up my pole. "I'm here whenever. Let's catch a few more before we have to go in."

And we do—we cast and reel and cast and reel and Anders doesn't say another word about his family.

But I don't stop thinking about them. About Kiley most of all, and wondering how on earth she could walk away from them. I don't know much about anything when it comes to love and marriage and kids and family, but I already know I'm going to have a terrible time leaving my new fishing partner when I'm done here.

THIRTEEN

Vindicated

Joe

"IT'S THE ONLY TIME CHAD AND I CAN GET AWAY WITH HIS KIDS for a family trip before the end of the year, J. We'll take them extra at Christmas, I promise. I'll make it super sweet for Anders. We'll hit up the Upper Peninsula and take him out on the slopes."

There are so many wrong things in that sentence, I take a full minute before I respond, squeezing the phone in my hand and pulling it away from my ear. Out of the corner of my eye, I see Anders and Lucy curled up together on the love seat, absorbed in some show on their tablet. I cover the phone speaker and tell Anders, "I'm gonna step out for a minute, bud. Just on the deck."

He nods his understanding, immediately returning to the screen held in his lap, and I move through my bedroom to the sliding door and slip through, closing it behind me.

"J?" I hear Kiley's annoyed voice call out. "Did I lose you?"

"I'm here."

"Oh, there you are. Okay. So where did I lose you? Did you hear the part about missing Thanksgiving? Not so much missing, really. Just postponing. I can take the kids Christmas through New Year's. Chad and I will grab them and we'll head to the UP. I found an opening at a resort up there . . ."

"Kiley."

"What?" Her voice is terse, but I know from experience the issue is not me. She's feeling guilty and she's taking it out on me while trying to overmanage another offer so that it's not so much "I'm not taking them" as "I've found something better!" She does this every time. Steamrolls that shit into the ground. I recognize I've played my part in creating this monster. For most of our relationship, I was the one leaving. She was left trying to navigate all the pieces on her own. I fully accept responsibility.

"You're asking me to walk back in the house and tell those two kids that the Florida beach vacation with their mom they've been counting down on the calendar—and I mean crossing off the days since May—is canceled, and instead, you're going to come here and take them skiing, something they've never done and I'm not sure Lucy can handle, over Christmas and New Year's, which, by the way, are *my* holidays this year and my family already has plans for them."

My ex is silent a beat and then she huffs into the phone speaker. "Jesus, J, dramatic much? It's no wonder where Luce gets it." I shut my eyes and clench my jaw to keep from snapping at her. It wouldn't do any good. To Kiley, Lucy isn't autistic. She heard the diagnosis the same as me. She sat in that tiny, cold office and spoke with the neuropsychologist the same as me. But somehow, she heard "abnormally difficult and prone to dramatics" instead of "autism spectrum disorder."

I take a deep breath and force my tone to be calm and steady. "Kiley. I really think you should at least talk to Anders.

I can give him the phone and you can break the news to him. Talk up the ski trip. Whatever you need to do, but he needs to hear his mom's voice. He misses you and hearing it's gonna be another month longer before he sees you is gonna hurt."

"You know I can't, J. He'll cry and then I'll cry and I can't cry right now. I'm in the car, about to walk into a showing. You're better at smoothing things over."

"Then call him later, after your showing."

"Please, J," she whispers, and I can feel myself caving.

I huff out a breath. "Fine, but you should call him soon. Really soon, Kiley. FaceTime so you can talk to Luce as well. She's not really into the phone, but she needs to see your face, too. Especially if you're gonna try to take her to a resort."

"You know, now that you mention it, I'm wondering if taking Lucy is a mistake. She's probably too young for a ski hill . . ."

"What the fuck, Kiley?"

"I'll talk to Chad," she says in a rush. "I'll see if I can convince him, but you know how he gets, and besides, it would be good for Anders to get some time without his little sister dragging—"

"I'm going to cut you off before you say something really awful about our child and I can't unhear that shit. I'll talk to the kids. You go to your showing and then plan to call them as soon as you can manage. Bye, Kiley."

I disconnect the call before she can say anything else and stand on my deck staring out into the woods, trying to calm myself down. I fight the urge to call and tell her I'll keep Lucy and Anders through all the holidays and to forget the entire ordeal. Experience tells me she hasn't made any plans yet. She's just throwing shit at the proverbial wall and seeing if anything will stick—if I will fight her. And experience tells her I won't. I want her to have the life she's always needed, and I don't want my kids hurt in the process. It's not their fault I fucked things up with their mom.

But I have full custody. Not because I won it, but because she gave it to me. She gets to see them a few times a year. We try to switch off holidays to make it fair, but mostly, I just wanted them to grow up knowing their mom. The problem is, knowing her, in the distant way they've been afforded, is not enough. And I'm not enough to cover both roles in the not-distant way. Anders is eight. He's still craving the scraps Kiley dangles, but for how long before he gives up? How long will I have to watch this play out, a knife twisting in my gut, over and over?

I get why she walked away from me. I can't fathom how she could do it to them.

⌣⌣⌣

Eventually the cold afternoon seeps into my T-shirt and bare feet and I walk back into the house, mentally preparing myself for the task of telling my kids the bad news. I'm met with the sound of three voices chatting it up in my living room and feel a wave of calm wash over me. *Maren's here.*

I step into the room and see three heads smushed together on my love seat. Maren's sandwiched between my kids. It's not surprising Anders is practically in her lap. The kid worships the ground she walks on. Between her taking him under her wing on her borrowed fishing boat and the fact that she lets him play with Rogers whenever he wants, she's his dream come true.

But I'm a little taken aback to see Lucy pressed into her other side. Lucy's expression isn't exactly adoring. She doesn't show that face to anyone but her big brother, and, on the very rare occasion, me, but she's content. She's touching Maren, voluntarily, and watching her closely. As I get closer, I can see Lucy has tucked her hand in Maren's.

"She likes to have her arm tickled," Anders says in a low voice. "Sometimes when she gets upset, I tickle her arm and she calms down. I think it smoothes her."

"Soothes," Maren murmurs, tentatively dragging her fingers back and forth over Lucy's small, pale forearm.

"Soothes," Anders corrects himself.

I clear my throat to get their attention and definitely *not* because I'm feeling suddenly choked with any sort of unfamiliar emotion.

I round the furniture, settling on the squashy leather ottoman opposite them. "Hey. Sorry I was gone so long."

"Dad! Maren's here!"

Maren and I both laugh. "Yeah, bud. Figured that one out. You two have fishing plans I forgot about?"

"Nah," Maren says. She's wearing a worn-looking long-sleeved shirt with the words GOOD NATURED emblazoned across the chest. It's covered in diagrams of various native plants. "The fish will get to live another day. I'm tired of breathing in varnish fumes and decided to take a walk. No surprise, Rogers dragged me this way." At that, I realize Rogers is lying at their feet on my rug. "Clearly," she continues, grinning, "he approved of getting away from the varnish fumes, too."

"I was just about to suggest grabbing some dinner. Want to join us?"

"Oh, that's okay. I didn't mean to impose."

"No imposition," I tell her and mean it. Anders tugs her arm and nods, energetically.

"Please come! We'll get pizza! Dad and I can share a large one and you and Luce can share a medium."

"Or we can decide on what to get as a family," I say without thinking. My eyes dart to Maren's expression, but if she hears my slip, she doesn't react.

"I love pizza," Maren agrees easily. "I need to drop off Rogers, though. What time do you want to head out?"

"We can be ready whenever. But why don't you leave Rogers here? He seems pretty comfortable on the rug. In fact"—I switch gears on the fly—"why don't we do takeout? If you wouldn't mind staying with Anders for a bit, I'll order us all dinner and Lucy and I can go pick it up."

Maren seems nonplussed by my change but agrees immediately.

"Sure. I, um, actually brought something that I was hoping Lucy, and Anders, too, of course, could help me with?" From the floor, she lifts an old plastic tackle box, holding it awkwardly in front of herself.

"Tackle?"

Pink highlights Maren's cheeks and she smiles self-consciously as she takes in the dual stares of my children. "Kind of. It's actually something I used to do with Fost when I was a kid. I was always losing all his best lures in the weeds, so he decided I needed to learn how to make them. I've seen Lucy's incredible artwork," she says, smiling down at my daughter before turning to my son, "and figured maybe Anders would want to try to catch a musky on a homemade lure . . ."

"You want to teach my kids how to make lures?"

Maren starts to shake her head, "Unless . . . it's a dumb idea? I know paint is messy, but . . ."

I cut her off and my voice comes out weirdly strangled. "Not dumb. Right, Lucy? Would you like to build with Maren?"

Lucy is already reaching both hands to the box. "Yes, please."

Maren squats down to place the box on the floor and shows Lucy how to unclasp the hinged top. "There aren't any hooks on these yet," she explains. "So they're safe to play with. I thought maybe we could start with some wooden musky lures. They're already carved, but you guys can paint them as realistic or flashy as you want. I have some newspaper to keep your table safe and bought some new paints. You don't even want to know what twenty-year-old craft paint smells like . . ."

Lucy picks up two different carvings and holds them up in front of her eyes. I can practically see her little brain designing the perfect detailing. I can't believe I've never thought of this before. "Can I talk to you real quick in the kitchen?" I ask Maren, and she stands up without hesitation, moving to follow me.

"I'm sorry I didn't ask first about the lures, I just saw Lucy's artwork on the fridge and thought maybe she would want to try—"

"It's perfect. I'm not upset. Well, a little annoyed I never thought of it myself, but that's beside the point. I just got off the phone with Kiley," I start, once we're safely tucked away. I lean against the countertop and cross my hands over my chest. "She was supposed to take the kids over Thanksgiving. I was going to fly with them down to Florida and she was going to fly with them back."

Maren mimics my stance, standing across from me, her left hip against the island, her arms in front of her. "That's . . . wow. Commitment. I take it from the past tense that something fell apart?"

I don't know why I want to tell her, I just know I do. It's been years of this, and I don't have anyone to talk to. I don't want to talk to my parents because they already have strong feelings where Kiley is concerned, and I inevitably end up feeling like I have to defend her bullshit to them. Most of my friends are married and live in other states. Liam knows everything, of course, but he tends to overreact. I don't need anyone charging in to fix things, I just need someone to listen.

Maren is here. Maren knew my ex. Maren takes Anders out fishing, and Maren was tickling Lucy's arm.

So I tell Maren and when I'm done, she scowls and lets out a slow hiss under her breath. The effect on my anxiety is an instant balm.

She speaks quietly, just loud enough that only I can hear. "Would Anders even want to spend Christmas away from home and Lucy?"

I groan, scrubbing at my face. "I don't know. I don't think so, but it's his mom. He's in this weird place between giving up on her entirely and clinging to any piece she tosses his way. If he does want to go, I don't think I could stand in his way. This might very well be the last year he would."

Maren takes that in, her expression thoughtful, and then uncertain. "I wasn't going to say anything, because I am very aware this is not at all my place . . . but Anders has been talking to me a little about things with his mom. Nothing, well . . . gah." She stops. Reconsiders. Opens her mouth, then pauses again, her expression pained. "Jesus, Joe, I am so out of my depth here. Liam would be better at this."

Doubtful. "Maybe, but I'm talking to *you*."

"To your detriment, I'm sure." She doesn't wait for me to respond. "Okay, whatever. Here goes. Anders asked me about you and Kiley, when you were younger. Which I'm sure I wasn't super helpful on that front, but I told him the truth. You and Kiley were super in love. Somehow, from that, he pulled out an 'until they had kids.' And I . . ." She trails off, seeing my face. I'm sure I look as stricken on the outside as I feel on the inside. "Shit," she said. "I told you I'm out of my depth."

"No, I need to hear this. Please."

Maren sighs and walks the two steps toward me. She reaches the counter, turns, and presses closer to me, side by side, her hip against mine, and she gentles her voice even further.

"I told him I didn't know a lot about love, but it was my experience that kids made love multiply, not divide. He told me sometimes he gets mad at Lucy. I told him that was okay, because I get mad at my brothers all the time but still love them. He liked that. It's not a crisis to be annoyed by your siblings, it's a rite of passage. Anyone can see that kid adores his sister. And for good reason! She's adorable. You have good kids, Joe. The best, even. You're doing a good job."

"Why do I feel like there is a 'but' in there?"

Maren nudges me with her hip. *"But,"* she emphasizes, "and this comes with the caveats that I have only been around six weeks and am not a parent and also puked on my boyfriend to get him to stop proposing to me—but Kiley *might* not be doing the best job by Anders."

I absorb this, careful to keep my tone neutral. "This is not news, but why do you think that?"

"Because Anders said he gets mad at his mom sometimes, too, but his tone was different, you know? There was an edge to it. And when I mentioned maybe he could call his mom, he shut it down. Completely. Which, actually, made me really think because for goodness' sake, *she* is the parent. She is *his mom*. If she wants to show him that he means something to her—that she misses him—*she* should reach out. Now, after what you just told me, I'm wondering if she grasps that."

I sigh and she gives me silence. That comfortable, companionable silence I've grown accustomed to with her. I churn over her words in my mind, hot anger for my kid mixing with remorse for the way he's been holding on to these feelings.

"I fucked up," I confess. "I've been letting her walk all over me out of guilt for leaving her alone so much when I was in the military."

"Okay, but you were in the *military*, Joe. Fighting for your country. Not on tour with your rock band."

Her words do little to pierce the walls of self-loathing surrounding me. "She felt disappointed and abandoned for years, and I didn't even notice. She was building a life separate from me, and I completely missed the signs. I just assumed she was happy to keep our home while I was away; I was a selfish asshole, off playing the hero."

"All of this sounds like a good reason to question a marriage, Joe. I get it. Maybe you stopped working as a couple. Though, I think you're being pretty hard on yourself, taking all of the blame . . . but that's neither here nor there. I'm not hearing anything about why she's distanced herself from her own kids."

"She's making me pay for it," I tell Maren.

"Well, that's the stupidest fucking thing I've ever heard."

A bark of laughter erupts past my lips, breaking the tension in the room, and Maren's face softens into a smile even as her cheeks turn bright pink.

"Sorry, but it's true. She needs to grow up, and this is coming from someone who just quit her secure career to refurbish a bait shop in the middle of nowhere."

I snort at this, laughter still clinging around the edges.

"You aren't dragging your kids through it, though," I say. "You have every right to mess with your career however you want."

She waves me off before tucking her hand under her folded arms again. "Maybe so. Rogers has gotten accustomed to cabin living, so I'm not completely messing things up. My point is, she can be mad about how things went down between you two, and she can be disappointed with the decade she spent supporting you. Still feels shitty to me, since, again, you were in the military and she had a thriving career and stable home, but whatever. I guess I'm biased." It feels like Maren is defending me? And I feel something loosen in the middle of my chest; something shaking my walls—but she's still talking.

"Since then, though, she's moved on. Right? Career, Florida, new husband, stepkids?"

"Right."

"So, yeah. Time to stop making you pay for it, I'm thinking. Time to grow up and decide if she wants a part in Anders's and Lucy's lives, on their terms and yours."

"So reading between the lines, you're telling me to man up?"

"What? How did you get—No. That's not what I'm saying. I'm saying *she* needs to man up. Or not man up," she backtracks, her brow creasing. "I hate that phrase. It reeks of misogyny. But you know what I mean."

"I do and I agree. She needs to grow up. But I need to stop letting her walk all over me and stand up for my kids."

"Oh." Maren slumps next to me, feigning a pout. "Well, yeah. I guess you do need to man up, then."

"Thanks, Mare. This was helpful."

"Really?"

"Don't be so surprised. You're good at this. I can see why Anders confided in you."

"I'm not so sure about either of you Cole men confiding in me, honestly. I think you both need a therapist." I concede with a tilt of my head. "But I'm glad it helped in the meantime."

"It did. I'm no longer ready to tear my hair out. I'm going to tell Anders the bad news after pizza. Like ripping off a Band-Aid, I'm thinking."

"I'll make sure to get the paints set up while you're out, then. For after dinner."

"We might have a battle there. I don't know if I'll be able to pull Lucy away from her plotting."

"She can stay, too, if that's okay. And if you have crayons and paper, I can try to convince them to sketch first and paint after dinner," Mare says with an easy grin. This close, given so casually, it nearly knocks the breath from my chest. It's the kind of smile that steals beauty competitions. The kind of smile that's won over my kids.

The kind of smile that could even win over my dead heart if it was on the table.

Too bad it's not.

"I'd better order the pizzas, then. Seems like we have a busy night ahead of us."

FOURTEEN

Dancing on My Own

Maren

As nice as my cabin is, the Wi-Fi there is nonexistent, so I have to check my email at the lodge. Which is why I am there, first thing, during "morning coffee."

Believe me, I would have avoided it if I could.

"Morning coffee" is exactly what it sounds like, except with old men. And listen, I love the older guys. But all of them at once is like a holiday dinner with twelve nosy uncles you haven't seen in a while, all up in your business and every one of them "knows a guy." Need something fixed? They know a guy. Need something looked at? They know a guy. Need someone to knock you up? Oh, they have a nephew once removed who has a very lucrative career as a dentist and you can barely tell his hair is a toupee. He's available!

So I try to avoid the lodge this early in the morning, but I'm also avoiding town ever since the whole Bryce ordeal, plus Simon and Donna have me booked nearly solid with tours, so my free time is limited. The weather has been unseasonably warm and there's been a huge demand for guided fishing trips while the temperatures last.

Every moment I'm not fishing, I'm either making slow but steady progress on the bait-shop-slash-apartment or I'm over at Joe's. The clock is ticking, though, in more ways than one. For instance, my savings won't last forever. The tours help to keep me from spending out of my reserves for the day-to-day living expenses, but the bait shop is a literal pit. I probably should have had the entire thing bulldozed to the ground, but nostalgia (and Joe) prevailed. There's a ton of history within those ugly paneled walls.

It's salvageable, but it's not easy or quick. I'm basically just shuffling shit from one place to another, but I've rented a giant dumpster that will be arriving this weekend, and Joe and his parents have offered to help me fill it. I think having all the old materials cleared away will help.

That's my first task this morning. Check my email. Confirm the enormous dumpster is arriving soon, and then call my best friend. I wish I could FaceTime her from Fost's place, but along with being a money pit, it's also a black hole for technology.

So I've taken dozens of pictures, covering every questionable inch of the apartment and the bait shop, and I've emailed them to Shelby and her husband, Cameron. Because while they play home renovators on TV, they're also the realest of deals. I've scheduled a FaceTime consultation five minutes from now.

I sip from my coffee (just because I'm not interested in being fixed up with any balding nephews doesn't mean I won't partake of the free caffeine) while waiting for my laptop to boot up, and then click on the email icon. I send all the junk mail to the trash folder, making a mental note to go through and unsubscribe from things as soon as I'm back in technology once more. My sleep-addled brain snags on a line of text that reads **Internal Job posting: Grand Canyon National Park.**

I click immediately, my heart giving a pang. Not a full-blown lurch, and not a racing, thumping beat, but a pang. I love the Grand Canyon. I would have to sell my place and move, of course, but do I really want to stay in Michigan anyway? The posting would be a lateral move, but because the park is bigger, there would be more responsibilities and I would be eligible for a step increase and raise.

The posting is new and will be up for a month, which is a long time and has me thinking they've created the position, rather than trying to replace an existing one. Not to mention we're heading into the holidays. I kind of doubt they'll be looking to fill it until after the new year. I catch my lip between my teeth, skimming the description and details.

It would be a fresh start without losing the progress I've gained in the last decade. I minimize the tab, instead of closing it. I need to think on it a little more. On the surface, it seems meant for me, but lately I've been questioning everything. I'm feeling completely off-kilter, and at my age, I definitely ought to have my shit together.

I feel like I'm basically taking a gap year, trying to find myself, while my friends are having babies and planning weddings, their careers taking off. Weirdly, I've never been jealous of Shelby or Lorelai and their individual fame. They've overcome so much and gone through hellfire to get where they are today. I couldn't be more thrilled for them.

But I am a tiny bit jealous of the look of contentment they both wear these days. It's as though the world could be crumbling to dust around them, and they would still be standing strong, weathering all.

Love. That's what they have, and I don't. It's probably why I stayed with Shane so long, despite my waning feelings. I wanted someone who would weather the storm with me the way Shelby has Cameron and Lorelai has Craig. But not exactly like them because while I adore those men for my best friends, they're not really my type.

Which is why I am leaving the tab open. For now.

Without much thought, or even really knowing why, I find myself idly following the steps to get to my old Musky Maren website. I told Joe the truth back when he asked me about Bryce Callahan. I haven't been back to my site since I stepped away from everything ten years ago. But being here, fishing again and, despite my best efforts, hearing that moniker of "Musky Maren" over and over . . . well, it has me curious.

I click on the site via the back door and scroll through my old pictures, squirming a little at how juvenile it feels. Like another era—another person. But, honestly, it's not as terrible as I imagined. Not that I want to repeat history, but I find myself feeling a little proud of baby Maren and her clear drive. I'm also kind of pissed that I allowed people like Bryce to chase me out of the space I created for myself.

I click around the time capsule of my very first and only attempt at my own business and chew my lip, trying to replace baby Maren with almost-thirty-four-year-old grown-up Maren. What would I do differently? Better? Would I want anything to do with YouTube and video content after all this time?

But then I notice a little icon in the corner. Messages. I have a contact form through the website that I never disconnected. I just stopped checking the email. I could access it through here as well, though.

I'd forgotten.

With a deep breath, I hover on the icon and click once.

My screen instantly loads with email addresses. I don't bother reading through them all. I have a pretty good guess from the subject lines what they contain. Most are old. Like close to a decade old, though there are a handful that trickled in over the years in between. My eyes snag on the most recent ones, however, and my stomach sinks to the floor. At least a dozen recent emails are clearly from Bryce. I don't click on the messages, but the subject lines tell enough . . .

> **MUSKY MAREN IS BACK**
>
> **I had this weird dream about you . . .**
>
> **Guided Tour Inquiry?**
>
> **Local Signing at Cole's Landing?**
>
> **PUT YOUR PICTURE UP . . .**
>
> **Are you really married, though?**😐

I immediately click out of everything and slam my laptop shut, my heart racing and a cold flush covering my skin. I swallow back the urge to throw up my breakfast. I can't believe this. Except, actually, yeah, I can. That's the difference between baby Maren and me. I'm aware. I know how men on the internet work. I know the way they think.

After a minute of deep breathing, I open the laptop again.

This is stupid. My reaction is stupid. I'm a grown woman and he's just a small man on the internet. I delete every message unread, log out of the site again, this time for good, and get up to pour myself a fresh cup of coffee.

Ten calm minutes later, my phone finally alerts to a Face-Time call. I tap my phone screen, smiling wide. "Hey, babe!"

"Hello, stranger!" Shelby says, peering close. "Are you even more tan? How are you *more* tan? It's October. And is your hair different? You look different. All glowy or something?"

I smirk at her theatrics and pop in my AirPods so I can hear her over the din of coffee time. "I spend every afternoon on the water, so despite my liberal sunscreening, my fisherwoman's tan is well developed. As for my hair, I haven't washed it in three days. And I haven't showered yet today. So perhaps the glow is oil? Residual sunscreen?" I shrug.

"Darn," Shelby mutters, her lips quirking mischievously. "I was hoping you were getting some from Hot Bartender Joe."

Despite my earbuds, I whip around to see if anyone heard her. "Shelby!"

"What? Are you denying he's hot?"

God, no. "That's irrelevant," I whisper-hiss. "We've already covered this. He's Liam's best friend."

"Oh, is Liam there?"

I roll my eyes. "Obviously not."

"Then I fail to see the issue. Not to mention, you're not thirteen anymore, beauty queen."

"Just because you're all sexed up on the regular," I whisper, looking around again to make sure no one's listening.

"I am, thank you. The belly has made things interesting, but Cam isn't afraid of being creative."

"Wonderful," I mutter.

"Oh, stop. You're happy for me."

I pretend to pout, but she knows me too well. "I am. So what about the pictures I sent?"

She waves a dismissive hand at the screen. "One minute. Cameron is on his way." She leans in closer. "So for real. What's wrong with Joe? You said he's a single dad. Divorced? Widowed?"

"Divorced," I confirm. "A few years ago. He has two beautiful children who I really, really like. Is that weird? I mean, I love my nieces and nephews of course, but I *like* Anders and Lucy."

"Not weird. I bet they adore you and Rogers. God, you're like a fairy princess brought to life. They're probably in awe of you."

"Hardly," I scoff. "But they don't seem to mind having me around."

"Okay . . ." She trails off, her hands spreading in the air in front of her. "I'm not seeing the issue."

"Cameron still not there?"

She pins me with a look, and I sigh.

"Fine. The issue is he's not interested in me like that. I'm basically his little sister. Also, I'm moving as soon as this rebuild is done. Gonna sell the bait shop and apartment as one. Just saw an available job at the Grand Canyon. Thinking of applying."

My best friend stills for a beat, processing. Or maybe the phone has a delay. Either way, I'm left fidgeting on my end, self-conscious under her assessment. Finally, she asks, "Did I miss the part where you said you weren't interested in him?"

Oh, for fuck's sake. "You're obnoxious."

Shelby beams. "That's what I thought. We'll table this for now, in that case." She turns her head to someone off camera and suddenly Cameron's big, burly, bearded face is centered in my screen.

"Cam!" I cry, thrilled to see him and not just because he's great.

"Hey, Mare. How're you?"

"Depends. What do you think after seeing my pics? Am I nuts?"

His grin doesn't change, but he says, "Professional opinion? You should have lit a match the moment they handed you the deed."

I drop my head to the tabletop and thud it once, twice, before lifting it again. "And?"

"And . . ." He looks at Shelby. "And I'm gonna let my wife give you our personal opinion, but I'll warn you, she's doing that thing where she gets all dreamy. She's usually right, but it's always more work."

"Maren," Shelby gushes, as if we haven't been talking all along, "it's got gobs of character. That antique till? Those built-ins behind the register? That alcove with the wide windowsill that faces the lake? Dreamy, babe. It's perfect. This is so totally worth it. I'm coming up. We both are. Two weeks from now. You said you're gonna clear out all the trash?"

I blink, stunned at this news. "This weekend. I guess I'm not throwing away the till, though."

"Don't you dare. Just the trash. The rusty wire racks, the plastics. But if there's any cool merch that's got a vintage feel, put it aside for me. I want to look through and make sure we can't incorporate it."

"You're really coming?" I check.

"Of course. You didn't think you were going to renovate without us?"

"Well . . ." I absolutely thought that.

"Maren Lorraine Laughlin, are you kidding?"

"No, but you're more than a little pregnant right now, Shelby. And at any given time you two have three different projects rolling. I just figured you were bus—"

"Not too busy for family," Cameron cuts in with finality in his tone. It's the tone he uses on projects when the deadline is closing in and someone double-booked the tile and cabinet guys. "You're like Shelby's sister. That makes you my sister and we make time for family."

"I know you have a big family already, Mare, but I don't." Shelby's eyes are watery, and my throat reflexively tightens. "You and Lore are it for me. So please let me do this."

Hell. "I would be honored. Besides," I tease, though my watery sniff probably ruins the effect, "I'm desperate."

Shelby claps. "Yay! Two weeks, then. We booked a villa already! I can't wait to check out this resort after hearing so many good things over the years."

I blink at her, shocked. "You booked a villa?"

"Well, Cameron wanted a cabin, but they were booked, and anyway, we'll have a lot of gear. Cam's packing a whole trailer of his tools."

"I have tools," I say with a sniff. Though, to be fair, probably not the quality or even the amount someone like Cameron needs. I took a regular hammer to one of the walls last night, and it did both too much and not enough damage to the bathroom wall.

Cameron grins, self-deprecating. "I like mine. It's nothing personal. A man likes his own tools."

"I can't believe this," I say, still feeling unbalanced. "I'll take you out musky fishing or something. I owe you."

"Family," Cam reminds me. "I'm not much of a fisherman, but I'd love to catch a musky."

"I'll find you one," I vow. "Thanks, you guys. I can't even tell you how much this means to me."

"Send pics after you've cleaned it out," Shelby says. "The

apartment, too. I want a clearer picture of what we're dealing with."

"I will."

"Love you, Mare."

I swallow hard. "Love you both, too."

ᒐᒐᒐ

I thought the giant driveway-sized dumpster was going to be overkill. After all, the bait shop is maybe five hundred square feet, and the apartment is barely double that. How much trash could there possibly be? Especially keeping in mind Shelby wanted the final say on anything "vintage" or that "fit the aesthetic," so that all went into an ever-growing pile.

I thought wrong. Old, stained carpeting that reeked of stale cigarette smoke was ripped up, closet doors with long-rusted tracks were yanked out, tiny aluminum sinks with leaky faucets and original cabinetry that held a thick coating of cooking oil and grime all went to the trash. Linoleum flooring that hid even more linoleum flooring underneath, and yeah, paneling. So much paneling.

And that was just in the apartment. Everything from the water-wasting toilets to the sun-faded buffalo-plaid curtains had to go and it took all day long. But I had help. Earlier, Donna and Simon came, and while Donna stalled things a little out of nostalgia (Fost's apartment felt like one of those historical exhibits in museums where they show a living room through the different decades, except it was just the 1980s), Simon was plenty of help when it came to pulling up flooring. In the afternoon, Donna left to watch the lodge and Simon went to take Anders and Lucy out for ice cream before keeping them for the night so Joe could put in a shift at the cabin with me. (Originally the plan was to have the kids at the house with us all day, but that was before we found the magical duo of asbestos and lead paint. We called Joe and told him to keep the kids at home and we masked up.)

Cameron was right. I should have lit a match and called it a day.

"I don't remember ever seeing Fost smoke," Joe says, rubbing his forehead with the sleeve of his flannel and making his hair stand up with sweat.

He does not look good sweaty. He *doesn't*.

I peel another nail from the paneling with the back of my hammer. It comes out of the particle board with a satisfying squeak, and I move to another.

"He didn't around us, but your mom said she remembered both him and his wife smoking like chimneys before she died of lung cancer. I'm thinking he stopped after that, but by that point, it didn't matter. At least to his walls."

"Basically have to take this down to the studs," he grunts.

I sigh. "Cameron's professional opinion was to burn it down."

Joe raises a brow over his face mask that clearly communicates his agreement.

"Shelby's an idealist, though. She said the bones are too good to set on fire. But she couldn't smell through the pictures. She may have felt differently if she stood where we are now."

"She's not wrong. The bones are solidly built, and the foundation is like new."

I grimace. "Maybe so, but I'm gonna have to wash everything in bleach water."

"We'll help," he offers, and while I want to argue, I can't.

Not because I need the help (though I do), but because I'm quickly learning that they would ignore me anyway.

"You guys have enough going on with the resort and Lucy and Anders . . . I don't want you to feel like this is necessary. I'm the dummy who is trying to make something out of nothing."

"And we're the ones who knew this place was rotting away after we moved Fost out and completely neglected it for years."

I don't respond. I just glare at him, which he pointedly ignores and carries another armful of toxic ceiling tiles out the door.

When he returns, he rocks his head from side to side, cracking his neck. "Let's wrap on this room and come back in the morning. It's getting dark and we need to eat."

I stand, pressing my hands into the small of my back and arching my spine. "Only a few panels left. I'll remove the nails and you cart them out. I'd offer to order a pizza, but I don't think we should eat here."

"How about you finish this, then I'll drop you off at home, you order a pizza, I'll shower at my place, and then come to yours to help you eat it. Dad and Mom have the kids for the night, but my fridge is empty."

"Works for me," I say, trying not to sound too happy that I'm not done seeing Joe today. I also don't bother thinking too hard about why that makes me happy. I'm dead on my feet. All I want to do is strip off these toxically dusty clothes, stand under a steaming-hot shower, and crawl into bed.

And yet, I'm not ready to say good night to this man.

It takes another thirty minutes to finish pulling out the rest of the paneling and for Joe to muscle it out the front door.

By then, it's full dark and my hands are raw, my fingernails are obliterated, and my shoulders are on fire. I doubt I'll be able to get out of the bed in the morning without a lever and pulley operated by my dog.

Joe moves room to room, shutting off lights and double-checking windows. Because after all this work, I'll be damned if I let this house burn down now. I follow him out the front door and lock it behind us, then we head to his car. I walked over here this morning, but I'm grateful to not have to do so now. At this point, if I saw a bear, I might let him take me.

I've never been in Joe's truck before. I've always felt like you can tell a lot about a person from the inside of their vehicle. It's like a microcosm of their life. Joe's Ford is no-fuss. Nothing modified or upgraded, but tidy and comfortable. It smells like him . . . clean laundry detergent and man. There aren't any fast-food wrappers, but there are multiple reusable water bottles of varying shapes and a car seat for Lucy in the back. The radio automatically hooks up to the Bluetooth on his phone and plays country music that I only recognize because Lorelai Jones is my best friend and, because of that, I pay attention.

Somehow, knowing he listens to edgy, obscure country music makes him even hotter. Which believe me, he did not need, where I am concerned.

We pull up to my cabin in no time and I stifle my groan as I drop down onto the gravel that leads to my temporary porch.

"You'll order pizza?"

"Yep. To be delivered. I'm gonna order after my shower, though. I have a feeling I'm gonna be a minute. If you're ready before me, let yourself in."

His frown is illuminated in the streetlight. "I don't like the idea of you showering without the door locked. Just text me."

"Joe. Okay, fine, I'll lock it. Rogers is in there, so he'll bark when you knock, and it will be fine. I won't drown, I'm just fucking tired."

"Should we skip tonight?"

"No!" I say too quickly and am glad the dark hides my pink face. "It's fine. I'm hungry. Go and come back."

Joe watches me unlock the door to my place and let Rogers out to pee. He does his business quickly and runs back to join me inside. After we're inside, I lock my door, muttering under my breath, and march straight to my bedroom, stripping off as I go. I might not burn down the apartment or bait shop, but I really want to burn these clothes.

Then I hustle into the shower, turning it to near scalding, and let it fall on my muscles, loosening me up from head to toe.

FIFTEEN

Hurt So Good

Joe

I PROBABLY SHOULD HAVE ORDERED TAKEOUT FOR ONE BACK AT my place, but I couldn't help myself. Besides, this is a thing friends-slash-brothers do. Liam would want me to make sure Maren's good after such a long and arduous day of work, and he'd expect me to pay for her dinner. If he were here, he would do it himself. Since he's not, it's up to me.

And anyway, my house is empty, and my kids are with my parents. I like my privacy, but the house is too quiet with them gone. So I take a quick shower and head over to Maren's cabin.

I'm reaching out to knock on the door right as the head-lights of the pizza delivery person pull down the resort drive. So I wait them out and pay while accepting the pizza before knocking on her door. Rogers barks as she said he would, but she pulls open the door in an instant. She's dressed in white cotton short-shorts with a blue floral pattern that reveal her yards of tanned legs and a matching cami with lace around the edges. In other words, she's in her pajamas.

Fuck. I did not need to know what her pajamas look like. Or that they'd be so fucking cute.

"Sorry," she says breathlessly, stepping back and letting me in. "I'll be right back. Just gotta grab something."

Thirty seconds later, she's draped a giant cardigan over her pajamas and pulled on thick fleecy socks. She's twisting her wet hair on top of her head as she walks back in and takes a long sniff, her eyes closed and her lips pressed together. "Mmm. That smells delicious," she says. "I have beer and water. What'll it be?"

"Beer."

She grabs two bottles, removing the caps. "Mind if we eat over the box? I don't think I can reach over my head to the cabinets right now. My muscles are deader than dead. Washing my hair was a mistake. I didn't even bother with conditioning, which means I might have to cut it all off tomorrow. The knots will be atrocious."

It's on the tip of my tongue to tease that I could have conditioned it for her before I mentally punch myself in the dick. *Liam.* Remember Liam. Her brother. *My* brother, for all intents and purposes.

Maren turns on the TV and we eat the entire pizza in one sitting, sipping our beers side by side on the couch, the box between us. When we finish, Maren drops the box onto the floor and pulls her legs up on the couch, her side pressing closer to mine from the action.

I lift my leg, crossing my ankle over my knee, and stretch my stiff arm over the back of the couch, my fingers accidentally brushing the hair at the nape of her neck. If she notices, she doesn't show it.

"Baseball okay?" she asks. "The Tigers are up for a wild card."

Neither of us mentions me leaving. I should leave. Instead

I nod and Maren lowers the volume and grabs a pillow. She tucks it against the back of the couch, but I grab it from her, place it against my thigh, and pat it. "This will be more comfortable. I won't bite," I tell her casually, without taking my eyes off the screen. As if my heart wasn't thumping in my chest. Because it shouldn't be.

But still. Older brother types can cuddle.

"Thanks," she says softly and immediately drops her head on the pillow. This close, the mouth-watering scent of her still-damp hair wafts up and I close my eyes, savoring it. It's been so long since I've smelled a woman straight from the shower. Eventually, I relax, too, sinking further into the couch and slipping a little to the side.

♩♩♩

I wake up to full dark and it takes me a moment to remember where I am. I don't remember lying down, but I'm stretched out full length on a couch in Maren's cabin. Her smaller form is tucked into mine, and mine is curled around hers. Her hair is smoothed under my chin, her warm breaths pulsing against my collarbone. The TV is off, but I can't remember turning it off.

I'm pinned into the cushion by her body and it's barely a beat before all of me realizes it. Maren makes a soft noise and turns in my arms, her back settling against my front, pressing tightly against me.

Oh *fuck*.

She wiggles her hips, her perfect ass sliding against the place where I am straining hard against the zipper of my jeans, and she gasps. Then she tenses and her breathing stops and she's definitely awake now.

"Oh god," she whispers and instantly starts to pull away. Without thinking, my hand darts out and captures her hip. "Don't."

If possible, she tenses further. "Don't what?" she asks, still on a whisper.

I squeeze her hip gently, then rub a soothing circle over her side, hip, and butt. Reflexively, I press against her again.

"Don't leave."

She hesitates and I can hear both our hearts thudding between us, waiting to see what she's going to say. She should kick me out. I should get up and let her go to bed. I should drive my ass home.

She reaches back for my hand and pulls it to her front, granting permission. Or maybe making a request. Either way, I'm gone.

I slide my fingers upward, over her midriff, teasing her rib cage and up in between her breasts before finally curling around one, cupping and palming it before circling a fingertip around her stiff nipple. I pinch it between my thumb and forefinger and she gasps, arching into my hand, which has the fortunate benefit of once again pressing her into my groin. She bucks against me, and I press a kiss to her neck.

It's been so long since I held a woman like this, I know I won't last. I'm this close to blowing my load in my jeans. I can't do that. I move the hand that's been trapped between us underneath her, curling up and capturing her other breast, doing my best to distract her, rolling and pinching and massaging until she's bucking wildly against me.

All this and I haven't even gotten into her underwear.

I move to remedy that immediately. "Can I?" I whisper

directly into her ear, even though we're alone, trailing my fingertips under her waistband.

"God, yes."

I slip in and cup her hard, finding her soaked and ready for me. She spreads her knees, pushing off the cushion and I slip my finger inside of her, coating it, and then drag it out slowly, circling her clit once, twice, before diving in again. I add a finger and she thrusts against my hand, her insides clenching against me. With my other hand, I squeeze and roll and tug at her nipple.

I swallow my groan, tightening against her and licking against the strained tendons of her neck, tasting her. Kissing her. Sucking her and marking her. I twist my fingers inside of her, curling them and rubbing rhythmically against the inner wall where I know it will feel the best. My thumb is circling her clit, my fingers are rolling her nipple, and my mouth is working just below her ear. I've never wanted anything in my entire life as much as I want to make this woman come apart in my hands. She's thrashing and bucking and her nails are digging into my thighs so hard I can feel them through the denim and it feels fucking miraculous. The way she's rubbing against me, I know I'm going to be driving home sticky and I can't seem to care. Can't seem to even process it. All I feel, all I know, is *her*.

And then she seizes up, her thighs clamping on my hand, her insides clenching powerfully against my fingers over and over and over, but I don't stop thrusting my fingers until she's done riding it out, fucking my hand and stealing my soul in the process.

She comes down and so do I and there's only breath and racing heartbeats between us. I slip my fingers out of her, and she lets out a soft whimper at the absence. That sound imprints on my brain in echoes—echoes that will haunt my sleep.

We lie there in stunned silence until our breaths even out and our heartbeats steady and I pull my hand away from her warm skin, and for the first time I feel the uncomfortably cold, wet stickiness in my pants.

Fucking hell, it's like sophomore year all over again. Liam would give me such shit if he . . .

Fucking hell.

Maren seems to come to her senses at the same time and sits up, then gets to her feet and walks to the bathroom without a word.

I sit up and rub my hands down my thighs, smelling her on me. All over me. I'm practically hard again, just from that.

I get up, walk to her kitchen, and run the faucet. I wash my hands and dry them, retrieve a glass from above the sink and fill it. Drink it. Fill it again, and drink that. Still, she hasn't come out. I put the glass in the sink and make my way to the bathroom door and tap a knuckle on it.

"Maren. You can't stay in there forever."

"Just watch me."

"Who will take care of Rogers?"

"Anders can." I hear her murmur and it sounds a lot like "Holy shit, *Anders.*"

"Maren, come out here, please. I'm going to leave, but I need to see your face so I know you're okay."

A beat, two, and the door swings open. "Of course I'm okay. I'm way more than okay. I'm thoroughly . . . *okay.*" In the dim light of the bathroom, I can see her flushed cheeks and messy hair. She looks thoroughly fucked, actually, but I doubt that's helpful to anyone but my ego.

"I don't know what to say," I confess with a wry grin. "I didn't expect that to happen, but I'm . . . I'm not upset it happened, either."

"Obviously, me neither. Though I feel like I owe you—"

I shake my head. "Believe me, you don't."

"But—" she starts.

"Nope. No. Let's just say . . . you don't. Okay? Trust me. I'm good."

"You're goo—" And then her eyes get wide and her lips form an understanding "oh" and her cheeks grow an even deeper pink.

"Yeah, so. I'm good. But I don't think we can do that again."

"Absolutely not!" she agrees. "My brother—and your kids! And, god, your parents. And my parents! And the job in Arizona—and I just got out of a relationship and—"

"Okay, okay," I cut her off. "Clearly we have more than enough reason to never do that again."

"Right."

"Right."

"Well. That was, um, exceptional."

I blink. "Really?"

Her brows scrunch together. "I thought so—didn't you?"

"Absolutely."

She beams, her shoulders relaxing. "Good. And we don't need to tell anyone about this. Like ever."

"Fuck no. Just between us."

"Great. Awesome. Phew!" she says, adorably pretending to wipe her brow.

I lean in, ducking close, and press a kiss to her forehead, holding it a half second longer than necessary and inhaling her scent into my lungs one last time.

When I pull away, her eyes are closed as though she's savoring the moment, too. I feel a twinge in my chest at the sight, but step back and break the connection, drawing the lines once more.

"Good night, Mare."

"'Night, Joe. See you when I see you."

I leave then, waiting to hear the deadbolt click into place behind me before getting back into my truck. I don't hesitate in her driveway. I drive home, let myself in, strip down, and get into bed. But I don't fall asleep for a long while. Instead I lie awake thinking that none of what just happened was brotherly in the slightest.

Still, I can't find it in me to care.

♪♪♪

If I'm honest, Cameron Riggs is a lot bigger than he seems on TV. I don't usually find other guys intimidating. After all, I was in the Marines and know my way around a bar fight. But that was *before*. Feels like another life altogether, even. Now I'm a single dad and I manage a vacation resort. I haven't done a bicep curl since before Lucy was born. My handyman skills start and stop at weekend warrior. I can at most fix a leaky pipe, but Cameron Riggs?

He can build an entire fucking house. From the ground up. And he learned to do it on the fly with cameras in his face.

Oh, and apparently he can sing and dance and was chosen as one of *People*'s Most Beautiful People the last two years running, along with his wife, Shelby Springfield, who was once America's pop princess and can rebuild a mid-century armoire with one hand tied behind her back. While six months pregnant.

At this point, I might as well assume Lorelai Jones cries diamonds and Craig Boseman has a literal Midas touch.

It shouldn't be a surprise. Maren has always been a knockout, even by knockout standards. Not that I'd have ever admitted it to Liam, but the fact remains. She could stop traffic. It's easy to forget up here, in the middle of the Northwoods, or at least compartmentalize, but she has her own version of magnetism. It's part of what made her YouTube channel so popular, and it's what drives the sales of her guided tours through the roof, even in the off season.

My point is, like attracts like and it's become absolutely, painstakingly clear to me in the last four hours that Maren belongs with a different kind of crowd. She fits in with Cameron and Shelby. She fits in with Lorelai Jones. She's one of them, even if she's not on TV or winning Grammys.

So what's she doing here? (Besides getting fingered on a couch by her older brother's best friend.)

She's fixing up her inheritance, selling it to the highest bidder, and then getting the fuck out of Dodge is what, and I need to remember that. This is temporary. *She* is temporary. (Even if the noises she made when she came apart on my fingers will remain branded in my memory until the day I die.)

I suddenly feel everyone's attention on me and realize they've asked me something.

"Sorry," I say, my face burning. "I was thinking of something else." Someone else. *Get your head in the game, Cole.* "Missed the question."

"Oh gosh," Maren asks, her auburn brows scrunched together. "Are we keeping you from something important?"

I glance at my watch. "Actually, I do need to run back to my place in about fifteen minutes to grab Anders off the bus.

But we're good for a few," I explain, motioning to Lucy, not wanting to disturb her. Lucy is curled in Maren's lap, drawing on her tablet. She's designing a lure, of all things. I know. I can hardly believe it myself.

"You can leave her with me," Maren offers, easily. "I'm comfortable and she seems okay."

I hesitate, but slowly nod my consent. "Want me to drop by your place after I grab Anders and pick up your pup?"

"Sure. He's probably getting antsy, and Anders is the only one who can wear him out. He knows where the fetch dummy is," she says. "If he wants, he can bring that and throw it off the dock out back for Rogers."

"Dinner?" I ask.

Maren's lips scrunch to the side and she dips her head, her voice soft, to ask Lucy, "Hey, girl, are you getting hungry? What should we get for dinner?"

"Dinner?" Lucy says, her blue eyes raising to Maren's face, her small fingers pausing their talented sketching.

"Yeah, what should we get for dinner?"

"Hot dogs," Lucy says.

"Hot dogs," Maren confirms, and then looks to Shelby and Cameron, who are watching our interaction with interest. Cameron is speculative, as if he's eyeing up a big project and wondering if the budget fits. Shelby is smiling, giving nothing away. "Do hot dogs sound okay to you guys?"

"Can we get cheddar dogs?" Shelby asks, rubbing a circle over her growing belly.

At this Maren laughs. "This is Wisconsin. You can get anything with cheese."

"No cheese, please," Lucy speaks up, her small lips in a pout.

"No cheese for you," I agree. "But we can get cheese for our friends."

"Okay," she says, still frowning. "No cheese, please," she whispers to herself and returns her attention to her drawing.

"You sure you're okay? This might take me a bit," I tell Maren. "If she gets upset, there's a bunch of PBS episodes downloaded on her tablet already so she doesn't need to stream anything. I keep her off YouTube. It's pretty unpredictable. There's an extra water bottle, too. She doesn't like tap water, even though I fill her bottle from the tap. Oh, and a snack," I continue, just remembering. "I packed her Goldfish crackers, but if she doesn't want them today, I am pretty sure there is an emergency Fruit Snacks in the inside zipped pocket. Oh, and an extra set of clothes in case she has an accident. She shouldn't, but new bathrooms sometimes intimidate her. She doesn't like the noise from the flush, so she'll ask you to flush it after she plugs her ears . . ."

"Actually, Luce, let's go potty now. Before I leave." I hold out a hand and Lucy scowls at me, shaking her head.

"Joe," Maren whispers. "She just went. Remember?" Her smile is gentle, and so is her tone. "We'll be fine. There will be *three* grown-ups here. If you count Cameron, which I barely do, because he's basically a giant kid. Regardless, we outnumber her."

"Two of those grown-ups are practically strangers to her."

"I won't leave her side," Maren promises.

"She's fine, now," I tell her, trying to find the right words, "but earlier—"

Maren shakes her head. "It wasn't a big deal."

My eyes widen in disbelief. It was a massive deal, actually. Maren came over this morning, like usual, to help with Anders, and Lucy was in the midst of a sensory overload. Maren made the mistake of unzipping her coat while approaching my daughter and ended up with a glass of orange juice in her face and a kick to the stomach.

I've never been more horrified in my entire life. Even if Maren comes over often enough that she's gotten to witness plenty of calm mornings, I can't keep myself from worrying we'll eventually scare her away.

"Okay," she admits. "It was a big deal, but I didn't take it personally, and as you can see"—she gestures to my daughter in her lap—"all's forgotten."

"How are you real?" I blurt, before shaking my head and scratching at my neck. "Sorry, it's just . . . she could've really hurt you over a *zipper*." In fact, I wasn't convinced she didn't hurt her, but Maren insisted she was fine.

"One, she didn't, I swear. Two, you already addressed it. It won't be the last time something like this happens, but I will do my best to remember her triggers. It's the best we can do."

I hesitate, but she's right. There's no secret cure for that kind of reaction. We can only do our best.

"*Joe*," she presses. "You've thought of everything. We'll be okay. Take your time. In fact, take a little extra. Maybe take Anders out for a cone or something special. It's still early. We don't need dinner yet. I swear I'll text you if there's an emergency."

I like the idea of taking Anders out for a little guy time. We haven't done that in . . . well, maybe ever? Lucy is okay with my parents, but only just recently and never without her big brother there.

"Okay," I agree, trying not to sound as reluctant as I feel. Maren raises a brow, and I know I'm caught. "It's not you," I insist. "It's just—"

"I know," she cuts me off. "But she's okay right now. She might not be another day, and that's all right. But for the moment, she is happy right where she is. So go."

I get out of my chair and then crouch to the ground, planning my words carefully. I don't want to make a big deal out of this and scare Lucy into realizing I'm leaving just in case she decides to care, but I don't want to sneak out, either. That can have other consequences. "Hey, Luce, I'm gonna go grab Anders off the bus. I'll be back soon."

"Okay, Daddy."

I stand before checking one last time. "Okay?"

Maren grins up at me, Lucy's attention back on her drawing. "Okay."

I grab my wallet and keys and try not to look back. This time it's not because I'm worried over my daughter. She's in good hands.

This time it's because I don't want to collect another piece of Maren's "temporary" and add it to my "forever."

SIXTEEN

Like a Prayer

Maren

MY BEST FRIEND WAITS APPROXIMATELY THIRTY-FIVE SECONDS after the door closes behind Joe before she hones in.

"What. Was. That?" she asks, impressing meaning into the words as if I haven't noticed the eyes she's been giving me since the moment Joe got caught zoning out and I talked him into leaving Lucy with me.

"I'm gonna go break apart that window seat in the main room so my wife can sand it down and make it pretty again. Don't mind me. I'm not here." Cam smirks over his shoulder at me. "Good luck!"

"Don't make it weird," I say to her, my eyes darting to the child in my lap.

"Obviously, I wouldn't. But Mare. Come on. You've been here maybe two months? You two act like you've been married for years!"

"What? No we don't!"

"Want me to grab the dog?" she asks in a poor imitation of Joe's deep voice. "What's for dinner? You get that kid and

I'll get the other . . ." She finishes in an even worse imitation of my voice.

I feel my face grow hot under her scrutiny. Okay, so maybe that does sound kind of domestic. "I'm just helping him out while I'm here. We're practically family."

"So you keep telling me. What's with the"—she pauses and then mouths the last words—*eye fucking*?

I straighten, my eyes darting down to Lucy, who is busy "braiding" my hair into twists. There is no amount of conditioner in the world that will save my hair after this.

Pressing my lips together, I consider my words carefully, mindful of young ears. "Shelby Springfield, you are evil. Did you wait for me to be confined before you decided to lay your twenty questions on me? Is Lorelai in on this?"

Shelby flips her hair over her shoulder and pats the top of her belly. "Maybe and definitely. So spill. You have no way out."

I sigh and Lucy mimics me, giving up on my hair and leaning her head onto my chest.

"I'm not staying."

"So?"

"So this is temporary."

"And I'll repeat, so?"

"So I'm not about to jump into a fling with a single father who also happens to be best friends with my older brother." I finish the last words in a rush and work to keep my breath steady, even though my heart is racing. This is the exact thing I have told myself over and over since the night on the couch two weeks ago. The repercussions are too much. I couldn't live with myself. There are too many factors.

"You already slept with him," Shelby says in a soft voice,

and I look down at Lucy, alarmed, but somehow she's fast asleep on my lap. Hell, now I really am trapped.

"I have not," I say in a near-pout. "But we did round a few bases like teenagers on my couch and it was possibly the hottest thing I've ever experienced in my life. Which is saying something because Shane was no slouch in that, um"—I glance down again—"area."

"I see."

"Do you?"

Shelby nods. "I do. That's a pickle."

"It is."

"You want more."

"Of course I do. But I doubt he does, and again, I'm leaving. There are too many strings attached for a fling, and anyway, I don't think I'm a fling kind of girl."

"Why do you have to leave?"

"What do I have to stay for?"

Shelby's gaze drops to my lap and mine follows it, but neither of us say anything. I know what she's thinking. It's crossed my mind. Well, more like it's crossed my heart.

But I can't put words to it. I won't. It's not my place. They belong to someone else.

And I belong to no one at all.

⌣⌣⌣

My brother calls just as I'm heading out to take Rogers on a misty early morning walk. It's my second phone call this morning. My family members back in Michigan are operating an hour ahead, and they have certainly been making use of the time difference to catch me.

My mom and dad called while I sat on my porch, sipping

coffee. They tag-teamed via the speakerphone, which I hate because there's always a weird delay, but they mean well. "I don't want to keep you for too long," my mom always says. As though speaking with my parents every week is an inconvenience. Being here, literal steps away from Simon and Donna Cole, helps. For example, I didn't have to rehash the weird final, *final* breakup with Shane at the lodge for my parents. Donna gave them the full scoop with all the not-so-gory details, so they only needed my verbal confirmation that it was as uneventful as they'd heard.

Liam, though. I could do without his checking in.

Normally I love talking to my brother, but right now, the timing is . . . not awesome. I don't know what the heck to say to Liam. We usually discuss work (I'm currently unemployed), or relationships (I'm currently unattached). I'm still feeling the repercussions of the time his oldest, closest friend finger-banged me on his couch, and yeah. Not telling him that one. I can't even fathom how that would go over. For me *or* for Joe. *Especially* Joe, who made it clear he wasn't looking for a repeat of said finger-banging moments before driving himself home with a very telling wet spot on his pants. I have no plans of repeating it and negative plans of ever sharing it with any living soul. Except Shelby. Who already told Lorelai, if the **DAYUM GIRL GET IT** text is anything to go by.

But apart from *them*.

So here I am, fervently trying to make idle small talk that is interesting enough to avoid the conversations I don't want to/can't have, but boring enough that he'll be looking for a way to end the call. I'm currently running through every character I've had on a musky tour in the last two months. I've already told him about Steve-O the Yeller and Drunk-as-a-Skunk Patrick and am trying to draw out a tale about Maggie, who brought a full Crock-Pot of mac 'n' cheese to share on the boat.

"I've been meaning to ask you," my brother interrupts and I stop short. "How's Joe doing?"

"Who?" I ask like a complete idiot, my heart thumping in my ears.

"Joe, Maren. Josiah Cole."

"Oh. Right. I know Joe."

"Yeah. Good." Liam chuckles into the phone. "How's he doing?"

"Joe?"

"Yeah. And the kids. How's he been? Do you see him much?"

"Oh." I swallow. I decide I can be honest. "He's . . . well. I guess he's okay. He works really hard. His kids are awesome. Anders is my fishing partner. He's almost as nuts about musky as I was at his age, if you can believe it." Liam grunts and I smile. "I know. And Lucy is a doll. She has tough mornings still, but she's adjusting to her special preschool well, and I even was able to keep her for a couple of hours the other night so Joe could take a break."

My brother is quiet a beat and I immediately want to walk back every word I've just said. Except I don't *know* what I've just said. Finally, he speaks. "I didn't realize you were spending so much time with him."

"Well, and the kids," I rush to clarify. "Mostly the kids, really. They're great, and Joe can use the help, and I'm here. So . . ." I trail off, cringing, painfully aware of how defensive I must sound.

"Be careful there, Mare."

"I don't know what you mean."

"I mean," he says, his tone colored with every shade of big brother in his arsenal, "we've been through this. Joe is a grown-ass man with two kids and an ex-wife. His problems are way over your head, kid."

"I'm almost thirty-four, not eighteen, Liam. Not that it matters, because I'm just being a friend, helping another friend— *your* friend, actually."

"You're thirty-three going on twenty-three, Maren. You don't have a job, or a place to live. Not to mention you broke off the only serious relationship you've had in years because it 'felt wrong.'"

He's not saying anything I haven't said to myself, but *wow*, it stings coming from him.

"I'm just *helping*," I repeat, my words sharp but measured.

"And that's good," he assures me, his tone mild, and I want to smack him through the phone for it. "I'm sure he appreciates any help he can get. I'm just warning you not to get in over your head with him."

"I'm not sure I know what you're implying."

"I'm not implying anything. I'm stating facts. Joe has a lot on his plate. Real things. Things you can't even begin to relate to. And the last thing he needs is you getting all involved, playing house, and then having your feelings hurt when he has to move on from this for the good of his kids."

I bite my lip, hearing his words and feeling the truth of them settle in my gut. And what I'm feeling isn't good. My brother is right. Mostly. His delivery leaves much to be desired, but I'm able to see past my defensiveness to the core message. Joe is not for me. His kids are not for me.

And I am certainly not for them.

"I need to go, Liam. I'm supposed to meet Cameron at the apartment," I lie, ready to end the call. Cameron may not be at the apartment yet, but I might as well head on over. The sooner I get this done, the sooner I can move on. Again.

♪♪♪

It's the off season but the bar is full tonight. We could say Cameron and Shelby are the reason, but that's only partly true. It's hopping in the lodge tonight because it's karaoke night. Well, okay, not officially. Because it's the off season, there's no such thing as karaoke night. But there is a mic and loud music and lots of drunk vacationers.

So while half of the seats are filled with resort guests hoping to casually rub elbows with the reality TV stars, the other half showed up because they knew Josiah Cole would be behind the bar.

I wish I was exaggerating. He's *that* beloved. And if he was dreamy at eighteen—tanned, arrogant, built like a quarterback—he's a sight to behold at thirty-eight. He's in a pair of low-slung, perfectly worn jeans, a light blue button-down with the sleeves rolled over his forearms, and a Leinenkugel's hat worn backward over his golden waves.

He's bobbing his head and swinging his delicious hips as he pours from the tap while an older regular named Johnny belts out "Fortunate Son" by Creedence Clearwater Revival. I'm late, because I didn't want to come. Shelby texted me as I was sitting on the edge of my bed, debating pretending I fell asleep early.

We've been working our asses off at the bait shop and apartment. It's not a stretch.

I didn't, though. Instead, I texted her back saying that I was on my way, slipped into my oldest cowboy boots, and walked out the door, not bothering to put on makeup or fix my hair. It's a high-ponytail-and-ChapStick night and that's that.

And beer. Multiple beers. If I'm going to survive this, I need alcohol.

"Hey! Finally!" Shelby says, finding me as I pull up a stool at the bar. "I was about to sic Cam on you! I thought you'd fallen asleep!"

"I thought about it. I'm pretty tired," I tell her. "I might just have a beer and call it."

"What?" Shelby's eyes are the size of Oreos. "Absolutely not. This is our last night and I've already convinced Cam to sing a duet with me. Two, actually. I picked 'I Got You Babe' and he picked 'Friends in Low Places.'"

Oh, for Pete's sake. This is what I get for being best friends with outgoing-celebrity types. *So much karaoke.* If only Lorelai were here.

"I'll just grab that beer, then," I tell her and shift to the bar, waiting my turn.

Donna serves me, as Joe is preoccupied with a couple of blond twentysomethings. I ask for my beer and a seat opens up next to me, so I motion for Shelby, and she and Cameron walk over. Ever the gentleman (plus, he's giant, so he barely fits on the stools anyway), Cam leaves the seats for the ladies and stands over our shoulders.

By the end of beer one, Donna kisses my cheek goodbye and Shelby asks me to save her seat so she can pick out an ice cream cone from the freezer in the corner where the Coles stock a variety of options usually found only on ice cream trucks.

By the end of beer two, Cam and Shelby have sung their first duet to deafening applause and several dozen phone screens recording them.

By the end of beer three, Joe is leaning against the bar in front of me, chatting with Cameron about how not to pass out in the delivery room. I'm pressed forward, and so is he, his forearm inches from mine. It's then that it happens. The moment I've been dreading since I hung up with my brother four days ago and decided to put some distance between me and the Coles, not for my sake, but for theirs. Joe is straightening from the bar at the sound of his name being shouted, and someone passes him a mic. He's laughing and I'm captivated by the way the little lines around his beautiful blue eyes crinkle. The fingers I have wrapped around my beer—a fresh one that Joe just slid my way without asking—squeeze tight and then slip around the condensation.

All it takes is the distinctive opening chords and my heart jumps straight into my throat. And the bastard knows it, too. He swerves to me and gives me a cheesy wink before opening his mouth to sing.

Fucking A it's Bon Jovi. Not just any Bon Jovi, either. It's the most romantic song of my childhood memories: "I'll Be There for You." It's all growly and hot as hell and I barely notice how the rest of the bar sings along, including my famous best friend and her husband, because all I can see is Joe. And he keeps smiling at me like he doesn't realize he's ruining me forever. I want to scream at him to stop being so fucking perfect. I want to jump across this bar and wrap my arms and legs around him and never let go. I want to run straight out the door and pack my shit and drive to Arizona and the Grand Canyon and beg them to hire me.

I want to stay here forever, watching him be this happy and relaxed.

Instead, I feel my face stretch into a grin that almost hurts, and I sing along. Joe notices my effort and his face changes, becoming impossibly lighter. I watch the tendons of his neck as he throws back his head and belts it like Bon Jovi before returning his gaze to mine and beaming at me.

Finally, he mouths, pointing at me, before picking up the chorus.

And suddenly I realize he's happy *because* I'm happy. Because he pulled this smile out of me. It's why he picked up the mic and sang Bon Jovi. He did it for me.

And I don't know what to do with that.

♪♪♪

I said I don't do flings. And I don't. I commit and am loyal and have no interest in casual.

But he sang Bon Jovi to make me smile. And before that he gave me one heck of an orgasm on my couch. And before that he took me out on his boat and gave me a really amazing day. And before that he convinced me to stay in a nice cabin at his resort for basically free and to take a job doing guided fishing tours, which I adore, and, well, I've had three and a half beers and I'm turned on as hell.

Still. This is very unlike me. I don't do casual. Like ever. I'm firmly a third-date kind of girl. No judgment, just it takes me a while longer to warm up to someone.

But it's as though I was born to be attracted to Joe.

I've been carefully avoiding being alone with him since my brother thoroughly warned me off—again—but after closing down the bar, Joe offered to walk me home, and in turn, I invited him to come inside. He barely closed the door before I had him pressed back against it, my hands in his hair, my tongue in his mouth, his fists in my shirt, his hips pressed against me. "Last time" be damned, he doesn't even protest.

"I want to kiss you," I tell him.

"You're already—"

I press the pad of my finger to his lips, cutting him off. "Not here." I rub my fingers where he is straining against his jeans. "Here."

"You don't have to do that," Joe insists, as I ever so slowly tease his zipper down. His tone isn't very convincing, if I'm honest. He's pretty out of breath for someone who doesn't want his cock in my mouth.

"Shh," I whisper, slipping my hand into his waistband. "If you don't want this, I won't do it. Otherwise, be quiet and let me taste you."

"Jesus fuck," he groans. "It's been years, Maren. I don't know if . . ." He trails off, seemingly at odds with himself. I watch his throat work as he swallows hard and my tongue darts out to lick at the place where his stubbled jaw meets his ear. "Please," he whispers, and I immediately comply, pulling him out of his pants and gripping him in my hand, thick and powerful. I sink to my knees right there. My mouth waters as I lean forward, my tongue darting out to the tip, circling it slowly. Then I lick up the slit, pumping my hand before taking him fully into my mouth and sucking hard. His head falls back against the door with a thud and he hisses, his hips bucking. He's gently fucking my mouth and I've never been so turned on.

I roll my tongue, hollowing my cheeks and wrapping my hand around his thigh, holding him to me as I work. I twist my grip and squeeze as I suck in and his breathing grows harsh.

"Maren, I'm going to—Oh fu—" He tries to reach for my

head, my shoulders, but I don't budge. I suck harder, giving him more of my tongue, more of my hand, all of my enthusiasm. My thighs are clenched and my underwear is soaking and my breasts are tingling and all I want is to hear this man come apart.

And a moment later, he does. I swallow him down before letting him go and resting my forehead against his hip, catching my breath. He's panting and slumped against the door, barely standing, so I gently tuck him back in his boxer briefs, then his jeans, and pull up his zipper. Finally, I rock back on my toes and push off the door to get to my feet.

"What just happened?" he asks breathlessly when I'm at eye level again.

I don't know what to say, feeling suddenly very sober and very calm. Content.

That has to be a good sign, right? Unless I'm not as calm as I think. I suppose time will tell.

Instead of responding, I shush him again, a tiny smirk playing on my lips, and press a kiss to his stubbly cheek. I reach behind him for the doorknob and twist it. He picks up on the hint and starts to move.

"Good night, Joe. Sleep tight."

He smiles at me in the dim light and walks through the door. "I expect I'll sleep like a baby, thanks to you. 'Night, Maren."

I close the door behind him, leaning against it. Feeling the throb in my core, I decide to head to bed. I'm thinking the memory of the sounds he made while I worked him with my mouth will be the perfect soundtrack to my own orgasm. I should sleep pretty well myself.

SEVENTEEN

The Boy Who Blocked His Own Shot

Joe

Fourteen years before, somewhere in the Middle East

I'VE BEEN SITTING IN THE COMPUTER LAB FOR NEARLY AN HOUR, *waiting for privacy, but Kennedy has three girls on the line back home that he has to email. I don't know how he manages it. Not just keeping them all straight, but having the interest of three girls. He's not much to look at, even in fatigues, and he's more than a little bit of a dick, but I guess to each their own.*

Finally he rolls away from the keyboard, stretching his fingers over his head with an obnoxious groan. "Done." He walks over to the printer, grabs up his pages, and dangles them in my face. "New spank-bank materials up and loaded."

"Nice," I tell him in a dull voice.

"You headed back? I'll wait for the reading if you want."

Not for the first time, I wonder if these girls know he takes their private emails and reads them aloud to the rest of the guys. That strangers hear their sexual fantasies and roar with laughter. Maybe they do and they don't care. It boosts morale or whatever.

"Go on ahead," I tell him.

"Does your girl know what an old man you are?"

He doesn't wait for an answer, and I wasn't going to give him one anyway. They all call me "Gramps." At first it was because my name sounds like something from the Civil War. Josiah Cole. But then it was because I have a fiancée that I've been with since we were in high school and don't mess around on her. Not even in theory.

Not my style.

Kennedy leaves and I'm finally alone. I don't check my email. I've already responded to Kiley and my mom tonight. Kiley's email was full of wedding-planning questions and her venting about work. Normal stuff that I responded to as best I could, even though I'm not really in the headspace to have an opinion about flower arrangements, and I can't even imagine what "strawberry jasmine mint" filling would taste like in a tiered cake. My mom's email had me feeling shitty, though that wasn't her intention. It was all about the resort and my dad and what my old friends are doing now that they've graduated from college and are moving away.

It's all good stuff. I'm happy for them. And usually that kind of news rolls off my back. I'm content doing what I'm doing. I was made for the Marines. I have a purpose and it complements my restlessness.

But there are moments, usually late at night, when everything is quiet and no one is attacking us and we're in that period of waiting, in between missions, that I feel the heavy press of homesickness.

I glance behind me once more before clicking on the search engine and typing in her name. Musky Maren. As expected, she's added new content. Makes sense—it's summer break in Wiscon-

sin. She's recorded videos in other states, on other lakes, but Wisconsin is where she says she feels at home. It's why I come to her website.

I click on the first video and settle back in my seat, adjusting the volume. The best part about Maren's videos is she doesn't talk too much. Even still, I sometimes mute the sound. I'm not interested in fishing tips. I just want to forget I'm in a desert for a while. I want to see the loons, painted turtles, blue skies, white clouds, and gently rippling waves. I want to imagine I can smell the wind kissed with pine. One time, Mare caught a mama black bear and her cubs swimming across the lake, and I just watched in rapt silence, my chest burning.

Today, I watch Maren. I've known her most of my life, but she's always been a kid to me. This time, I'm struck with how grown-up she looks. Mature. Long reddish-brown hair tucked under the brim of a baseball cap, the ends tossing in the wind. She's in shorts and a simple tank. Tanned limbs and relaxed smile. Freckles dotting the bridge of her nose and scattered across her cheeks. She looks like summer.

I do the math. I turn twenty-five in a few months' time. So she must be what? Nineteen? Twenty? I grin to myself, thinking of my best friend Liam, her oldest brother. I bet he's shitting himself, trying to fend off the punk frat boys sweating after her.

I don't envy him the job.

On-screen, Maren's face splits in a wide, beaming smile and she stands, yanking up her pole and reeling for all she's worth, her hands a whir of movement. I click on the volume in time to hear her excited squeal. There. That sounds like the Jig I know.

A splash of water later and she's holding up a giant northern pike, deftly removing the hook and snagging her fingers in the gills, careful to avoid the needle-sharp teeth. I watch her, from halfway across the world, leaning back in my chair, my arms folded across my chest. She's telling me about the fish, the bait she used, the conditions of the water, all in an enthusiastic, breathless way that just bleeds happiness, and I feel it like a missile strike to my solar plexus.

She's brought me home.

ᒎ ᒎ ᒎ

I don't have the first fucking clue what I am doing—I only know I don't want to stop.

I haven't so much as hugged a woman I wasn't related to in three years, and suddenly I'm making out on couches and getting head in darkened hallways from Maren Laughlin. Maren, whom I've known since she was in diapers. Whose brother has been my ride-or-die for thirty-plus years. Whose brother will shoot my dick off if he finds out it ever touched his sister's perfect mouth.

My eyes roll back in my skull at the mere memory of her tongue curling along . . .

Christ, I'm in trouble.

It's not like I planned for this to happen. In fact, I'm not even sure I know exactly what *is* happening. I know I like to be around her. And my kids like to be around her. And she seems to like being around us. Her friends are a lot, but in a good way. Her family loves me like I'm one of their own, and I love them. I'm unattached and so is she. I'm an adult and so is she. Maren loves the resort and the lake as much as I do.

All the boxes are checked, and yet I'm not sure what they're checked *for*, exactly. Are we friends? Are these benefits? Are we dating? Should I ask her out? It's been twenty years since I've asked a girl, a woman, out. So long that it *was* a girl, but now would be a woman. I have no idea if that's even how it's done anymore.

And I have no idea if she wants that. She's leaving as soon as the work is done and she sells the bait shop and apartment, despite the way she seems to be growing attached to me and the kids. She had been fitting into our lives seamlessly nearly from the beginning, so much so that I hardly knew it'd happened until her friends arrived and she'd taken a step back, inserting space between us.

Then, I really noticed. And I didn't like it. I wasn't sure if I'd done something to scare her off. Let's face it, I'm not exactly a prize over here, between the ex and the ready-made family, and Maren's got the entire world open to her. She's gorgeous and sweet and generous and patient and outgoing and has this ability to suck everyone into her orbit and set them spinning.

What if that's all this is? Magnetism. Gravity. Chemistry.

Am I just a desperate jackass, panting after her like that idiot Bryce Callahan? Like all those guys who used to stalk her YouTube channel and jack off to her pictures?

I'd almost convinced myself to let her be. Let her finish her job and move on wherever the wind takes her next. It would be for the best and I could chalk it up to being lonely and pathetic. But then last night, when she'd looked off, I sang Bon Jovi because I hoped it would cheer her up. I couldn't help myself. I only wanted to bring playful, happy Maren back. And it worked like a charm. She lit up like a house on fire.

And then she devoured me in her cabin. Literally. My head is still spinning. I've never come so hard in my life.

We need to talk.

Or maybe we don't. She doesn't seem to want to with all

her sexy shushing. Maybe this is what dating is like now. Was that a hookup? Are we hooking up?

This is the kind of shit I usually talk to Liam about, but . . . for obvious reasons, that's off the table.

Which is why I asked Cameron Riggs to meet me for coffee this morning. I told him I had some renovation questions and needed his advice at one of the villas. Which isn't a lie, since we're renovating them this winter. It's just that I already have a reliable contractor on board for that.

Cameron shows up in his truck. I jump out of the golf cart and immediately hand him a steaming cardboard cup of black coffee. He looks a little worse for wear after last night's impromptu karaoke, but is still beaming good-naturedly like a happy fucker who knows he's won the lottery in life.

I open the villa door and we step into a large open space, the kitchen to our left and the living room to our right. Cameron immediately looks to me for direction.

"Actually, I lied about the renovation advice, but don't worry," I hastily assure him. Dude is huge and I don't know him well enough to be sure he wouldn't punch if he felt cornered. "I'm not ambushing you. I do need advice on something, just not construction."

Cameron leans against the granite-topped island and sips his coffee, at ease. "Ah. I've been wondering. Hold on a second." He pulls his phone out of his pocket and immediately starts to scroll.

"What are you—" But I can already hear the distinctive tone of a FaceTime call going through.

A man's voice drawls in a harried southern accent. "Riggs, I already told you to call Arlo about the tux. You're barking up the wrong tree with this linen-pants thing. I don't give a shit if you wear swim trunks, just get your ass there in time to catch me when I pass out after Lorelai appears at the end of the aisle looking like god's gift to, well, me."

Cameron shakes his head at the screen, laughing. "Save your breath, *Huckleberry*. I already worked it out with your best man. I'm not calling about that. I have someone here who needs our advice. He's in love with Maren."

EIGHTEEN

Please, Please Let Me Get What I Want

Joe

THE VOICE ON THE OTHER END, HUCKLEBERRY, I SUPPOSE, GIVES an easy grunt of understanding before saying, "Oh. Am I finally meeting Joe?"

I choke on air, rasping and hacking as I hear Cameron say, "Yeah. It's Joe."

"All right. Let's hear it."

Cameron sets the phone down on the island, facing both of us, and motions for me to begin.

"First of all, I'm not in love with Maren."

"Debatable," Cameron says.

"Sure, man." Huckleberry, who I'm assuming is Craig Boseman, Lorelai's soon-to-be husband, says this in a way that communicates he doesn't believe me in the slightest.

"I don't understand what's happening here," I mutter, embarrassed. "I didn't even tell you I needed to ask about Maren in the first place, and I definitely didn't mean for you to involve . . . *Huckleberry*."

"You can call me Huck, or Craig."

"Nice to meet you."

Cameron smirks from his place against the counter. "Oh, so you really brought me here to talk about construction?"

"Jesus, fuck. Fine."

"It's all right, Joe," Huck says in a patient tone. I take some time to look at him on the screen. He appears to be in some office. He's very normal looking. Scruffy beard, T-shirt, a pair of black eyeglasses. "You're talking to the only other two guys on the planet who can relate to falling in love with one of these three remarkable women. Welcome to the club."

My mouth opens and closes a few times before I shake my head and put down my coffee and make the decision to roll with it. It's not like I have anyone else to talk to about this shit.

"Fine. Okay. So I'll just jump right in. I like Maren. And I think she might like me. Hell." I cringe. "I sound like a middle-schooler." I straighten and swallow, starting again. "I have *feelings* for her and sometimes I think she might have feelings for me, too, but I can't tell."

"Riggs?" Huck prods, removing his glasses and motioning to the screen with them.

"I haven't talked to Maren, but they do an awful lot of eye fucking."

I choke again. "What?"

Cameron shrugs. "What do you mean, *what?*"

"Christ." I rub my palms against my eyes. "Never mind, I don't think I can do this."

"Joe. She's worth it. We've all been there. Literally been there. I had an anonymous erotic poetry account that I used to flirt with Lorelai, and Cameron learned how to build houses just to have sex with Shelby."

"That's an oversimplification." Cameron frowns at Huck on the screen.

"We don't have time for the 'It all started when I was a tap-dancing eleven-year-old' version, Riggs."

These guys are idiots. I sink down onto the sofa in front of the island, facing them.

"I need to talk to Maren. I know this. Beyond the, um, eye fucking or whatever. I'm just . . . out of my depth. It's been like over twenty years since I've done this," I tell them. "I have no idea how this works nowadays. Do, um, I ask her out on a date? Or something?"

Cameron straightens, grinning wide. "That's a good start."

"It's just . . . we've hooked up? A few times?" My ears feel like they are on fire. This is humiliating.

"Okay," Huck says, gesturing with his glasses on-screen again. "And how was it?"

I roll my eyes. "Hot as hell. Obviously."

He grins. "That's good."

"Right. That's probably the reason for the supposed eye fucking, though I'm still not sure Cameron's reading that right."

"Shelby sees it, too," Cameron murmurs as if that settles it. Which I guess it kind of does.

Huck clears his throat. "I'm not sure I understand the issue."

I slump back against the sofa. "I don't, either."

"You like her?"

"*Like* her," I say, emphasizing *like*. "Yes. Very much."

"So what's holding you back?"

"I've known her family my entire life. Her brother is my best friend. That's one issue. She's also kind of hot and cold with me. I think she's interested and she's great with my kids, but she's younger than me and I don't even know if she wants kids, let alone mine."

Cameron purses his lips. "That's getting ahead of yourself, don't you think? You haven't even had a date."

"That's the thing, though!" I point out, agitated. "I can't even consider a date unless we're on the same page because our families and my kids are deal-breakers. Her not staying here is a deal-breaker. Which is completely selfish, I know. How can I ask any of that of someone without a first date? Let alone someone like Maren?"

Cameron's face falls into something more serious. "I see."

"You do?"

"Absolutely. That's a lot," he confirms easily.

Huck asks, "What do you mean, 'someone like Maren'?"

I blow out a breath, my fingers tugging at my hair out of frustration, trying to find the words.

"Like, she's everything. Maren is beautiful inside and out. She's . . . she calms me. When I'm with her, it feels like home. She gives me that. It's comfortable, but she's also the sexiest woman I've ever known. I don't know how that's true, because growing up, I barely noticed her. Maybe she was just too young. But now it's like she can walk in the room, and every part of me notices. Before I even see her. I feel her there, and I want her, but I also just want to be near her to talk to her. To make her laugh. She laughs, and it's like . . . stupid."

"Stupid?"

"I mean, I'm . . . stupid. For her, though. And in general."

"Totally in love with her," Huck agrees. "Sorry, man. You're in it now."

I don't argue. I'm not ready to concede, but I can hear myself. "So what do I do?"

"Man." Cameron is laughing. "I have no idea."

I fall back against the couch cushion again, defeated.

Huck says, "I think you need to talk to her. But for all the reasons you already mentioned, I get why that's difficult. It's a lot of pressure really early on."

"And she isn't planning to stay."

The room is silent for a long minute, with Cameron sipping in contemplation, Huck lost in thought, and me in misery. Until Cameron brightens.

"Ask her to stay."

I try not to sound doubtful. "You think?"

The big man shrugs. "Can't hurt. The apartment and bait shop are nearly fixed up to sell, but she seems pretty cozy here. Ask her to stay through the holidays and let things progress, naturally. Hopefully, time will give you more perspective. Both of you."

The idea has merit. It's low stakes in the way that she can say no and that would be my answer, or she could say yes and we can spend more time together and see where it leads. Maybe I can even ask her on a date.

"That's not a terrible idea," I tell him after a beat.

"For what it's worth," he tells me, straightening off the counter, "I do think she likes you. She watches you nearly as much as you watch her. I'm hardly an expert—it took me a decade to work my garbage out with Shelby—but I do know it all came together when I made the decision to stay. You just have to have the guts to ask."

I nod. "I can do that. She's worth that."

"She is," Huck confirms. "They all are. Okay, now that that's all worked out, I have to go—I have Annie Mathers in the studio. Nice to officially meet you, Joe. Keep the first weekend in February open."

Huck disconnects the call and I look at Cameron as he puts away his phone. "February?"

Cameron grins. "His wedding."

ʃʃʃ

When I decide to do something, I have to do it immediately. Now is late, yesterday would have been better. Cameron and Shelby left hours ago, and Maren told me she'd be at the apartment, painting her new, unpaneled, Sheetrocked walls. The late-October sky feels heavy, overcast, and smells like snow. Before I know it, the lake will be frozen over, and the ground will be hidden under a layer of ice and white. If I were Maren and wrapping up on things here, I would plan to leave before that happens.

So I'm asking her now.

Despite my talk with Cameron and Craig earlier, I'm still feeling awkward as fuck about this. Even with the kissing and flirting and spending time together over the last few months, it's easy to convince myself that I've somehow misread things and am about to make a massive misstep. In other words, I'm freaking out. And it's important to point out, I haven't freaked out about anything in years. I don't do freaking out. I get shit done, staying calm and cool. Collected. Freaking out gets you killed in the Marines.

"It's just a question," I say under my breath. "It's not life and death. You've held a live grenade in your hand. This is cake in comparison." On that happy note, I knock on the door before pushing it open.

"Hey, Joe!" Maren calls over her shoulder. She's paint-flecked and adorable in a pair of stained work overalls. There's a space heater on the floor behind her, humming as it warms the room, and soft country music playing from somewhere.

It's cozy because it's her. Maren makes every room she's in feel like that.

I shake off the nonsensical thought and wipe my sweaty hands down my jeans.

"Hi, I thought I could help. My mom is getting Anders off the bus today and Lucy is napping over there."

Maren's eyes widen in happy surprise. "That would be awesome! We'll get this room done in no time, then. There's an extra roller over there. I can finish the edges and you fill in behind me?"

"Sure."

I grab the roller and pour some paint in a plastic tray, taking my time so I don't spill. Then I start zigzagging my way along the wall she's already finished edging. We work in companionable silence for a long time. My nerves all but disappear. In fact, the repetition and the company calm me. And that in turn gives me the confidence to ask, because no one else has ever had this effect on me. My entire life, I've operated on high alert. Constantly aware and ready for anything at a moment's notice. Until now. Now, I feel . . . settled.

That has to mean something.

"Cameron said you were about finished," I say, careful to keep my tone neutral. I continue rolling the paint, not looking in her direction.

"Just about," she agrees. "I'm waiting on appliances to arrive for the apartment. Shelby helped me pick some basic but sturdy options. And I need to order custom shelving for the shop, but Cameron drafted some measurements and calculations for me, so it's just a matter of finding something I like.

I'm thinking another month for shipping, but all the hard stuff is done."

"A month," I say, refilling my roller and dabbing the excess off. "That's well into November. Think you'll stay for Thanksgiving?"

I hear her brush pause in its strokes before picking up. "I hadn't thought of it, actually. Maybe? Got room for one more around the Cole table?"

"Always," I answer sincerely. "The kids would love it, too. Especially after Kiley bailed. It'll give us something extra to celebrate. A special guest this year."

Maren pauses again and I look up at her, meeting her eyes. "That's a very kind thing to say, Josiah Cole."

I shrug. "I meant it." I hesitate before laying it all out there. "You could stay for Christmas and New Year's, too."

"Oh." Her brows scrunch together. "I thought the kids were going to be with Kiley over the holidays. Don't tell me she's already canceled that, too?"

I honestly have no idea what my ex will do. "Not so far, though I wouldn't put it past her. But I was actually thinking you could stay and keep me company." I clear my throat. "Just, you know. Me. Without my kids."

This time Maren puts down her brush. She drops to one knee to steady herself and runs her fingers along her denim-clad legs, in a smoothing motion. Her head is tilted to the side and she studies me for a long beat. I refuse to shift or fidget, meeting her gaze straight on. Something else I perfected in the Marines. Being still. Waiting.

"You're asking me to stay?" she asks, her voice soft but clear.

"Yes."

"With you."

I nod. "With me."

I wait for her to ask me why. I don't have an answer if she does. Not one I feel like I can freely give her anyway. But she surprises me. She seems to know what I can't say.

"Okay. I'll stay."

I blink and can't help myself from checking. "Really?"

Her perfect mouth spreads into the sweetest smile I've ever had the privilege of seeing and something catches in my chest. "Yeah, really."

I pick up my roller and dip it in the paint, licking my lips and turning back to the wall. "Good."

A half second later I hear her brush resume, too. "Good."

NINETEEN

Girl

~~~~~~~~~~~~~~~~~~~~~~~~~~~~~~

Maren

Lorelai: Well, well, well, how the turntables have turned.

Maren: Oh please.

Shelby: BAHAHAHAHA

Lorelai: I'm just saying someone was feeling pretty sure of herself back in Nashville when I was going through my own crisis. All "love makes people idiots" and HERE WE ARE.

Maren: That doesn't sound like me.

Maren: *Mariah Carey I don't know her gif*

Shelby: You know you can just use the gif right?

Maren: Says the person who needed to be taught how to social media.

Maren: And yes, I do know that but the cell reception is spotty here and gifs take for the fuck ever to load.

Lorelai: So anyway, he asked you to stay.

Maren: He asked me to stay.

Shelby: And not just for the kids either. He asked you to stay with HIM, specifically.

Maren: Yeah.

Lorelai: How are you feeling about this? Last we talked you were ready to hit the road.

Maren: Against my better judgment, I feel okay about it.

Shelby: What does that mean?

Maren: . . .

Maren: It's . . . just that I talked to my brother and he kind of warned me off Joe. Again. He said some things, brotherly things, that weren't wrong but also not completely right about Joe being this divorced, single dad and me being . . . me.

Shelby: Explain what "you being you" means.

Lorelai: FUCKING LIAM

Maren: Ha. Right. Fucking Liam. He just reminded me that I am basically unemployed and just broke up with my first serious boyfriend and I'm almost 34 and just like, idk. Floating along. He thinks Joe needs someone better.

Shelby: He said what????

Lorelai: I'm sorry, but WHAT. THE. FUCK. There is no one on earth better than you.

Maren: Shelby—it was implied. The subtext being "he needs someone, opposite of you."

Maren: Lorelai—you're sweet.

Shelby: So that's why you were all weird before we left.

Maren: Mostly, yeah.

Lorelai: Okay, but he asked you to stay, so . . .

Maren: Oh, I also gave him a blowjob. So whoops.

Lorelai: !! Before or after he asked you to stay?

Maren: Before he asked me to stay, after Liam warned me off, and after he sang Bon Jovi to me.

Shelby: THATTA GIRL

Lorelai: Can I just say, I love that Bon Jovi is your kink. It's so surprising but also somehow not?

Maren: Is it Bon Jovi or Joe singing Bon Jovi? Either way, he brought me to my knees, literally.

Lorelai: Presumably with your staying, sex is on the table . . .

Shelby: On the counter, in the bed, in the boat . . . oh! On the bar!

Maren: Wow, that second trimester really hits different, doesn't it?

Lorelai: You do know you can't get pregnant again, right? You have to wait until this one is born.

Shelby: Ha ha.

Shelby: If someone could get a pregnant woman pregnant again, it would be my husband and his tree-trunk thighs.

Maren: So if we're keeping track: he got me off and then I got him off and now I've said I will stay through the holidays for no good reason except because he asked and I am helpless against his charms.

Maren: And perhaps more concerning, I am also helpless against his children's charms.

Shelby: I don't blame you. Anders is his dad in miniature and practically worships the ground you walk on. Lucy has everyone wrapped around her finger and I mean that in a good way. She's tough, but she's worth it.

Maren: *sigh* Exactly.

Lorelai: Before talking to Liam, did any of this concern you?

Shelby: Oooh. Good question.

Maren: I guess not, no. Things have been happening very organically. Like, I didn't even really notice how close we'd gotten until Shelby and Cameron came up for their visit.

Lorelai: Then I think you tuck Liam's warning away and see where this is going. You're an adult and so is Joe. If you or Joe have reservations, then you can talk it out.

Shelby: Agreed. And for the record, I saw no red flags.

Lorelai: Oop, sorry, babe. I need to go. Huck just enacted the holy trifecta: glasses, wine, and Willie Nelson.

Shelby: Don't do anything we wouldn't do!

Maren: That list is getting shorter by the trimester!

♪ ♪ ♪

The weeks after Joe asks me to stay pass quietly, sweetly. Joe and I get to know each other better every day, and everything I learn makes me a little wilder for him. He's thoughtful, intentional, orderly (nearly to the point of obsession), and surprisingly terrible at anything remotely handy. The man could run twenty miles in the hot desert sun with a hundred-pound pack on his back, but when it comes to wiring an electrical outlet, he's hopeless.

I like it. It makes him seem more human. Since I was a kid, chasing after him and my brothers, I always put him on a pedestal. The great Josiah Cole: handsome, athletic, brilliant, and popular. He might still be all of those things, but I'm the one who plumbed the bathroom in my apartment. Correctly. The first time. While he stood over my shoulder and handed *me* my tools.

I've never felt needed, and it turns out, I really enjoy being depended on. It suits me down to my bones. My entire life I've been on the receiving end, and I don't even think I meant for it to be that way. More like, people took one look at me and my wall of sashes and glittery crowns, and just . . . did things for me. It may have been flattering initially, but over the last few years it's worn thin. It's blatantly obvious people aren't doing it out of the kindness of their hearts, but rather because they think I'm not capable—that they've never believed I was capable.

Case in point: Shane. My old bosses at the parks. My advisor in college who talked me out of grad school. My parents. My brothers.

But Fost never treated me that way.

And Joe has never treated me that way, either. Perhaps he would have if he had even an ounce of energy to spare outside of his kids, but whatever the reason, I'm grateful. It's given me the opportunity to discover my own potential. My pop-up fishing guide business is thriving, the apartment and bait shop look practically unrecognizable from Fost's days (and not at all in violation of health codes), and I can pour beer from the tap with minimal foam.

Everything has been awesome, besides one teeny-tiny little hiccup. Joe and I haven't so much as kissed since that (highly enjoyable) hallway BJ. And honestly, was that even a kiss? Technically, I suppose. It's been so long, I don't recall. Clearly this is something that needs to be rectified, but one, his kids are always right there.

And two. His kids are always *right there.*

We could probably ask his parents to take Anders and Lucy for the night, but that would require us to admit to them that we're something to each other, and also that we want to spend the night together. And telling his parents would be the same as telling my parents, and I don't care how old I get, I'm not sure I can do that. Some people have that kind of relationship with their moms. I'm envious of that elusive *Gilmore Girls* closeness. As far as my mother knows, I'm still a virgin. As far as my father knows, I don't shave my legs.

You can see the conundrum.

Today is Saturday, and it's another warm one. El Niño, maybe. Or climate change. Whatever the circumstance that's gifted us with a sunny, nearly sixty-degree day in November, I'll take it. Anders still hasn't found his musky and Lucy needed to get out of the house. Or rather, we all needed to get out of the house because Lucy needed anything but what we were giving her.

So we bundled up and jumped in Simon Cole's old glittery Lund fishing boat for the afternoon.

It's also worth noting Joe's not much of a fisherman. To be fair, I'm one of the best around, but still. Another thing he's not brilliant at that just makes me like him more.

Lucy stopped fishing thirty minutes ago and is busy organizing all the plastics in my tackle box by color. I'm going to have to redo everything later tonight, but it's worth the sacrifice to grant Anders even a few more minutes of fishing.

The kid's been getting nibbles on his line. We're slowly drifting along the shoreline, and I know this is the spot to make it happen. No one else has a line in the water. I had Joe reel in a while ago, even though, let's face it, he wasn't gonna catch anything. But still, if on the off chance he did, it would kill Anders to have his dad find a musky before him, especially since his dad isn't the one who has been obsessively seeking a fish for the last three months solid. I'm concentrating on keeping us near the shore and ready to jump with a net.

"Pull up," I tell Anders when we start to edge around another bog. "I'm gonna motor us back around. How's your bucktail? Want to swap out lures?"

Anders makes a face, reeling in, the gloss of his navy-blue manicure flashing in the sun. It matches mine and coordinates with our June-bug-colored lures, specially designed by his little sister. Obviously, matching your manicure with your lures isn't a requirement to be a successful fisher-person, but we think it adds a little something extra. "I don't know," he eventually says. "What do you think?"

I shake my head. "My gut is saying keep it. It's a good one. The colors are perfect and if you've already gotten some hits . . ."

"This is our last day, though . . ." Anders fidgets, roughly rubbing at his nose with the palm of his hand the way he does when he's anxious. Poor kid is losing hope.

"This season," I finish. "Last day this season. You have your entire life ahead of you. I didn't catch my first musky until my thirteenth birthday! And you're already a way better fisherman than me."

"I didn't catch one until I was an old married man, kiddo," Joe offers, passing Lucy more plastics. I wonder where he even found those? But then I see my backup tackle box is open next to him. He gives me an apologetic half grin, half wince.

Hearing my sigh, Anders raises his gaze to meet mine and he rolls his eyes lightly. "That's because you suck at fishing, Dad. Sorry, but it's the truth."

That has me hiding my snicker in my shoulder.

"Don't say 'suck,' kid," Joe chides good-naturedly. "Though you may have a point."

I take the boat in a slow, wide turn, pulling us parallel to the shore again. "Drop in as soon as we pass that point, Anders."

The little guy takes a deep breath, gripping his reel. "Okay."

I turn off the motor, content to drift. The breeze is enough to carry us and anyway, I'm crossing everything I have that this is the pass that does the trick. First, I check on my young partner, but there's nothing to comment on. His form is perfect. All that's missing is the fish on the line. Then I turn my attention to his dad. His form is also perfect, but in a completely different way. He's leaning back in his seat, his long legs crossed at the ankle over the edge of the boat, content to watch his kids. There's this small almost-smile on his lips that I've secretly coined his "Anders and Luce smile" because it's the one he wears during these unguarded moments with his kids. The ones in between the rushing around, the discipline, the providing, the serving.

A garbled shriek pulls me out of my daydreaming and I'm on my feet and at Anders's side in half a heartbeat.

"I got something!"

His pole is bowing and bobbing. "Yeah you do!" I don't have to tell him to yank up and set the hook. He's already there and reeling in as fast as his small hands can manage. I reach for the net, watching the line. "Don't let it go slack," I remind him, gently prodding the pole up. "Steady. You're doing amazing." I see a glint of silver in the water and Joe gives a mighty whoop, his feet smacking the boat as he surges to stand.

"Lucy, come look!" Joe shouts. "Anders has a big fish on the line!"

On the other side of Anders, I see Joe, juggling his phone in one hand and Lucy on his hip in the other. I'm worried he's gonna drop his phone in the water, but I suspect he wouldn't care one bit.

After probably the longest two minutes of his entire life, Anders babies the line close enough to the boat to see what he's caught, and it's a doozy of a musky. On the smaller side, but perfect for a first effort.

Definitely bigger than anything his dad ever caught, I'm sure.

"Holy moly, kid!" I shout while dipping in the net and expertly scooping the fish, bait and all. "You did it!"

"I did it!" he screeches, jumping up and down, finally letting loose and looking exactly like the little boy he is. I press my lips together, holding in my emotion, and lay the net on the bottom of the boat. I instruct Anders on how to unhook the fish and the best way to carefully hold it and keep it from further harm. Joe snaps a hundred pictures of Anders with the fish, and then Anders and Lucy. Anders holds his fish, and Lucy, her face a study in stoicism, holds out her hand-painted lure. I'm so proud of them both, I could burst. Instead, I take Joe's phone so he can get a photo with all three of them. After, he reaches out a hand.

"Your turn."

"I want one with you, Maren! So we can frame it on the wall at the lodge," Anders says, his eyes pleading. As if I could ever tell him no.

To anything.

"Yes, please! My fishing partner and protégé!" I drop to a squat next to him and wrap my arm around his shoulders and beam. I'm not sure whose smile is bigger.

We quickly release the musky, and it wastes zero time darting away.

"I'll see you next year," Anders vows solemnly and I laugh, getting to my feet. I hold out my hand for a high five but Anders dives in for a hug.

"Thanks, Maren," he says into my waist, and I swallow back a fresh sting of tears. I'm not usually this emotional. Definitely not while I'm fishing. It's Anders. It's gotta be. This kid makes my heart squeeze. Looking up, I meet Joe's eyes and that's all it takes for my tears to spill over.

He doesn't laugh at me. He doesn't even say a word. He just nods in a way that says, *I know. It's a lot.*

Eventually Anders lets go and the moment is over. I sit in the back of the boat with the kids while Joe drives us back to the resort and his parents' dock. We carry everything straight to the lodge so Anders can share his catch with his grandparents. They ring a giant bell over the bar and write his name on the board, even though his musky is a good deal smaller than the rest of the big ones caught over the course of the season. Joe jumps in the kitchen to make a couple of celebratory pizzas and Donna makes the kids Shirley Temples from the bar with extra cherries. The lodge empties out early, so I take the liberty of changing out the college football game on the TV for some big-screen cartoons. I grab a spot at a table and Lucy climbs in my lap, slumping back against my chest, happily slurping her pink drink and getting more than a little bit of it down both of our fronts. Her small body is warm and wiggly, and she smells like sugar and sunscreen. She offers me her straw, jabbing it in my face. Anders laughs at the way I jerk away, startled.

I grin. "I guess I zoned out." I gently push the cup back toward Lucy's lap. "No, thank you, baby."

Anders watches us and sips from his own drink. Eventually he says, "I'm surprised she lets you call her that. She always yells at Dad saying, 'I'm not a baby!'"

"She does?" I look at Lucy and tap her shoulder to get her attention. "Is it okay if I call you 'baby,' Lucy? Do you want me to stop?"

She shakes her head. "I'm *your* baby."

Eyes wide, I look to Anders for help, but he shrugs.

I don't know what to say. It's on the tip of my tongue to straighten her out, but that feels needlessly cruel, and I'm not sure how much relationship nuance Lucy is capable of understanding. Besides, I started it. I called her "baby" because that's what rolled off my tongue.

Oh Lord. I need to talk to Joe about this.

"Okay, then," I finally whisper, squeezing her little body to mine for a brief second and then letting her go and sighing as I lean back into the rest of the seat.

TWENTY

Heaven in Hiding

Maren

November 18, 2024

Maren Laughlin,

I hope this email finds you well. I am writing to inform you of an opening at Grand Canyon National Park (South Rim) for the position of EDUCATIONAL PROGRAM DEVELOPMENT. We came across your résumé and thought your experience and educational background would be a good fit.

Below is a description of the position and general overview of salary and benefits for the position. The position will remain open until January 1, 2025, and applications will be accepted until that time. Thank you for your consideration. We look forward to hearing from you.

Sincerely,

Madeline McEwan

Human Resources and Recruitment

National Parks

*** Attachment ***

I skim the attachment, barely taking it in outside of recognizing that I am qualified and that a month ago I would have been interested. Okay, maybe two months ago. Who am I kidding? Three months ago. In that short space of time between puking on Shane's shoes and seeing Joe on the shore in front of Fost's place.

So basically the car ride from Michigan up, over, and across to Wisconsin.

I close out, but don't delete the email. Despite my lack of interest and promising Joe I'll stay for the rest of the year, my brother's warning still echoes. I mean, what even am I to Joe? Really? Because right now, I know deep down that if I left, I'd be breaking my own heart. And I might be breaking his kids' hearts, but kids are resilient. They have short memories.

But what I can't figure out is how it would affect Joe. Would it break his heart? Is his heart even on the table? When he asked me to stay, I didn't press him for answers. I could tell, instinctively, he wasn't ready to give them, and anyway, I was too much of a coward to hear them.

But it's been nearly a month and I'm not sure I should settle for anything less than that.

Well. Okay, I might be tempted to settle for sex if it was on the table. The man is driving me wild with his forearms dusted in golden-blond hair, his wide, warm, calloused palms, the flash of his dimple when he's laughing at something I've said.

(I am so aware of how that sounds. I'm not saying I *would* settle for it. Just that I'd be very tempted. If I can't have it all, couldn't I just maybe have some?)

My phone buzzes on the glossy bartop beside me with

a text, so I close my laptop and put it away to think about another day.

> **Liam:** HEARD YOU'RE STAYING UP THERE FOR THANKSGIVING.

I snort at the all-caps message. My brother isn't that old. After all, he's the same age as Joe, but in texting years, he's basically a baby boomer. I'm convinced it's because his kids are tweens. Something about having middle-schoolers ages you extra.

> **Maren:** Yep. I thought I told you?

> **Liam:** I DON'T REMEMBER.

> **Liam:** DONNA AND SIMON INVITED US ALL UP FOR THANKSGIVING. MOM AND DAD TOOK THEM UP ON IT.

I blink at the message, my stomach sinking. Oh god. My parents are coming here. In less than a week. Gray dots appear on my screen.

> **Liam:** JESS AND I ARE BRINGING THE KIDS UP TOO.

I swallow back my growing dread, my fingers hovering over the keys to say . . . what? It's not like I can just not respond now that he knows I have my phone with me.

> **Maren:** You are?

There. That was neutral. My parents and my oldest brother and his wife and his kids. All of them. Here. In less than a week.

> **Liam:** WELL YEAH. MIGHT AS WELL.
> TWO OF MY FAVORITE PEOPLE IN
> THE SAME PLACE.

I can feel my heartbeat in my throat and immediately feel guilty for my reaction. This is my family. I love them. I can't wait to see my nieces and nephews. And my mom and dad. And sure, Liam. At least Jess is coming. I love my sister-in-law. She makes me feel less insane in a house full of big brothers.

But I was looking forward to a quiet holiday with Joe and the kids. And I'll have to explain about my brother's warning to Joe. Which will either irritate him or turn him off. We're never going to have sex at this rate.

> **Maren:** Awesome! Can't wait to see you!

I flip my phone over and ignore the buzzing of my brother's response, dropping my head into my hands with a groan.

"Bad news?"

Speak of the devil.

I whimper, thudding my head on the bar.

"It can't be that bad."

I straighten, huffing my bangs off my forehead. "My parents and Liam and his entire family are coming up next week for Thanksgiving. Your parents invited them."

Joe blinks, frozen. Eventually, he thaws enough to say, "I see."

"And I should probably tell you now, Liam warned me away from you last month and actually like two months before that, when he was up here. So, well before you asked me to stay. Obviously, I ignored his advice."

Joe's expression darkens and his blond brows crush together. "He did *what?*"

I continue. "I don't know, Joe. Was this"—I gesture between us—"a bad idea? Is it even worth it? I've been trying to be patient and let you work out whatever you need to work out. Like, I realize you're divorced and a veteran and Lucy is autistic and Anders has mom issues and your ex is . . ." I trail off, coming up empty, before deciding on, "Whatever. That's a lot, but I don't feel like it's too much. I swear. I can handle it. If you want me to, that is."

"I do want—"

I cut him off, because I don't want to lose my courage to see this through. "I want to sleep with you." He closes his mouth with an audible snap, his jaw muscle ticking, and I press on, unsure of what is transpiring behind his determined blue eyes. "I mean, not *just* sleep with you. I don't only want that, though if that's all you can offer, I'd probably consider it, but I *do* want more than that." I exhale, exasperated. "What I mean is, I'm not *just* here to help with your kids. Though I love your kids and want to help with them. But I also like you. Granted, we still need to get to know each other, but I am *very* interested in you. And also very attracted to you. Are you interested in me? In that way?" By the end, my voice has climbed to near-squeaking proportions. Very uncool, not-at-all-confident-sounding squeaking. My beauty pageant vocal coach would die at this shameful display.

I hold my breath, feeling my heart thud in my ears and my stomach clench. He doesn't respond right away, and I'm just about to take it all back when he reaches across the bar and grips my chin between his thumb and fingers and tugs me closer, immediately sealing his soft, pliable mouth over mine.

Holding my breath for so long has me parting my lips in a gasp and he takes that opportunity to thrust his tongue in my mouth, kissing me long and luscious and deep. His fingers move from my chin to the back of my neck and twist in my hair and I'm practically standing from my stool to get closer to him. After a while—a long while—he releases me, pressing his forehead to mine, slightly out of breath.

His voice is rusty with emotion. "I am very interested in that way. In all the ways, Maren."

"Okay," I whisper, my eyes searching for the truth between his.

"I'm so interested," he presses meaning into the word, "I can barely sleep. I can barely eat. I put my shirt on backward yesterday and wore it that way until my mom noticed. I . . ." He swallows, hesitating. "I jack off more than a teenager, thinking of your mouth. Your body. The way you smile at me across a room. The way your hair smells." He releases me and steps back but is still close enough for me to hear his low words. "Yeah, I love how you treat my kids and, make no mistake, you've been a lifesaver these past few months. But that's not why I asked you to stay. I asked you to stay for *me*. It feels selfish and I know you could be anywhere doing anything, but I want you here, with me."

I sink back in my stool and grip the edge of the bar to keep from slipping to the floor and quirk a smile. "Soooooo, you're telling me you're interested."

He chuckles deep and the sound skitters across my skin like a live wire, setting my hormones into overdrive. "I'm telling you I'm interested."

"Well, in that case, I'm gonna let you tell my brother."

"Or, counteroffer, we don't tell your brother until after

Thanksgiving and he's back in Michigan. We'll play it cool around our families, just as we've been doing."

I frown. "Does this mean we have to wait until then to have sex, too?"

He looks up at the clock on the wall and shakes his head. "Fuck no. We're closed. Give me ten and I'll walk you home."

A giddy little zing darts between my legs. "In that case, I accept your conditions."

TWENTY-ONE

Take Me Home Tonight

Joe

I CAN'T CLOSE THE BAR QUICKLY ENOUGH. THANK GOD IT'S November. We're in that lull between fishing and snowmobiling season when the lodge sees little business after the sun goes down. After grabbing my coat from the hook in the kitchen, I hesitate a step. I consider shooting my parents a text, checking in on the kids, but they have them for the night and it's after Lucy's bedtime. I tuck my phone away.

They're *fine*. I know they are fine.

I'm the one who's not fine, and for the first time in years, I'm putting my kids second, just for the night, because this is important. Maybe the most important thing I've ever done.

Christ. She thought I didn't *like* her? That I would only keep her around for my kids' sake, and she was okay with that? What kind of signals had I been sending?!

It's clear I need to set several things straight and fast.

Well. Not too fast.

I shove my keys in my pocket and stop in my tracks at the sight of Maren, perched on a stool, her hair tucked behind her ear, a backpack on the floor next to her. She's got her bottom lip tucked between her teeth.

"Ready?"

She wrings her fingers, looking uncertain. "I am, but are you? I feel like I've just laid a lot at your feet and maybe I've pushed you. Nothing needs to happen today. I know you have a lot going on and—"

I give myself a mental shake. *Minutes.* I left her alone for maybe two minutes and she's already questioning herself. How is it possible this woman doesn't realize how sexy she is? And cute? And sweet and brilliant? And just how lost I am for her?

I stalk toward her, eating the distance between us in three steps and placing my hands on the bar on either side of her slim frame.

"I've never been more ready for anything in my life. Are you having second thoughts?"

She searches my face for the truth. "Not at all, but as much as I try to unhear what Liam said—"

I raise an eyebrow and press even closer. "New rule. Not one more word about your brother tonight."

She licks her lips, and I can feel the heat of her body mingling with mine. "Good call."

"Now," I tell her, "you have two options before you. I can go down on you here, or I can go down on you in your bed, but I am going to taste you either way."

Her eyes flare and her breath catches. "Have you ever done that in the bar with, um, *anyone else?*"

"Never. This would be a first for me."

Her eyes shut of their own accord and her head falls back, baring the soft skin of her throat to me. I immediately dip forward for a sample, my tongue tracing a path from her jawline to her ear.

"Here, please," she decides, already breathless.

I step back to the door, turning the lock with an echoing click and shutting off the lights. It's still plenty bright, but at least from a distance, it's clear we're closed. I tug her forward off the stool and make quick work of removing my top layer, an old flannel shirt, and laying it over the top of the barstool. I turn to Maren, reaching for the zipper of her jeans while capturing her mouth and kissing her. It's only been minutes since our last kiss, but I can't get enough.

She tastes phenomenal.

She wriggles out of her pants, and I slip her underwear all the way off, before lifting her and placing her on the stool. I drop to one knee before her. Then both. Her hands are already twisting in my hair, and I place a kiss on the inside of her thighs, spreading them wide. It's dim, but my fingers lead the way, trailing up and in and along, finding her warm and petal soft, wet and ready for me. I don't waste time, pressing in for a long, slow lick, curling my tongue and circling her clit over and over, drinking her in. I lap at her, wrapping my arms around her thighs and anchoring myself close enough to fuck her with my tongue. If I thought her mouth was delicious, this is like sampling the finest delicacy. *Maren, Maren, Maren,* on my lips and around my tongue. Over and over, until she's bucking wildly, her hands tugging painfully at my hair. I swallow a grunt, huffing a laugh at her enthusiasm, and she hisses at me, "Don't you dare stop."

As if I could.

I don't answer her with words. Instead, I wrap my lips around her clit, sucking hard as I plunge two fingers into her core, curling them. It's barely a beat until she cries out and clenches against me, her thighs holding me captive as she rides out her orgasm. I gentle my efforts, place soft, open-mouthed kisses at the apex of her thighs, slipping my fingers out. Eventually her legs fall open, releasing me. Her grip loosens, her fingers caressing my hair. Coaxing.

I get to my feet, hiding my grimace at the twinge in my knees reminding me that I'm not twenty and also that our floors are hard.

Maren doesn't miss a thing, even in the dark.

"You all right there, old man?" she teases good-naturedly.

I groan, but it's only half-serious. "I'll survive. It was worth it."

"I'll say."

"Should we go home so I can ice my knees?"

Maren's eyes twinkle in the moonlight as she presses a kiss to my lips. "Come on. I'll take good care of you."

♪♪♪

She doesn't lie. I barely remember to shut the door behind us at her place because she's already dropping clothes as she dances across the space to her bedroom. I kick the door shut with my booted foot before chasing after her, working at my own buttons.

I'd planned to play it cool whenever I thought about the unlikeliness of me being lucky enough to ever get Maren Laughlin naked. And while such planning was a more recent development, it was all-consuming. Which is why it was so important to go down on her first. Besides the fact that I really wanted to, I *needed* to. It's been years since I came inside a woman's body and much longer than that since I've been this out of my mind over someone.

Kiley was my first love. My first everything. I would have walked through fire for her. We grew up together until we grew apart. I don't regret one minute of our relationship, but this is different in every possible way.

I'm a grown man. A father. A business owner. I know what I want and what I need, and those things are one and the same in the woman standing before me at the foot of the bed, fully nude and effortlessly beautiful. She steals the breath from my lungs and the thoughts from my head. She holds me up and knocks me on my ass.

She tugs my T-shirt over my head and traces my chest with her fingers, dragging them down toward my waistband. There's a single bedside lamp lit, and I fight the urge to cover my midsection. I'm healthy, but I'm far from the athlete I used to be. Long, *long* gone are the days when I used to lift weights on top of two-a-day football practices.

Then Maren presses her mouth to my chest, her tongue darting and circling across my skin, and every uncertainty disappears. I help her remove the rest of my clothes until I'm standing before her, hard as a rock and completely exposed.

Her lips curl in a soft grin, made even softer in the low light. "Josiah Cole, naked in my bedroom. If you'd told me back then . . ." She trails off, shaking her head, and I can't help but laugh.

"You'd have run away screaming."

She tilts her head and giggles. "You might be right—I was pretty young. But grown me is freaking the fuck out about it."

I step closer, reaching my hand into her long, auburn hair

and tucking the waves behind her ear before slipping my hand down her neck and cupping it there. "You wouldn't know it looking at you," I say quietly. "You look collected as always. Meanwhile, you've got me shaking in the knees."

"How is that possible? You just made me come harder than I have in . . . well," she says, and smirks, "since the last time you made me come on the couch. You have nothing to worry about."

"Let's just assume we're both nervous. It's been a long time for me and you're, well, *you*. Beautiful, thoughtful, genuine you."

"And you're everything I didn't think I wanted but now I don't know if I could live without."

I release a long, slow, heavy breath. "This isn't just sex."

She shakes her head.

I decide that's enough talking and pull her against me, kissing her hard. I take my time, my tongue dancing with hers, my hands pressing her impossibly closer until every part of us is connected so completely I can't tell who's who and the only sound is our shared breaths passing back and forth.

I back her up until her legs hit against the mattress and she falls with a soft *umph* and I crawl over her, careful not to crush her, but she's already grinding herself against me and licking at my lips. I match her hunger and every reservation is gone. All that's left is her and me and it feels right. So totally right.

Her legs are a cradle around mine and I'm straining against her right there, so close and so ready. She's soft and wet and I am shaking with the effort to hold myself back from taking her in one powerful thrust. I force myself to slip down her body, sucking one of her perfect, raised nipples in my mouth and swirling my tongue.

"Oh god," she says, holding my head to her breast. "Oh god," she repeats. I lean on one elbow, using my free hand to cup her other breast. Maren, it needs to be known, has spectacular breasts. Round and full and so soft I could bury myself in them. I need to taste the other, so I do, sucking, rolling, and nipping it gently with my teeth, so that she's whimpering and writhing under me. My cock twitches against her thigh and I'm brought back to my own needs when her thighs slip apart even further as she opens herself up to me. Without thought, I'm lined up at her entrance, nudging against her soft core. She bucks, agonizingly slow, and I start to black out around the edges of my vision at the sensation.

She puts a hand against my chest, and I snap back to attention.

"I've got an IUD, but I also have condoms if you would feel better."

I blink, trying to focus on the words coming out of her mouth. "I haven't been with anyone since Kiley."

"It's been since Shane for me, but I was tested four months ago at my regular appointment."

Good enough for me. "No condom, then."

She drags herself against me, controlled and sensual. "Oka—" but I'm done playing and cut her off with my thrust, sliding in to the hilt on a groan. Her legs clench against my hips and she wraps her heels behind me, but I barely notice anything outside of the way her body has opened for me, a silky embrace that has my eyes rolling back in my head and my hips snapping in and out. I try to slow down, but Maren tightens her hold. "Harder. Hard as you want."

"But I don't want to go too fast," I grit out, already feeling the thread of my self-control slipping.

"I'm so close, so, so—Joe. Don't stop—" And then she's crying out, her entire body curled against me, clenching, from the inside and out. I barely last one more thrust before I'm following her over the edge, turned on by the intensity of her orgasm thrumming through us both.

I collapse over her, rolling to one side so as not to suffocate her, and she buries her face in my shoulder, wrapping her arms around my neck. Our breaths slow to steady, and she kisses the place where my shoulder meets my neck. I rest my head against hers, hearing our heartbeats between us.

We don't speak, but it doesn't feel weird. It never does with Maren. Her fingers run a path down my shoulder to my elbow and back and I can't stop myself from kissing her. Her forehead, above her ear, her fingertips, her cheek. I suspect before the night is through, I'll have covered every inch of her with my lips.

Eventually, when our hearts settle, she goes to clean up in the bathroom. I pull on my boxer briefs and crawl back into bed. She didn't ask me to stay, but I hope she does.

She comes back to bed, dipping to the floor and picking up my T-shirt and then pulling it on. "Do you mind?" she asks. "I don't sleep well naked. Especially in November."

"I don't mind, but I feel like I should warn you that if I wake up to you in my shirt, I'm gonna want to take it off you, maybe with my teeth."

Her eyes grow wide before she turns off the light and slips under the covers, lacing her fingers through mine and curling into my side. "Promise?"

♪♪♪

Liam Laughlin shows up a day early. He's the kind of guy who is the life of the party and loves a good prank. He gets off on surprises. I knew that. Maren knew that. We should have expected he would pull a stunt like this, flying in a day ahead of his family and renting a car to show up at my door at ten A.M. Tuesday morning.

On the one hand, his timing was thoughtful. My parents had already gotten Anders to school and even dropped off Lucy at her preschool. I'd finished my morning run and breakfast. On the other hand, his timing was bullshit because I was in the middle of wishing his younger sister a very, very good morning in the shower, with my tongue.

At first we ignored his knocking. But soon my phone started ringing on the bathroom counter, and finally my Apple Watch buzzed with his repeated notifications.

Maren drops her leg and gently pushes back my head, her smile frustrated but genuine. "It might be the kids."

I curse, scrubbing at my face and then checking my watch, before cursing again.

"No. Not the kids. Your brother."

"Liam?" she shrieks, and I shoot to my feet, shushing her.

"He's here. Outside."

"Oh my god," she says, shutting off the water. "Oh my god, oh my god, oh my god."

"Want me to get rid of him and come back?"

She glares and I can't say I didn't expect that, so I reach for my towel and pass her the other one.

"I'll go answer the door. Stay here. I'll try to get rid of him."

I quickly rub at my skin, then wrap the towel around

my hips and march to the door, opening it a crack. "You're early!"

Liam's hazel eyes, the exact same shade as Maren's, take in my dripping-wet hair and towel and comprehension dawns. "In the shower? Sorry, man. Should have guessed."

"No problem. But I need to rinse off, still. Want to meet for coffee in thirty?"

"Is it cool if I just wait here? I drove a rental."

My breath stutters for a half beat and I try to cover it up, rubbing my hand through my sopping hair. "Right. S-sure. Yeah. Just, uh, make yourself at home. Here's the remote." I hand him the TV remote, feeling stupid. "Be right out."

I make my way back to my room and the bathroom— taking in the space as I go to make sure there are no hints of Maren spending way too much time in my home—to where Maren is standing in her towel, looking cold and . . . well, like someone whose orgasm was interrupted by her big brother. "I'm sorry," I whisper, and I turn on the shower to muffle our voices. "He's still here. I couldn't think of a way to get rid of him."

"So what am I supposed to do? Sit in here all day while you two catch up?"

"No! Of course not. I closed my bedroom door. I told him I had to rinse off to buy some time. You can go out and get your clothes and sneak out my sliding doors." I wince, hearing myself. "Jesus, I'm sorry. That's so—"

Maren cuts me off, frazzled. "What if he catches me?"

"He won't."

"He almost did!"

I step closer to her and wrap my arms around her shoulders and kiss the top of her head. "I like you," I tell her. "A lot. I want you and I need you, and he's not going to talk me out of that."

"But you said you wanted to keep it a secret from him."

"I do," I tell her, pulling back and searching her eyes. "But not because I'm afraid he'll change my mind, or because I think he has any say in my life whatsoever. I want to keep it between us for a little while because it's new and less complicated this way. Between our families and my kids, I already have so much pressure on me to not fuck this up. I want to spend some time with you before opening the floor up for discussion. When we do tell everyone, I want us to be a united front."

"Oh," she says into my neck, and I can feel some of the tension ease from her shoulders.

"Yeah. *Oh.* So if he sees you slipping out the back, fine. But I'd rather he not. Besides, sneaking around the next few days might be kind of hot."

She steps back, considering. After a pause, she hikes her delicious smirk back in place. "I see your point."

"Yeah?"

"Lucky for you, I happen to have always had this fantasy about sneaking around behind my parents' back on vacation with my secret older college-aged boyfriend."

"That sounds oddly specific."

She lifts a slim, tanned shoulder, still glistening with water droplets, and I fight the urge to lick them off. Her eyes read my distraction and she trails a fingertip along her collarbone. "I have a vivid imagination. Fooling around in a bar after hours is only the tip of the iceberg."

And I'm instantly hard even though I just came not thirty minutes ago. Her eyes dip to where I am tenting my towel and she smirks again.

"Definitely a secret, then," I tell her. She dresses quickly before pressing a quick, closed-mouth kiss to my lips and shuffling past me, peeking out the sliding door to make sure the coast is clear, and then steps out.

I decide to make use of the water since it's already on, turning it ice cold and stepping in, freezing out all thoughts of my sexy secret girlfriend before I go hang out with her brother.

Huh. Guess it's not so far off from her fantasy after all.

TWENTY-TWO

White Flag

Maren

I'M DRESSED AND READY FOR COMPANY BEFORE MY BROTHER SHOWS up, Joe in tow, to *surprise* me. Thankfully, Rogers causes such a ruckus when Liam knocks on the door that it isn't obvious I was expecting him. I do give him shit for heading to Joe's first, though. After all, he's *my* brother.

That afternoon I take him by Fost's place and show him the renovations. He seems impressed by what I've managed, with the help of Shelby and Cameron, and even (begrudgingly) admits he would've had to hire a contractor for almost all the non-electrical work were he in my position. I deserve a medal for graciously swallowing my snarky response to *that* statement.

Then we head to the lodge, where Donna and Simon sing my praises, showing off the musky record board and highlighting all the late-season catches I'd facilitated on my recent guided tours. So many that I've started daydreaming about making it my full-time gig. Moving into the apartment myself maybe . . .

You know, being my own boat daddy.

It feels like progress, and for a short while, I start to imagine a little respect shining in his eyes. But it must be a trick of the light because just as quickly he makes some crack about "unemployment suiting me" and how he wishes he could just "shirk all his responsibilities and take a gap year." Around a dinner of takeout at the lodge that evening, he grills me on my plans. This is a good time to point out how not even my actual father has been this high-handed. Like ever.

It's exhausting.

I've managed to shift us from taking up space at the bar to a shorter table in the dining area. Joe's dividing his time between helping Donna pour cocktails at the bar and lounging on the raised hearth of the unlit stone fireplace beside us.

"Joe," my brother shouts across the lodge, gesturing with his beer (that *I* bought, mind you), "help me out, man. Tell her. She can't live at the resort forever. She should be looking for new jobs! They won't hold her old position indefinitely." I stifle my eye roll because they already filled it months ago, but let him rant. "She needs to stop acting like a teenager and get back to the real world."

While my brother's attention is on Joe, I raise a sly, humorous brow, crisscrossing my arms over my chest. Considering *he's* the reason I'm still here and not applying for new jobs, I'm eager to hear how he's gonna play this.

Joe doesn't disappoint. Ever, I imagine (while inwardly sighing like a lovesick preteen). "First of all," he reminds Liam, "I've been living at the resort forever, so it'd be pretty rich of me to say anything about that." My brother has the audacity to chortle. *Chortle*, I tell you. "And didn't her ex-boyfriend get the promotion over her? So he'd be her new boss?" Joe shakes his head and looks at me. "No thanks. I wouldn't go back, either. *They don't deserve you.*" My stomach does a little swoop. The good kind. He continues, turning his attention back to my brother. "And she's not living here for free, you know. She's brought in tons of business to the resort with her guided tours, and fixing up Fost's place is a smart investment. Properties up here go for a premium."

Joe contemplates a small beverage napkin in front of him, finally crumpling it in his fist before meeting my gaze. "I'm sorry, I didn't mean to speak over you like that. You can speak for yourself." He spears Liam with his cool blue eyes before getting up to retrieve and clear away our plates. "It's time for me to grab the kids from my dad. Want to see them?" he asks us both, and I do, but I also feel like maybe this would be a good opportunity to give him and Liam some time. Not to mention, I could use the quiet to process the way Joe just defended me to my brother. To his best friend of thirty-plus years.

I didn't need it. He's right, I can speak for myself. But it still felt nice to have someone in my corner for once. Lorelai would have loved to be a fly on the wall for that. Shelby, too. Adolescent crush aside, she would give anything to see Liam getting put in his place. As it stands, I'm a heartbeat from spontaneous orgasm.

"I'll come," Liam says, not missing a beat, getting to his feet. "Mare?"

I shake my head and stretch my hands over my head with a big yawn. "Nah. I need to get back to Rogers. Take him for a long walk. Think I'll go to bed early before the whole family descends on us tomorrow."

I can feel Joe's eyes on me, but I don't meet his gaze out of fear I'll reveal too much in front of an audience. I can always text him before bed.

♪ ♪ ♪

Turns out, he texts me first, right as I'm crawling into bed with a cup of hot tea and a spicy romance Lorelai insisted I read about a horned and horny demon and his fated Valkyrie mate.

I've learned not to mock it before I try it when it comes to monster porn.

> **Joe:** Just checking in. Do I need to apologize?

I put down the book and tea, puzzled.

> **Maren:** What on earth would you have to apologize for?

> **Joe:** I'm not sure. You just seemed off when you left earlier. Did I come on too strong to Liam? He didn't say anything, but if I did . . .

Oh.

> **Maren:** Oh jeez. No.

> **Maren:** Honestly, that was really nice. Thank you for sticking up for me.

> **Maren:** I was annoyed with my brother. For the things he said and for interrupting our shower. Perhaps my "off" was just "sexually frustrated."

> **Joe:** . . .

Joe: I could fix that, you know.

A delicious tingle zips through me, curling my toes under the quilt, and I grin into my phone screen.

Maren: OH I KNOW

Joe: I never realized how your brother talks to you . . . I'm sorry. When you said he warned you off me, I thought you were exaggerating, because . . . well . . . you're the catch, Maren. YOU.

I fan my face, feeling suddenly too warm.

Maren: He means well. He wants the best for you. You're like a brother to him.

Joe: He's literally your brother, though. You're being generous.

Joe: Proving what I just said. You are the catch. 😊

I slump back with a sigh. There he goes, being all cute and supportive and wonderful and . . . well, absolutely correct. Again.

Maren: It's complicated.

Joe: Yeah.

Maren: He's a good brother to me, too. He just doesn't realize I've grown up, and I guess I see his point.

Joe: I don't.

In my mind, I can clearly picture Joe's bland frown, furrowed brow, and darkened eyes, and I wrestle with the urge to stand up for Liam or defend his actions somehow. They've been close for so long, this feels wrong.

Maren: The last thing I want is to be a wedge in your decades-long friendship. I appreciate what you said more than I can express. It meant the world to have someone in my corner, whether I needed it or not. I really like you, if it's not already super obvious.

I bite my lip, gauging how much more I should say.

Maren: But you're going to have to trust that I can handle my brother and not get involved.

Joe: Eventually we're going to have to tell him about us and I'm not gonna put up with his talking to you like that.

My belly does the swoop thing again at his reference to an *eventually*. *Eventually* implies long term. Future. *More*. I really, really like the sound of more. Still, I hate the idea of getting between them.

Maren: We'll see.

Joe: Maren . . .

Maren: You're right. Eventually, if it comes to that, we'll address it.

Together. For the time being, though, I'm hoping he'll start seeing me for the woman I have become and realize I'm capable of making solid choices, including who I sleep with and want in my life.

Joe: I suppose that's enough. For now.

Joe: For the record, I really like you, too.

Maren: I'm starting to get that.

Joe: The orgasms not proof enough?

Maren: Is there a limit?

Joe: Not with you, there's not.

Maren: Gah. There you go. Turning me on again and being all sweet.

Maren: Good night, Josiah.

Joe: Sleep tight, Jig.

꙳ ꙳ ꙳

I love my mom. I really do. She's whip smart, still rocks her curves at sixty-eight, and, relatedly, makes the best stuffing in the world. She's fantastic and I hope to be half as good a mom as she was to me when I was growing up.

That said, I wish she would leave already.

It's been ten hours, but she sized up the tension between me and Joe in minutes. MINUTES. Maybe seconds, honestly. After all, it only took her minutes to come up with an excuse to pull me aside in the kitchen and begin her interrogation.

"And just how long have you and Josiah Cole been together?"

I shriek, shushing her and watching the doorway for anyone who could have heard us. No one comes in, thank god, and I round on her, whisper-screaming in response.

"How on earth?"

She leans a single generous hip against the countertop and plants her hand on the opposite hip. "Maren Lorraine Laughlin, are you serious? I am your mother. I grew you and pushed you out of my body." She gestures between her legs, and I grimace. In her eyes, I'm a virgin until the end of time, but she has never held back on the gory details of any of our births. She's a complex woman, my mother.

"First of all, it's very new and very secret. And second, Liam will murder us both if he figures it out."

My mom rolls her eyes with breathless chuckle. "Please. That man wouldn't know a duck if it quacked in his face. He still thinks Rosie likes boys."

I press my lips together to hide my smile. My fourteen-year-old niece's sexuality is a nonissue. No one in our family ever has or ever will care either way, including her dad. But we're waiting for her to feel comfortable coming out to us. It's the worst-kept secret, second only, apparently, to me and Joe.

"Be that as it may," I tell her, patiently, "I'm not ready for anyone to know and we're being careful because of Joe's kids."

My mom doesn't respond for a long minute, but then she gives me a soft smile, tugging on my ponytail like she did when I was little. "Okay, baby. I won't say anything. But, just so you know, I've always thought the world of Josiah Cole and he couldn't do better than you."

"Really? You don't think I'm . . . I don't know, too immature?"

My mom's forehead creases in bewilderment. "Maren. You were born with a middle-aged soul. How else could Fost have handled you out on his boat morning, noon, and night? You're a nurturer. It's no surprise to me that you would find someone with a ready-made family in need of extra love."

In a split second, relieved tears surge to my eyes and my vision grows blurry around the edges. I reach for my mom, wrapping my arms around her shoulders and pulling her tight. "Thank you for saying that."

She strokes my hair the way she used to and chuckles softly in my ear. "Goodness gracious, you're squeezing the life outta me. Did you really think I'd feel otherwise?"

I don't respond, just squeeze her even tighter before letting go. I turn and pull some sangria out of the fridge, along with a tray of pre-sliced fruit, and twist the bottle top off with a crack. "I think I could use a glass of this. Want to join me?"

♪♪♪

That was hours ago, and as much as I appreciate having my mom's support, I still need her to leave. She's too smart. Not only that, she and my dad decided to share my cabin, since I had the extra room, and let Liam and his family take their cabin after they decided to show up last-minute.

This is taking the vacation fantasy too literally. I'm thirty-three and being cockblocked by my parents in the room next to mine.

> **Joe:** I'm sorry. Want me to call you? I was in the military. I'm not half bad at phone sex.

The mere thought of Joe's low voice in my ear while I imagined his hands . . . Through the wall, I hear the bed my parents are sharing creak. Nope.

> **Maren:** I can't touch myself while sharing a wall with my parents. Gross!

> **Joe:** How did you survive being a teenager?

> **Maren:** That's different. They didn't know then.

> **Joe:** Speaking as a parent, they absolutely knew.

> **Maren:** UGH. That's not helping.

> **Joe:** Okay, okay, I'll work on it. We'll figure something out. Besides, it's only four more days.

> **Maren:** FOUR MORE DAYS

> **Joe:** Maren. I went three years without before you turned up.

> **Maren:** Fair point. But that was before you knew what it was going to be like . . .

> **Joe:** Okay, okay. I'll figure something out.

I bite my lip, thinking he's being far too reasonable about this. I take out my hair tie and rumple my hair, lying back on my pillow before lifting my sleep tank in an artfully sexy way. I take a selfie, then hit send. There's a beat of radio silence and then the gray dots.

> **Joe:** holy shit I think I just spontaneously combusted in my pants

> **Joe:** I'LL FIGURE SOMETHING OUT TOMORROW

> **Joe:** I hope you don't think I'm deleting that picture.

I belatedly stifle my gasp, then stare, frozen, at the wall, listening for signs that they've heard. Jesus. I wonder if there is another open cabin this week?

> **Maren:** You have to delete it! What if your kids find it?!

> **Joe:** I'm sorry, I can't think straight right now.

> **Maren:** Joe!

> **Joe:** Who needs food? Water? Sustenance? Not me. I have photographic evidence that the most perfect breasts exist.

I giggle, and then I type, **You're ridiculous.**

> **Joe:** I'm lucky is what I am. Good night, Mare.

I groan.

> **Maren:** Night, Joe.

TWENTY-THREE

Tolerate It

Maren

I'M NOT THINKING WHEN I HEAD INTO TOWN THANKSGIVING morning, at least not about anything other than black olives. My family can't do a holiday without at least two cans of black olives on hand, but apparently, the Coles are indifferent. Indifferent, I tell you.

Thank goodness I checked with Donna before the local grocery stores closed for the day. My nieces and nephews would likely riot. They're practically feral.

So that is all that's on my brain as I stroll into the Safeway, with its 1960s music, glaring halogen lights, and nearly empty aisles. There is exactly one checkout in operation, and I give the cashier my friendliest, most bashful greeting as I hurry past her, immediately seeking out the olives. I definitely feel like everyone should have holidays paid for and off, and yet . . . olives. I'm the problem, it's me. My eyes are on the signage above the aisles, and I walk straight into a wall of human with a surprised *oof.*

"Ope! Sorry!" I blurt.

"Musky Maren!"

Dammit. My midwestern smile teeters, slips, and flops to the floor, swimming away.

"Heyyy, Bryce." My tone is irredeemably dull. "Good to see you."

"You're in town!"

"I am. With my family."

His face is sweaty and flushed pink, eyes widening. "At Cole's Landing, I bet!"

The way he thinks he knows, or, I suppose, the way he *does* know if his now-deleted message on my website was any indication, makes my skin crawl unpleasantly and I just want to get out of here. He's still beaming at me.

"How long're you around? I've been thinking! Maybe you could come to the hardware store and sign some gear. We could let the public know, set up a booth . . . You could even stay at my house. My wife wouldn't mind. Plus, she likes to visit her parents down in Green Bay every weekend . . ."

I interrupt that unpleasant train of hospitality, not at all interested in hearing where it was headed. "I don't really do that anymore, Bryce. Haven't in years."

"Oh, but for old times' sake." He presses in closer, lowering his voice to effect an intimacy we didn't share. Wouldn't share. "We used to have a chat room, 'Musky Maren's Men,' back in the day. I bet I could call up the Maren signal and they'd all be on their way on a moment's notice. I told them I knew you . . ."

I'm already shaking my head, fisting my hands to keep the tremors from taking over. "I really need to get going. It was nice seeing you again," I lie, automatic politeness rearing its ugly head.

I make it back to the car and shake out my fingers, inhaling and exhaling, slow and steady, before turning over the ignition and reversing out of my space just in case Bryce was on his way out. I'm ten miles out of town before I realize I don't have the black olives.

↓↓↓

I don't have to dress up for a family Thanksgiving, but I want to. I rarely have the occasion to take it up a notch in my daily life, and I want to look nice for Joe. Therefore, I tell my parents I'll meet them over at the Coles' and take my time blowing out my hair until it falls in soft layers down my forehead and midway down my back. I apply real makeup, brightening up my eyes and darkening my lips to a pretty coral. I didn't bring a whole lot of winter clothing with me since I hadn't planned on staying this long, but I'd found a sweet long-sleeved cranberry dress online that fit snugly around the waist, then flared and swung around my knees. I layered it over a pair of thick black tights and heeled black booties. To finish it all off, I slip a bunch of silver bangles up my arms and a few sterling rings on my fingers. By the time I'm all put together, I've mostly shaken off the encounter from this morning.

I have lots of experience in denial. I worked that angle for the entirety of Musky Maren. But time and age have given me lots of perspective. I realize now that if something feels instinctually bad, it's bad, and also, I don't owe anyone any part of me. Not even the public parts. Not even the ones I freely gave access to at one point.

It doesn't matter what happened in the past. It doesn't matter if they weren't actually threatening my safety. *It doesn't fucking matter* if they were/are nice guys (or girls, but let's be honest, my audience was primarily men).

I don't owe them anything. Even if I decided to go back to my channel tomorrow and started filming new content. I still don't.

Because that's the issue, isn't it? They think because I'm a public figure, or I was a public figure, I'm asking for the attention. And I am. In a way, anyway. I was asking for strangers to watch and enjoy my content. But that doesn't give them carte blanche to the rest of my life. That doesn't excuse them digging into my personal space and inviting themselves inside. There's a boundary, and for whatever reason, the men I knew who were and are public figures haven't had that boundary challenged the way the women I know have.

So I've moved past the encounter, but I'm also plenty angry and frustrated at the way it took me out. And I'm newly determined to not let that happen again.

I'm even more determined when I arrive at the Coles' sans black olives. Which, in all my righteous fury on the drive back, I'd completely forgotten about all over again.

"You had one job!" my brother teases, the moment I put down my purse and press a kiss to my mom and dad's cheeks and hug Donna and Simon.

I roll my eyes at him, plopping down on the couch between Anders and my nephew Caleb, who are absorbed in the original *Home Alone* movie.

"You smell good," Anders says, leaning in.

"Thanks, kid."

"Auntie Mare always smells good," my twelve-year-old nephew Caleb says, and I grin. Compliments from little boys are harder to earn and therefore worth at least twice as much as any others.

"Thanks, other kid," I tell my nephew, elbowing him gently.

"Seriously, how'd you forget?" Liam carries on. "Mom said you went to town this morning and everything."

I shrug a shoulder, pretending to watch Kevin McCallister's enormous family wreak havoc around his enormous house the day before they were supposed to leave on an enormous vacation in Paris.

"It's not that big of a deal, Lee," my sister-in-law Jessica says, exasperated. She shakes her head and gives me a friendly one-armed hug. "He's just grouchy because this means he can't put olives on all his fingers and pretend he's an olive monster like he's still ten," she tells me.

"Maybe," my brother agrees, tipping his beer toward his wife. "But still. She was there. I just don't understand how she could forget such an essential item. It's not Thanksgiving without the olives."

"I got sidetracked! It happens. It's a holiday! Yeesh."

Joe takes that moment to walk in, Lucy on his hip. He looks his usual laid-back handsome, wearing a robin's-egg-blue V-neck sweater over a white tee and sinfully tight-fitting jeans that hug his thick thighs and trim waist. His wavy golden hair falls across his forehead in a soft swoop and tucks behind his ears. "What'd I miss?"

"Maren, Maren, Maren," Lucy says, her small arms reaching for me. I stand and take her, then settle her in my lap and immediately fuss with her knit jumper to smooth it over her knees the way she prefers.

"Hey, baby," I whisper. "How're you today?" She doesn't answer but plays with my bangles the way I knew she would.

I let her remove a few and then turn to my brother, filling Joe in on my latest indiscretion.

"Oh no," Joe says to me, grinning, his tone deadpan. "Not the olives."

I quirk my lips in response.

"I just want to know how she could possibly go all the way into town and not pick them up. Such a space cadet! This is what I'm talking about, Mare." My brother is ranting, and a tingle of unease starts at the nape of my neck. "You're so used to only taking care of yourself. You're like a college student."

My grip on Lucy tightens, but I don't say anything. This isn't the time or the place, and anyway, he's just blowing off steam. I know this. He's probably on his second beer and feeling loose. Not to mention, his buddy is here. So he's showing off. I know this, I know this, *I know this.*

It's not about me.

"Christ, Liam. It's just olives. Get a grip. Need another beer?" Joe asks, a bite to his suggestion, and I close my eyes, holding my tongue.

"Today it's olives, but what will it be tomorrow? *Oh, I forgot to turn in that job application?*" Liam snorts against the mouth of his bottle.

"Fine. I didn't forget," I blurt, my heart racing far too quickly for the situation. "I was at the store, in the black olive aisle, when I ran into a guy that was a fan of my old YouTube videos and the encounter unsettled me. I ended it quickly, returned to my car, and was halfway home before I realized I hadn't grabbed the olives."

"Are you okay, Maren?" Anders asks softly next to me. Clever boy.

I smile at him. "I am. It was silly, really. Nothing to be worried about."

"Bryce Callahan?" Joe asks, appearing for all the world to be relaxed, ankle over knee, beer in his hand, settled back against the love seat, his tone even, but I know better. His eyes are something else entirely.

I nod.

"Unsettled you how?"

"He's just extra familiar," I answer my brother. "It's nothing."

"Obviously it was something if you left empty-handed," he points out.

"It *was* something," I concede. "Now it's nothing. I'm already over it. This is part of being a person in the public eye. Comes with the territory."

"But you stopped being in the public eye years ago," Jessica says, her expression concerned.

"I told you this stuff would follow you."

I meet my brother's eyes. "You did." Like fifteen years ago, but sure.

"That's not right," Joe insists.

"What do you know about it? It's not like you've ever seen the videos . . ."

I release a long, slow breath and pray to the gods of holiday dinners and Stove Top Stuffing for patience.

Joe takes a long sip from his beer, his eyes on my brother as if to answer. Which, based on the utter silence that blankets the room, I guess it is.

This. *This* is exactly what I was worried about.

I get to my feet and try to turn and place Lucy on the couch, but she doesn't relax her grip. So instead, I readjust her on my hip, and she lays her head in the crook of my shoulder, her breaths puffing against my neck. A warm feeling settles over me, calming me. I carry her toward the kitchen.

"You don't have to answer that," I say to Joe, low, as I pass near him. "In fact," I address the group, "I'm leaving the room and I'd appreciate it if you all could not talk behind my back about how disappointing I am."

When I aim my attention in Joe's direction, I nearly stutter at the intensity in his gaze. "I'm just gonna take her into the kitchen. I've got her."

I watch his Adam's apple bob before he nods. "I know you do."

TWENTY-FOUR

Lover Lay Down

Joe

I WATCH MAREN WALK OUT, MY DAUGHTER CURLED IN HER ARMS, and notice another set of eyes following her. Anders.

He looks at me, worry written into his features. I pat the love seat next to me and he comes straight over. "Is she okay?"

"Yeah, bud. I think so," I tell him honestly. "But if you want to check on her in a few minutes, I bet she'd like that."

"What's gotten into her?" Liam asks the room at large, his expression so clearly baffled, I'm tempted to punch him for being so dense. She literally just asked us not to talk about her and it's like the words rolled right off his stupid back.

I'm saved from responding by Jessica. "I think, dear husband, your baby sister is sick of your shit."

I grunt into my beer, finishing the bottle.

Liam scowls. "She's my sister. It's my job to harass her."

"I don't harass my sister," my son says simply. He looks put out with my oldest friend, and for the first time since entering the room, I want to laugh. Straight from the mouths of babes, or however that old saying goes.

Liam doesn't reply, but he does tip his head in my direction. "Have you really seen her videos?"

This I can answer. So I do. "Not in years, but I liked them when I was homesick and overseas. She filmed up here and it reminded me of what I had to come back to."

Liam blinks. Eventually, he says, in all sincerity, "I hadn't thought of that. That's cool, man. I'm glad you had them, then." And I want to wring his thick neck for the double standard. She's somehow asking for the negative attention for making the videos, but he's glad I had them when I was homesick. I try to remind myself of how he made home-cooked meals the entire two weeks he stayed with me after the divorce. Pots and pots of mashed potatoes for Lucy. The way he woke up early to get Anders to kindergarten when I was too hungover to move.

But the argument falls short this time. As much as I appreciated everything he did for me and my kids, he's failing his sister big-time and I'm over it.

I know I'm treading a fine line here. "They were nice videos, Lee. Classy. Cute. She knew her shit. Still does, if our record amount of guided tours this fall are anything to go by."

His jaw ticks. He probably wants to argue but doesn't dare. Not to me. It was my choice to join the Marines, sure, and I don't regret it, but we all know that while I was sweating my ass off and getting shot at and under threat of getting blown up in a desert on the other side of the world, Liam and our other friends were living the cushy frat life.

"I'm gonna go check on Maren," Anders says, pushing off the couch. He leaves and Liam watches me with another discerning look. I decide to let him wonder. I may not be ready to confess my feelings for Maren, but I'm not going to hide anything, either. Besides, Liam won't ask. He'll do backflips in his mind trying to figure out what's happening between Maren and me, but us being together wouldn't be on his radar. To him, it's more likely I'm a yeti and she's a Chupacabra and we're opening a mythological wine and cheese shop than us sleeping together.

"Your kids really like my sister," he observes. Jessica snickers into her sangria and I am positive she's caught on already. I'm also positive she won't say a word. She's having too much fun. She winks at me over her glass, confirming my suspicions.

"She's likable," I tell him. "Now. Another beer?"

Liam drains the last ounce in his bottle, holding it out to me. "Thanks."

ʓ ʓ ʓ

It takes quite a bit of finagling to get Maren alone, but it turns out I have an ally in Jessica and even Maren's mom. I let it be known that I need to work at the bar the Friday after Thanksgiving, and they start planning their Black Friday shopping trip to Green Bay. My mom offers to take my kids along. Then Jessica asks if the bar will be busy.

"Probably," I tell her offhandedly. "It's a big snowmobiling day." (I have no idea if this is true, but it could be and that's enough.)

"Oh, man. Do you really need Maren, then?" she asks in a raised voice, putting on a pout as if I've just ruined her day. She's laying it on a little thick, but I appreciate the effort.

"Oh, um," I stutter, apologetically. "Yeah, I do. Sorry."

"Aw. I was hoping to catch up, but I understand," Jessica says, smoothly. "Maybe drinks tomorrow evening when we get back? Gosh, it'll be after dinner, though."

"Uh, that would be nice," Maren says, glancing at me.

"I'll have drinks ready," I assure them both. "You just call ahead, and I'll send the snowmobilers on their way."

And that's how I managed to get Maren alone, all day, the day after Thanksgiving. Or how Jessica managed it, rather. After everyone pulls out, a little after breakfast, I knock on her door, practically giddy. She throws it open, flashing me a bright smile, and wraps her hand around the back of my neck, pulling me against her. In no hurry, we make out against her door, and aside from the interrupted shower the other day, it's the best start to a morning I've had possibly in my life. Sure as hell beats anything I woke up to in the Marines, and while I love my kids more than air, Maren's soft curves are singularly incomparable.

When we break apart, breathless (her) and hard (me), I tell her to get her coat.

"Tell me we're not really working at the bar all day," she says, grabbing her jacket and slipping her arms in.

I pull the sides of her jacket closed and zip it up, tugging her so close my lips tingle against hers. "We're not. I have plans for you, just not here. Though"—I grimace—"I do have to open the bar later this afternoon. After four should do it." I had to make a compromise to add some validity to our story.

Maren beams up at me, her hazel eyes shining. "So I have six uninterrupted hours?"

"Oh, I plan to interrupt you," I tell her, touching my tongue to her lips and then nipping slightly. "Repeatedly."

♪♪♪

"Close your eyes," I say, leading her by the hand into the boathouse. Well, it's not really a boathouse. It's more of an old, empty kayak and canoe storage space, but we've always called it the boathouse, the way we call the place where we clean fish the fish house. We walked here, so she has some idea of where we're going based on the amount of time I've had her crunching over the newly snow-blanketed path. "Stand right there," I say, stopping her just inside the enclosed entrance. "And give me one second."

The space is empty except for the large quilts and pillows layered on the compact dirt floor, four space heaters pumping out comfortably warm air, about a hundred unscented candles, and a picnic lunch. I start lighting candles, creating a cozy glow outside the bits of sunlight shining through the tiny cracks in the roof and walls.

"You aren't starting a fire, are you?"

"In fact, I'm starting a lot of them. Go ahead and open your eyes," I tell her. Then I spread my arms wide. "Surprise!"

"Oh my god," Maren whispers, her fingers pressed to her still kiss-swollen lips. "You made me a sexy picnic in the *boathouse*."

I'm grateful for the dim lighting, because I'm positive my cheeks are red. I was going for effortless, but the amount of work I put in to appear like it wasn't that much work . . . well. Let's just say it's clear Anders isn't the only one smitten with Maren. "I did. Hopefully it's not too cold. This would probably be better in the summer, but . . ."

"But the bugs would be terrible," she finishes pragmatically, and I relax. Because of course she gets it. She spins slowly, taking it all in. "I should know," she tells me. "I spent many a summer day hiding in here. The spiders, in particular, are atrocious." Her face glows in the candlelight and steals my breath straight from my thrumming chest. "This is incredible.

No one has ever . . . This is like my childhood dream come true. How did you know?"

"I pay attention. Growing up, if you weren't on Fost's boat, you were in here. I thought it might be romantic? Kind of? I'm out of practice."

She shakes her head. "Josiah Cole, I don't know what to say."

"Well, that makes the two of us. I'm always speechless around you," I blurt, feeling my face heat again. I clear my throat. "Want some wine? Leftover turkey?"

"Is there leftover pie? Really, I just want pie."

"Pumpkin and pecan. And I grabbed Cool Whip, though it might get melty."

"We should probably hurry, then. One of each, if you don't mind. I don't think I'm ready for wine yet. I had plenty yesterday."

"Coffee?"

She hums her assent and I pull out a thermos and pass it over.

Maren cracks open the thermos and inhales the steaming aroma with closed eyes. I cut us a couple of slices of pie, divvying them up on paper plates and laying them on the blankets. Then I walk over to the speaker in the corner and hook it up to my phone's Bluetooth, turning on some music. Something folksy, slow and melodic. We dive into our dessert and talk in low tones about yesterday's dinner, the bar, the resort, our families, my plans for the villas. Whatever comes to mind.

Time passes and we've crept closer, side by side on the quilts, both of us reclining on our elbows, barely a foot of space between us. The candles sputter and cast flickering shadows on the walls and the wind whistles through the cracks, but the heaters keep the space cozy enough that we've laid our coats aside. Maren listens intently to my daydreaming of what I want to do with my parents' legacy, occasionally offering her valuable opinions, because she knows these lakes and this area almost as well as I do. They mean just as much to her. It occurs to me I never had that with anyone else, outside of my family. Kiley liked it up here, but it wasn't ever special to her. It wasn't home, at least not any more than any other place the Marines moved us.

And when I ask Maren about her run-in with Bryce Callahan, she tells me all of it. The entire time, I have the primal urge to haul off to the hardware store and punch him square in the face, but I don't. I listen. She has enough people talking at her, telling her what she should and shouldn't do. I don't want to become another spewing voice. Firstly, what the fuck do I really know? It seems to me that she's worked it out for herself, and besides, she knows I have her back. If it came to that.

Which is why I ask, "Could I talk to him?" She blinks and I worry I've offended her. Dammit. "Not to threaten him or anything," I rush to clarify. "And not like you can't handle him. You absolutely can. But from what you're saying, it sounds like he freaks you out. I don't give a fuck about black olives, but clearly he shook you up."

She presses her lips together, and I can tell she's considering her words carefully. I'm about to take back my offer when she speaks in a quiet voice.

"Would you come with me?"

"Of course," I tell her without hesitation.

"You're right," she tells me, shaking her head with a sad kind of smile. "He freaks me out. It's probably nothing, but something about him makes my skin crawl. But if I send you to talk to him instead, I'll still be afraid to see him in town. I need to confront him, but I think it would help if you were there beside me. I'd feel safer and, I don't know, stronger."

"Any time. You say the word when you're ready and we'll go together."

What with work, her brother, and renovating and selling her inheritance, she doesn't need me to guide her hand. She's a powerful woman who knows her own mind and it's sexy as fuck. But there's a small piece of me, one I'll admit out loud only upon threat of death, that feels good knowing I make her feel safer. Stronger, even. Hell. My back is straighter just thinking about it.

I'm embarrassing.

Maren changes the subject, and we talk about Christmas, and she wiggles even closer, relaxing and leaning her head on my shoulder as we stare up at the flickering ceiling, whispering about what I want to give my kids.

Kiley and I married so young—met so young. She wasn't good for me, and I definitely wasn't good for her. I feel almost guilty now, because being with Maren doesn't feel like work. I don't have to learn how to fit with her. We just . . . are.

Is it too easy? Or is it just easy because for once I'm getting it right? Like running on a windy day, and you're struggling against hills and strong gusts trying to push you back down the hill, and suddenly you turn, and the breeze is against your back, carrying you along and cooling you.

My life turned and there was Maren.

"Oh! I love this song!" Maren says, jumping to her feet and scrambling to the speaker to turn it up. "Lorelai got me hooked on Gabby Barrett a while back." She turns to me, holding out her small hand. "Dance with me, Joe."

I pretend to think about it. "Is dancing in the boathouse part of your fantasy?"

"Only the literal culmination."

I get to my feet and like everything so far, we fit together so easily. Like two pieces of a puzzle clicking into place. She tucks her head in the space between my neck and shoulder, and I wrap my hands around her back, low. Her fingers twist in the hair at the nape of my neck and mine tangle in the hem of her soft sweater. I spin us slowly and she sways us side to side, our feet shuffling against the dirt floor in a quiet march that matches the thudding of my heart, the beat whispering to me in the dark.

Her arms tighten around my neck, ever so slightly, pressing her even closer against me. So close, I can feel her breaths mirroring mine. I close my eyes and inhale the scent of her hair, painting it in my memory. Another song starts and we don't stop. Nothing short of a train plowing through the walls could make me let go of her.

A door crashes open, startling us both.

A train or, apparently, Liam. He stands in the doorway, the bright light burning through the dim space and making me blink fiercely against watery eyes.

"Hey, man, I thought I heard something. Oh shit. Sor— Wait, Maren?" He starts to back out but, just as quick, steps in again, his brows crashing together. "What the actual fuck is going on here?"

TWENTY-FIVE

If You Could Only See

Joe

MY VEINS HAVE ICED OVER. I'M LEFT GAPING OVER MAREN'S shoulder. Unbelievably, she squeezes tighter, clinging to me and burying her face in my neck. I don't know what's happening when she brushes a kiss against my cheek and pulls back, her eyes capturing mine for a brief moment. They're teeming with unspoken things, but before I can hope to decipher them, they dart away.

She turns to Liam. "Hey, Liam. We were dancing. That's all. Just a dance."

"Like hell *that's all*. What is all of this? I thought you two were working in the bar. I stayed back to help—" And then he approaches, towering over Maren and getting in her face before I can even blink. His voice is low, but I hear him loud and clear in the darkened space. "I told you to stay away. What are you thinking? He has kids. He's just gotten over a divorce! I can't believe you—"

"Hey!" I yelp, cutting him off and jumping between them, putting my hands against his chest. "What are you talking about? Don't be an asshole, Liam."

"*I'm* the asshole?" He sputters, incredulous. "You're the one hooking up with my baby sister!"

"She's not a kid, you dick!"

I feel more than hear Maren's sigh against the back of my neck.

"And that makes it okay? Is this why you sent your kids away? For a piece of ass?"

I shove at him. Hard. "Don't call her that! And don't you fucking dare talk about my kids. You don't know anything."

He shoves me back, but I keep my footing. "I know what I see. I'm not stupid. I know you're going through it, man." He flings his hand out, gesturing to Maren behind me. "But this ain't it."

I'm seeing red. "What are you talking about? Going through it? I'm through it. I've *been* through it!"

"Aaand this is my cue," Maren says in a soft voice behind me. She comes around my side and stands there, taking in Liam and me. "I told you I won't get in the middle of you two. I refuse. You've been friends for too long. But . . ." She looks at her brother. "Give Joe some credit, Liam. He's a fantastic dad. This place is doing so well under his management. Open your eyes and your mind and take it in before you make snap judgments." She turns to me. "I promised you New Year's Eve and I stand by it. But I think it would be best to give you both some space." I open my mouth to protest, and she places her fingers across my lips. "Honestly, I could use some time to think, too."

She grabs her coat off the floor and leaves out the door we walked through only hours before. Before sharing pie and smiles and our dreams. Before the thermos of coffee and the slow-dancing and the gut-deep realization that she is everything.

And now she's gone.

"I'm not done talking to you—" Liam says, turning on me, but I slash my hand between us, cutting him off.

"We're done, though. I'm done. And I need to get this cleaned up and open the bar for tonight. So you can see your way out."

"She's my *sister*, Joe. Even if she was good for you, she's off-limits."

I don't respond, just blow out candles and pile them up by the door.

"She doesn't know the first thing about kids or being in a real relationship. She's practically a kid herself."

I pack up the picnic, stacking our paper plates and laying the empty thermos carefully in the basket.

"Not to mention, she's apparently got stalkers that will be following her for the rest of her life from those stupid videos. You don't need that around your family."

I drop the blanket and let my hands fall to my sides, facing him squarely. "How is it you claim to care so much about your sister, yet you can be such an enormous dick to her? Seriously. It's borderline abusive."

Liam laughs me off. "Right."

I don't even crack a smile. I can't. "I'm serious. You call her names, you belittle her, you take every opportunity to push her down, and still she loves you! She looks up to you! Always has! It makes me sick to think of it now. The way you've always treated everyone else better than her. Are you jealous? Is that it? I can't think why, but what else could it be?"

Liam's smile slips.

I press on. "I really like her. She's special. She's good with my kids without even trying. She cares about this place. She makes me feel good and it's simple between us."

"What did she mean about promising you until New Year's?"

I exhale. I suppose there's no point in keeping it secret now. "There is *something* between us. I've felt it from the first, *months* ago," I emphasize before the vein at his temple bursts. "Give me some credit, man." I roll my eyes. "And it's been growing gradually, but of course it's complicated. With my kids and the renovations she's been doing . . . so I asked her to stay through the holidays. To give us a chance to get to know each other, without the pressures of time or family or jobs. A chance to see if there is something real between us."

"And?" His tone is terse.

"And . . ." I exhale, trying to find a way of putting it that conveys how serious this is for me but also not sharing anything with Liam I haven't already told Maren. Which, at this point, could fill a twenty-six-volume encyclopedia set. "I don't know," I eventually hedge. "It was going pretty well until about fifteen minutes ago."

"That's on me," he says, sounding contrite, but not enough, if you ask me.

"Yeah," I tell him. "It is."

"If she really cared, she wouldn't let me get in her way."

"Oh, fuck off," I tell him. "She hasn't let you get in her way, you've forced yourself in. What's the deal with you warning her off me like I'm made of glass?"

"I just . . ." He sputters, turning red. "You've been through a lot, Joe. Coming back from the fucking war and your wife leaving. Lucy . . ." He trails off in the way everyone does when they talk about my kid. The way that annoys the shit out of me. Well. Everyone *but* Maren, that is.

"That's all just life. And don't you ever talk about my kid like she's something I'm going through. She's not a tragedy, she's my child."

"I'm sorry," he apologizes quickly. "You're absolutely right. That was uncalled for."

"I'm fine. We're all fine. But Maren makes me better. And I want—" I swallow. "I want to be able to do that for her, too. So you coming in here, spouting off bullshit about her not being good enough or me being too fragile, just proves you know nothing. Be mad at me for sleeping with your sister." Liam's vein pops again. "That's warranted. I'll own that. But you don't get to tell either of us we don't deserve to be loved."

Liam is quiet for a long minute, and I know he's trying to calm himself down after my revelation. I respect his effort. I never had a sister, but I imagine it sucks feeling like you have to protect them all the time. Eventually, he says, "Want me to talk to her?"

"For me?" I scoff. "I'd rather you fuck off and let me handle this my way. But for yourself, for *her*, yeah. You better fix it. And quick."

He picks up the blanket and hands it to me before walking over to the speaker and turning it off. "This is not me giving my approval, by the way."

"Don't care."

"And I don't ever want to hear about you two having . . ." His voice strangles and he shudders. "Sex, ever again."

"Deal. Though I would advise calling ahead next time you decide to surprise either of us with a visit."

"Fucking fuck, are you serious? The shower?"

I shrug, but do nothing to minimize my shit-eating grin.

It's hard to tell in the dimly lit boathouse, but I think he's turned a little green. "You're an asshole," he says, but he doesn't mean it. "You better not hurt her."

I straighten, widening my stance and crossing my arms over my chest. "I won't, though that's real rich coming from you."

"For what it's worth, I'm sorry."

I pack up the candles, now that they're cool, and turn off the space heaters. "For what it's worth, I don't give a shit until you make it right with Maren."

ᔑ ᔑ ᔑ

She never shows at the lodge that night and her mom tells me she's left, passing me a note that I tuck into my pocket without reading. "She'll come back," she says, her smile sympathetic. "She left all her stuff and asked us to take care of Rogers for her. She found a flight out of Green Bay to Nashville. Spending a few days with Lorelai and that sweet fiancé of hers will be good."

There's a pang in my chest as fear squeezes inside of me. She'll be back. She said she would. I trust her. But Nashville is far, and what if perspective makes her change her mind about me? About us? What if she goes there and finds someone else? Or there's a job opportunity she can't turn down? What do I tell my kids?

As if she reads the thoughts straight from my head, Maren's mom adds, "She said goodbye to Anders and Lucy and told them she'd be back in a few days. She seemed completely normal. They weren't concerned."

So it's just me, then. I sigh and wipe at the already shining bartop. "Thanks for letting me know."

"She'll be back," she repeats.

I nod.

"Joe." I stop my obsessive wiping and meet her gaze. "She'll be back," she says, impressing feeling into each word individually. "I know my daughter. She's not running away."

"I don't know. I've been left before, and this feels the same." As soon as the words leave my mouth, I wince at how pathetic I sound.

"It's not," she promises. "She wanted to give you and my idiot son time to work things out without her being put in the middle. You can't blame her for that."

"I don't," I assure her quickly.

"Good. Read the note. It'll help." She flashes a grin so like her daughter's that it makes my chest ache. "Now," she says, scooting onto a barstool and folding her hands on the bar in front of her. "I have to tell you, I've fallen in love with your children. Fair warning, I plan to spoil them at Christmas."

This makes me smile as I place a cardboard drink coaster in front of her. "You'll have to get in line behind my mom, but I won't argue."

"I am sorry about Liam."

I'm already shaking my head. "Don't mention it. He's fine. He's an idiot, like you said, and he needs to apologize to Maren, but for my part, as long as he doesn't interfere with my trying to convince her to fall in love with me, I don't care."

Her grin spreads into an all-out blinding smile. "Don't give up on her."

"No, ma'am. Now what can I mix you up?"

♩♩♩

Joe,

Stop your spiraling, old man. This isn't what you think it is. In fact, I'm guessing this will hurt me a thousand times more than it will hurt you. You probably won't even notice I'm gone. As for me, however, I will miss you every second.

But this is important. I didn't expect ... you. Do you ever feel like we just jumped directly into the middle of things, skipping all the bullshit? In a way, I'm grateful. It's been so simple, and I happen to really like simple.

And I really like you.

Maren

⌥⌥⌥

If Maren's plan in giving me space was to show me just how bat-shit crazy I'd go without her, it's worked like a charm.

Nothing's changed. I still run every morning on my treadmill before drinking a steaming cup of coffee on my cold deck. I still pour Anders's cereal and make sure Lucy's elastic waistbands don't have any tags in them. I still argue with my dad over wanting to replace the appliances in the villas with more expensive yet more environmentally friendly alternatives. I still tend bar and laugh with guests, churning out more business for the busy summer months ahead.

Yet, despite all of the things I'm still doing, everything has changed.

Because Maren's not on the deck waiting with her own coffee to greet me after my run. And Maren's not there next to Anders at the breakfast bar, asking him about school and showing him updates from fishing message boards. And Maren's not there sketching new lure designs with Lucy and convincing her to try a different brand of mac 'n' cheese. And Maren's not there to giggle at my dad's antics when he argues with me, meeting his eyes over my exasperated head. And Maren's not there to charm the old guys at the bar, promising to help them catch the fish of their life next summer when the lakes open up again.

It's different because now there is a Maren-shaped hole in my life. Even Kiley calling, letting me know when she's planning to pick up both kids for Christmas, doesn't feel like the miracle it should.

"Aw, man," Anders says when I hang up the phone and relay the news to him. "I was kind of hoping to spend it with you and Maren, here." As soon as the words leave his mouth, he straightens and flashes me a guilty look.

I reach out a hand, placating. "None of that. You feel how you feel. I'm a little disappointed, too, but we got you for Thanksgiving. We'll pick another day before you leave to pass out presents and make it special."

"After Maren gets back," he checks.

"Of course." I try not to look worried because it hasn't even been a week. In fact, Liam just left two days ago. We talked things out over a couple of beers and it's as fixed as it can be until he talks with Maren.

"Okay. Can you take Lucy and me shopping so we can pick something out for her?"

"Do you have an idea what you're looking for?"

"There's a musky lure she was drooling over. She said it's in town."

I nod and my phone vibrates, since I put it on silent when I laid Lucy down for a nap.

Maren: Flying home tomorrow. Think you can pick me up?

I don't even check my schedule. I'll make it happen.

Joe: Absolutely. What time?

Maren: I'll send you the flight details. Early afternoon, so it won't interfere with getting the kids to school.

Maren: I miss you. And them.

Maren: "Miss you" isn't really a strong enough phrase, but I don't have a better one. "Desperately miss you," maybe.

Joe: We miss you too. Especially me.

I hesitate and type again.

Joe: Was that enough space?

Maren: Too much. I was ready to come back days ago, but the flights were expensive, and Lorelai wanted to show me around town a bit.

Joe: You could have called.

Maren: I know this won't make sense, but I couldn't. I needed to miss you. I needed the time to think about missing you and what it meant.

Joe: That makes sense. I'm not mad.

And I'm not. I've been a lot of things: pouting, hurt, frustrated, and lovesick . . . but never angry.

Maren: Lorelai is calling me down. We're headed out to dinner for my last night. See you tomorrow?

Joe: Tomorrow. Good night, Mare. Have fun with your friends.

Maren: Give the kids hugs for me! I'll see you tomorrow . . . I said that already. I know. I just . . .

I grin.

Joe: I know, too.

Maren: Good.

TWENTY-SIX

What Kind of Man

Maren

(Earlier that same week)

I'D BARELY BEEN IN NASHVILLE FIVE MINUTES BEFORE I STARTED having regrets about leaving him. And missing him. God, how I missed him. Pathetic. Stupid. Rash decision.

But it was the right choice. I know it was because I thought, before I left, that I could leave. That I could walk away and take another job in another state and be fine. If Liam pressed the issue or the kids didn't approve of me, or Kiley was an unbearable pain in the ass . . . I could start over, unscathed.

I thought wrong.

"You're head-over-ass in love with him," Lorelai says, smirking behind a glass of expensive red wine. We're sitting opposite each other on stylish, navy crushed-velvet sofas in the upstairs apartment of the duplex she shares with her fiancé, music producer Craig Boseman. She's curled her denim-clad legs under her and leans effortlessly against a squashy pillow. Her long black hair is gathered in a messy topknot and her face is bare of makeup. This is the Lorelai that I miss so much sometimes, it makes my chest squeeze. I'm so incredibly proud of her and all she's accomplished in taking back the reins of her career and facing down all the naysayers in country music who thought she couldn't overcome being unjustly canceled, dumped, and left unemployed. Obviously. And I adore Craig. He's her perfect match in every way. Soft to her hard, down-to-earth when she is flying high, and unrelentingly loyal.

That doesn't mean I don't wish she still lived just across town.

That said, I no longer live across town anyway. Which is why I'm here. Because as my best friend so aptly observed, I moved to Wisconsin and fell for Josiah Cole and now I need Lorelai's specific brand of straight talk.

"I am," I admit, before gulping my own glass of wine and making a face at the arid sweetness. My palate isn't quite as sophisticated as theirs. Lorelai and Craig love to tell stories about the early days when they drank cheap beer on grungy floors because they couldn't even afford furniture, but it's hard to remember back when they weren't as successful as they are now. Craig even named his massively popular recording studio On the Floor Records as an homage to his modest beginnings. They're very down-to-earth and well-adjusted and all that, but when it comes to their wine, they're straight-up snobs. "Head over ass," I rasp. "I think I have whiplash, it happened so fast. Like a car wreck, except I'm both the car and whatever the hell I've crashed into."

Lorelai whoops as Craig enters the room, his lanky form settling on the couch beside her. His hand curls around her bare foot and he beams at me, his clever eyes twinkling behind his eyeglass frames. "That's the perfect description: a car wreck," he says with a tilt of his head. "Mind if I borrow it?"

I glare at him. "If you make my life into a country song, I will murder you."

Lorelai snorts and pats his knee. "Too soon, babe. She's still in the shocked-as-hell phase."

"Ugh. That makes it sound like the stages of grief."

"It's not that different." She starts ticking off on her fingers, still holding the glass. "Denial, anger, bargaining, depression, and finally acceptance." She shrugs. "Sounds like love to me."

Craig groans theatrically. "You need to stop. This is scream-ing three chords and the truth. Y'all are killing me."

"Is this what it's like for you two all the time? Like, is every argument fair game for songwriting?"

Lorelai thinks. "Hm. Now that you mention it . . ."

"I don't know about arguments, but definitely foreplay," Craig admits, without shame. "Actually. Yeah, arguments, too. But there's a statute of limitations. Except instead of it being about not using material after so many years have passed, we have to wait to use it until both parties are over it."

"Usually after a minimum of five orgasms, at least three of which have to happen via tongue."

I sputter, the wine I'd just lifted to my lips dribbling down the front of my pajama top.

"It's in the fine print," Lorelai says.

Craig hands me a napkin. "Signed and notarized and sealed with a blood vow, I believe, wasn't it, honey?"

I catch my breath in time to roll my eyes. "Jesus H., you two. I think I'd rather stay in a hotel."

"Oh please," my best friend says. "We haven't argued in weeks. Don't be so dramatic."

"Can we focus back on my problems, please?"

"Of course, but remind me again what the problem even is?"

I narrow my eyes and take another sip. It goes down more smoothly this time. "I'm in love with him."

"And?"

"And I've never been in love before! This sucks!"

"Putting aside the alarming nature of that interesting tidbit considering you nearly married Shane, why does this suck? Joe seems great and so do his kids. You love Wisconsin and the resort, and I've never seen you so all-around-glowy and happy . . ."

"I didn't nearly marry Shane."

Lorelai waves a hand as if my statement is a gnat buzzing around her stemware. "Technicality."

"My brother is—"

"No thank you," she butts in. "Liam doesn't factor in this conversation."

"But he does! They've been friends longer than I've been alive."

"Then it's between the two of them, Mare."

"Not if it ruins things between them forever. I can't be the cause of that."

"I'm with Lorelai on this one," Craig speaks up gently. "I've . . . Well, okay." He turns to Lorelai and his face folds into a grimace. "I didn't tell you this because I didn't feel like it was my place." He turns back to me. "I spoke with your Joe a month or so back. Cameron Riggs called me up so we could give him a pep talk, if you will."

"WHAT?" Lorelai screeches, but she looks surprised more than angry. "Why?"

Craig still speaks to me. "He was freaking out a little . . . kind of like how you are right now. He really likes you, obviously, and he wanted to ask you to stay, which he did. Which is why I think it's okay to tell you this. He already asked you to stay and you did, and furthermore, you seem happy with your choice?" he confirms.

My entire body has gone still, but I manage a wooden nod.

"Right," he says. "Because you're in love with him. And you're worried that you fell in love and he's gonna snatch it back."

I nod again. "Something like that," I whisper.

"He won't. He didn't ask you to stay on a whim, Maren. I don't suspect Joe is the kind of man to do anything on a whim. He's got a lot more at risk here. He can't leave; you can. He's got a ready-made family; you don't. He's given his heart to someone before and they stomped on it; you've been fortunate enough to do the stomping in the past."

I inwardly wince at the truth in his words. "You sound like Liam."

"Yeah, babe, this isn't the motivational speech you think it is," Lorelai tells him.

His grin is soft and warm and 100 percent Huckleberry, and I'm reminded how this man managed to hook my fiery best friend. "But it *is*. Just hear me out. Joe knew all of that going in and still asked you to stay. He decided you, Maren, were worth the risk and he was up for the challenge. And you agreeing to stay proved you were willing to let him try to convince you."

"But that makes it sound uneven. Like I'm—" *The catch.* That's what Joe had said, wasn't it? *You're the catch, Maren.*

My heart races and my face flushes and my hand sweats around the stem of my glass. "He said I'm the catch."

"You are," Lorelai confirms softly. "He's absolutely right."

"So is he, though," I tell them. "He's funny and charming and smart and handsome and he's this amazing dad and a thoughtful son and boss and friend . . ."

"Sounds like a perfect match, then."

"But what about my brother? And the kids' mom? And my job?"

"No idea, but it's been my experience that those kinds of things are better tackled together than apart."

"But I just got here."

Lorelai shakes her head. "That's not what I meant. Honestly, I'm of the belief that it's healthy to miss someone. It's a great litmus test to see if it's real."

"I already know I miss him."

"Give it a few days. Make it really burn and then we'll kick you out. Just imagine what the sex will be like." She waggles her eyebrows and I groan.

"There it is."

"Am I wrong?"

I remember the way Joe and I were interrupted in the boathouse and how it'd been days before that with our families in town and I feel a little twinge that makes me squirm and flush.

"You aren't wrong," I grumble, tipping back the last of my wineglass. I stand to put it in the sink. "I think I should probably get to sleep. It's been a long day." Hard to believe dancing in the boathouse had been this morning and now I'm here, without his arms.

Why did I do this again?

Right. Missing him. And thinking. Yeah. Well, that worked like a fucking charm.

I round the back of the couch, blowing kisses to my friends, and take myself to the guest room where I don't check my phone, knowing innately that he won't text me. He's going to give me the time and space I requested because that's the kind of guy he is.

The kind who thinks I'm the catch.

Well, when I get home, it'll be my turn to convince him he's *my* catch.

♪♪♪

The return flight I chose when I booked my tickets is for a five-day trip and it's torture. At least four days too long, but I'm not that financially secure to where I can just book another flight, and I didn't pay for the insurance to swap things around. After two days, my brother calls. I don't pick up, and I don't call him back right away. I'm all for taking the high road, but I'm not above letting him sweat it out a little, first.

A day later, there's a knock at the door and low voices. Lorelai calls my name. For a split second, my heart jumps straight into my throat, thinking it's Joe.

I practically sail into the living room, but it's not Joe. It's Liam.

He looks jet-lagged and uncomfortable. Not only did he have to fly here, I imagine he's a little flustered at having to knock on Lorelai Jones's front door. I wonder how he got her address? I'm thinking he groveled to Lorelai. Despite this, he perks up when he sees me. "Maren! Hi!"

I bite back a smile at how out of place he looks, but don't offer to let him in. Not yet. "Hello, big brother."

"Good to see you."

I raise a brow, leaning against the doorframe and crossing my arms over my chest. "Is it?"

"Of course it is. Listen, I'm sorry for giving you shit about the olives and that other stuff, you know, with Joe."

"Woooow," I tell him, dragging the word out. "You flew all the way to Nashville and that's the best you got?"

"Yeah, well. I'm not sure how I feel about it all, to be honest, but I'm trying."

My tone is dry as sea salt. "How gracious of you. Well, if that's all . . ." I straighten off the doorjamb and reach for the handle.

"Come on, Mare. Don't be like that," he tries, but I cut him off.

"No, really. It's fine. You don't have to be okay with it. I just can't believe you came all the way here for that. You could have called."

"All right, look, I am," my brother admits in a rush, putting his hands out to stop me from closing the door in his face. "Okay with it, I mean. Do I want to hear about you two in the shower ever, ever again? Fuck no." He shudders and I gasp out a laugh.

"Oh god."

"But I deserved that. Is it weird? Yes. Do I think you might be awesome for each other?" He sighs, dropping his hands to his sides in a placating gesture, and I hold my breath. "Also yes."

I exhale.

"I'm sorry for being a dick. I'm sorry I made you feel like you were anything less than extraordinary."

"You made me feel anything *but* extraordinary, Liam. The complete opposite of extraordinary, even."

He looks stricken. "I'm sorry. I didn't—" He shakes his head. "I shouldn't have done that. Admittedly . . ." He stops and glances around, lowering his voice. "This feels weird, can I come in?"

"Not yet," I tell him. "Admittedly?" I prompt. He rolls his eyes with a huff and shifts his weight.

"Admittedly, maybe I'm a little jealous and I have been projecting."

My mouth drops open at his confession. "Jealous? Of what?"

"Of your freedom. I may or may not be going through a little bit of a midlife crisis. Or something. Hell, kid. I'm thirty-nine. Forty, next year."

"And you have so much to show for it! A hot wife who, confusingly, adores you. Two incredible children who look up to you, an amazing career that pays you stupid amounts of money . . ."

"Right. I know. Thank you." He grimaces. "And I'm grateful for all of it. I wouldn't change it for the world. But you? You can go anywhere and do anything you want. You're still at the beginning. If you wanted to pick up and fly to Fiji tomorrow and follow the migration patterns of the yellow-bellied crochet lizard—"

"That can't be a thing."

"Doesn't matter! You could anyway."

I open the door wider and hold out my arm. "All right. Come in."

He walks in and sits, perched on the edge of the couch as

if he understands his position is still precarious. Smart man, my brother.

I sit across from him, on the arm of the other couch. Lorelai gets up from the table with her laptop in hand. "I'm just gonna go send emails in the other room."

I smile at her gratefully and return my attention to my brother. "You're right. I do have that kind of freedom. I could technically fly off somewhere and start over. I *did* fly off to Nashville, not to start over, but to give you and Joe some space, and I realize my own privilege in that.

"That said," I continue, "I don't want that freedom. I don't *want* to leave. I want to settle down and be still. I want to belong to someone. A few someones, even," I admit, thinking of Lucy and Anders. "I wasn't looking for that and I certainly wasn't trying to find it with Joe. But . . ." I shrug.

"But you found it with Joe," my brother finishes.

I nod.

"Have you told him this?"

"Not yet."

"You should."

"I will."

"I'm sorry again for how I made you feel. I really didn't mean to hurt you. I wasn't thinking."

"Thank you."

Liam slumps onto the couch finally, gazing around. "This is a little weird, huh? I assumed a country music star's house would be . . . bigger."

"You should see our cabin," Lorelai says, coming back in the room. "It's little more than a shack and it makes this place look like a palace. Is it safe to come back in now?"

"Yeah, you missed all the gory stuff."

"Oh, I heard every bit." She flashes a wink at my brother. "You staying the night, Liam?"

"I can get a hotel . . ."

"No need. There's another guest room in the downstairs apartment. Why don't you get freshened up and I'll take you both out for dinner."

A few minutes later Liam leaves to unpack and get cleaned up downstairs and Lorelai returns from showing him around.

"Well." She fans her face. "He's back to being cute again since he got his head out of his ass."

For the first time in three days, I laugh.

TWENTY-SEVEN

Never Tear Us Apart

Maren

JOE IS WAITING, STANDING OUTSIDE HIS TRUCK IN THE PICKUP lane. It's freezing and I'm jet-lagged, but the moment I see his tousled blond hair sticking out from beneath a knit hat, I'm running. I drop the handle of my rolling suitcase with a clack against the pavement and he braces, reading my intention in time to catch me. I wrap myself around him like a koala bear and pepper his face with kisses before he captures my mouth in a deep, hot, wet kiss that sings all the way to where my core is pressed against his.

"Was that enough space?"

"Too much. Never again," I say breathlessly as his nose brushes my neck and sends little zings of electricity through me.

"Way too much," he agrees. "Next time I'm stowing away in your suitcase."

I slip to my feet, but not out of his arms, and look him in the eyes, feeling caught. "I won't do that again, Joe. Ever."

His eyes fill with emotion and his Adam's apple bobs before he shakes his head. "You don't have to say that. It's okay.

I understand why you left and it's okay to need your space to think. You don't owe me any—"

"No," I tell him, shaking my head and standing on my toes to plant a soft kiss on his lips to keep him from saying what he's about to say. "It's not okay. I'm not saying I didn't need to do it because I did this time, but I don't ever need to do it again. I won't leave like that."

He nods, releasing a shaky breath. "Okay."

"You're a catch, too, Joe. You're *my* catch."

The corner of his delicious mouth quirks in amusement and his eyes take on a glittery quality. "Is that so?"

"It's very so."

"I come with extras," he reminds me as if I needed the reminder.

"I can't wait to see them. I missed them."

The quirk spreads into an all-out smile. "Okay, but I was kind of hoping to make a slight detour by the boathouse before letting everyone know you were back. We have some unfinished—"

I cut him off with my lips, curling my tongue in his mouth and slipping my hands into his back pockets, bucking against him.

He pulls back just enough to speak. "I'll take that as a yes."

♪♪♪

This time, Joe leaves the picnic basket at home, and I practically pounce on him the moment he kicks the wooden door closed and tilts the latch to secure it. This isn't about taking our time. We've wasted enough already—*I've* wasted enough already. Five days? Bless past Maren's little insecure heart. She's dead to me. I climb him like a tree, tangling my hands in his overlong hair and wrapping my legs around his hips. Thankfully, he's up to the challenge, chuckling low as he grips the backs of my thighs, holding tight and pressing in and using my own weight against me in super-interesting ways. Ways that make me want to get my PhD in physics just so I can understand how it's possible this man has such a talent with simple friction. I'm convinced it's something he learned in the military. Whatever it is, it's made the name of every man before him leak straight out of my brain.

Thank all the stars he has mercy on my clit and lays me down on a pile of quilts, immediately getting to work on the too-many buttons of my shirt. I should have planned better. Worn a T-shirt. Or better yet, those tear-apart jogging suits that were popular when I was a kid.

There is something to be said for just how incredibly sexy it is to have your clothes peeled off your body by someone who looks like he might combust with every inch of skin revealed. It's not something I've given much thought to, happy to pull off my own clothes in the heat of the moment, but Joe is taking his time. Carefully unwrapping me like a gift. He undoes the button on my jeans, placing a kiss where the silver fastener used to be. Then he pulls on the zipper, following his torturous progress with his lips, his breath, his calloused fingertips. Heat blazes through me and I have to consciously work to keep my hips still.

He peels my jeans down my thighs, and I wriggle free in an effort to speed us along, until I'm left only in my bra and underwear. Impatient, I hook my waistband with my thumbs and lift, but he reaches out with his palm, laying it flat across the sensitive skin below my belly button and pressing gently.

He tsks lightly and his lips are curved upward as his eyes dance in the candlelight. "Not yet."

"Guh."

He laughs, crinkling his crystal-blue eyes, and starts to remove his own shirt, pulling it over his head in that super-attractive way that musses his hair, the way I figure all men were taught when the teachers separated the classes for the puberty talk in fifth grade. Girls got a stick of deodorant and the thickest sanitary napkin they'd ever see. Boys learned how to tug their shirt off in the hottest way possible.

I reach for his zipper, and he lets me. Thank god. It's not easy going. He's already straining against the denim, which of course only revs me up more. While I'm distracted, he performs some kind of magic that has my bra slipping down my shoulders, even though I swear he hasn't moved his hands, and suddenly his hot mouth is covering my nipple. His tongue is swirling and pulling and all coherent thought has left my brain. I am composed only of hot, spiraling, staticky molecules and vibrating particle sensations. Molten lava races through my veins and my breaths pant into the space between us. His fingers find my other breast, gently tweaking and cupping me, and even without the ability to think I'm climbing his lap and straddling him. I haven't managed to remove his jeans, but I've made enough progress that I can still slide myself against him. Up and down, circling my hips and inwardly congratulating myself when he gasps, his mouth releasing me, the cold air hitting the damp heat and causing me to shudder from head to toe.

His fingers grip my hips, pulling me against him as he lifts up and there's that delicious friction all over again. My thighs tremble and my insides clench as he drags against my most sensitive spot. He drops his forehead to my collarbone and I hold him against me as we rock.

With a sudden groan, his fingers slip into the waistband of my underwear and he swiftly pulls down. I take his hint and slide to the side, pulling them off the rest of the way and throwing them god knows where. He's hurriedly losing his pants and boxer briefs in one fell swoop and I grin at the first glimpse of loss of control I've seen from him.

The knowledge he's as desperate for this as I am fuels me impossibly higher.

He takes a deep breath, working to calm himself, and I take him in. All of him. He's beautifully built. Solid and thick, strong in a way that's beyond attractive. Not in the way that I can count his abs. In a way that I can count on him. Protective, thoughtful, aware, and dependable.

Head-over-ass in love. That's what this is.

He crawls over me and it's like I might lift from the blankets, his pull is that consuming. He doesn't check if I'm ready. He knows. His fingers drag from my knee, up my thigh, and press into my hip, asking for permission. I fall open and he takes me in one thrust, filling me completely. I arch against him, desperate to feel more, more, more. He works me slowly, dragging out and diving powerfully, never looking away from my eyes. I'm lost in his gaze, in the feeling of him covering me inside and out. The coiling that started with his mouth on my breast curls and tightens. I can barely move, barely contain it. My breaths turn to whimpers turn to reckless gasps and I'm undone.

I explode in flames and cries and he does, too, thrusting deep and holding there as I close around him and he pulses in me, as connected as two people could possibly be. My fingers press gouges into his skin, my mouth muffled in his tense shoulder. Eventually, his blue eyes flicker open, and his lips spread in a dazzling smile. I lick my lips, lowering my eyes from his powerful gaze to his stubbly chin. Where it's safe.

"I think . . ." I give myself a moment. The chance to check—to make sure it's not the orgasm speaking. But I know it's not.

I try again, shaking my head back and forth on the pillow. "I'm going to tell you something and I don't want you to feel like you have to say it back." I lift my eyes, searching his. *Be brave, Maren Laughlin. For once in your life, be the one who leaps first.* "I love you."

I swallow back the explanation on my tongue—the urge to fill the silence with caveats or a light-hearted joke, feeling my face heat and realizing with even more embarrassment that we're still connected. He's still inside of me and I couldn't have picked a worse time.

"Um," I say, not even knowing what words I'm looking for. "Like I said, you don't have to. I mean, maybe pretend I didn't say that. The last thing I want is to make you feel . . . like. I know you have a lot to consider and I'm not exactly who you probably—"

"Maren. Be quiet a second, will you?"

My mouth slams shut. His expression is unreadable, but his eyes feel gentle on me. Like they are caressing the planes of my face and memorizing them. Which is probably a good sign. Hopefully.

I open my mouth and he narrows his eyes and I close it again.

Finally, he speaks. "I have been in love with you since the

first morning you showed up at my house and made Anders lunch. Maybe that doesn't sound romantic, but you need to believe me when I say it is. It's the most romantic thing I've ever experienced in my life. You paid attention. You noticed and you didn't wait for an invitation. You just came over and filled the hole I didn't even realize was there. For my kids, sure, but in me as well."

His face gets all blurry around the edges and my throat is too tight to speak, so I lift my head and press a kiss to his lips. A kiss he deepens, and we lose ourselves in each other all over again.

TWENTY-EIGHT

I'll Be There for You

Joe

I HAVE WOKEN UP TO MAREN IN MY BED EVERY MORNING FOR eleven days in a row and I'm not sure I'll ever get used to it. It feels like she's always been there but also brand-new. You learn so much about someone when you sleep next to them. For example, Maren snores. These soft little puppy snorts. And her hair is a goddamn hazard, long strands tangling around me like a delicious fishing net. She doesn't like to be cuddled in her sleep, but somehow her feet will find their way to mine, or her fingers will hook in my waistband as if to assure her subconscious I haven't left.

That I'll never leave.

If asked, she's not a fan of morning sex, but she's perfectly happy to wake up to my fingers or mouth teasing out an orgasm first thing and is even more happy to reciprocate. I've always slept in my underwear, adding maybe a tee in the winter, but Maren has a surplus of cute nighties. Cute, not sexy; though on her, with those legs, it's all sexy.

She drinks coffee in the morning, hates running and prefers

yoga, likes cooking and reading so-called spicy romances, and loves my kids.

And, unbelievably, she also loves me.

Despite our sleeping together every night, she still has her place. Anders is smart and likely realizes she's been staying over, but he hasn't said anything. It's not that we were hiding it exactly; it's just that, well, I was trying to give him, *them*, time. Which would probably have been easier to do if Maren was sleeping at her place, but I'm also selfish. It took one night of her accidentally falling asleep at my place after making love before I declared myself addicted to waking up with her warm softness curled beside me. The next night, she brought Rogers's pillow and an overnight bag.

So we decided to tell the kids together. At our early family Christmas. We decided to wake up and do presents just like we would if it was actually Christmas Day, and Maren and Rogers spent the night. For the first time, she didn't shower and rush to get changed and try to make it look like she came over super early. Instead, we left my door open and let the kids barge in and wake us up.

Anders yelped with joy and smashed in between us, hugging us both as we made a *cuddle sandwich* around him (Maren's words, not mine). Lucy was more reserved and reacted very little. But not like she didn't care. It was more like she couldn't understand the big deal. Like Maren had always belonged.

I'm not sure which reaction I loved more, to be honest.

We spent the morning in our PJs and robes, sipping coffee and (not too) hot cocoa and stuffing our faces with the cinnamon rolls Maren made. We ripped open presents and watched *Home Alone* for the third time and took naps on the couch.

Later, my parents came over and were zero percent surprised by Anders excitedly shouting in their faces that Maren and I were together.

Apparently, we suck at playing it cool.

We stuffed more food in our mouths, opened more presents, and when it came time for bed, Maren didn't hide the fact that she was staying the night when Anders and Lucy asked her to read *The Polar Express* to them in bed. It was . . . Simply put, it was the best Christmas I'd ever had.

Followed by today, which will absolutely rank as the worst.

The phone rings at seven P.M. Kiley has had the kids for exactly ten hours and so when I see her name on the screen, I just assume it's the kids calling to say good night. Or maybe Kiley asking about Maren, since I wouldn't be surprised if Anders told her first thing.

I was wrong on both accounts.

"Hello?"

"Thank fuck you answered," Kiley says, and I blink because she isn't the kind of person to cuss, usually. Especially not around the kids. "Hold on." I hear a lot of commotion on the other end and then muffled silence.

"What is it? Are the kids okay?"

"By okay, do you mean safe? Yes. They are safe. Technically. But I'm about to lose my ever-loving shit with Lucy and I just got a phone call from the resort manager, who said if I can't make her be quiet, they'll have to ask us to leave."

I immediately tense and Maren, who is across the room, walks over, settling on the couch beside me, her brow pinched with concern.

"Is she crying?"

"She's . . . I don't know. What do you call it when she's

screaming and crying and flailing like a toddler? She's completely unhinged."

"She's not unhinged, she's autistic. She's probably had a sensory overload. What did you do today?"

"It's a fucking resort, J. What do you mean, what did we do? We did everything. Went swimming and did a ski lesson, ate lunch, swam some more. I was trying to tire them out. Anders was practically asleep in his dinner."

"Jesus, Kiley. Did you listen to anything I said? I sent you her schedule. I told you to take it easy with her. She needs downtime every day. That's too much for a little girl. One activity. One. And a nap, or quiet time with her tablet in a dark room."

"I'm not pandering to a four-year-old, J. You and your new girlfriend might let her run things over at your place, but I refuse. And anyway, it's too late for that now, so what do I do with her?"

I bite back the flurry of responses churning inside me. Kiley loves to throw my schedules in my face, acting like I'm a pushover, letting our child lord over me. For a while, I agreed with her, but then I realized I do what needs to be done for Lucy to be successful now. It might look different as she gets older; in fact, it probably will, but this is the only way I know to give my child peace.

The fact that Kiley refuses to do the same and it turns into an emergency time and time again, well . . .

(Also, the fact that Kiley just threw my "new girlfriend" into the mix isn't relevant, but I tuck it away anyway for further discussion later, because I don't love her tone.)

"Take her into a cool, dark room where it's quiet. Offer her the tablet. Or let her crawl in your lap. Sometimes she likes to listen to your heartbeat."

"She won't let me near her. No one. Not even Anders. You have to come get her."

My voice strangles in my throat. "What?"

"I can't do this. She's going to ruin our family vacation. I should never have let you talk me into including her."

"Including her?" I can feel my blood pressure rise with my volume. "Including her? She's your child! I shouldn't have to talk you into spending time with your own child."

"I'm not arguing over semantics, J. Just come and pick her up."

"If I pick her up, I'm picking Anders up, too," I tell her, and it's not a suggestion. Maren is already sticking her socked feet into her boots and grabbing our coats.

"You don't have to—"

"Have them packed and ready to go," I tell her. "We'll be there in an hour." I end the call and chuck my phone so hard it skitters across the table and thuds onto the floor. I reach over and pick it up.

Maren holds out my coat, not saying a word. Woodenly, I put it on, and she holds open the door. She holds out the keys, and at my stare she gives me a small smile.

"I don't know where we're going. You'll have to drive." I take the keys, and then tug her hand, gently. She folds into my arms and squeezes me tight. "Let's bring them back home."

I swallow hard and let her go. We round the car, get in, put on our seat belts, and then I sigh. "Thank you," I whisper low. She doesn't respond, just takes my hand in her lap.

〰〰〰

I can hear Lucy before I'm even out of the car. Next to me, Maren tenses and curses under her breath. I march up the walk to the villa Kiley told me was theirs, and Maren trots along behind me, catching up as I bang on the door.

It swings open almost immediately.

"Dad!" Anders runs into my arms, burying himself in my coat. "Maren!" he says a moment later, his eyes wide.

"Hey, kid," she says softly, cupping his face. "All packed up? Or do you need help?"

"I'm ready and I packed up Lucy . . ."

He trails off as his mom comes to the door. Kiley looks frazzled and, by the drink in her hand, maybe a little drunk.

"Well, well, well, Maren Laughlin all grown up." Her smile is cool, but not confrontational, so I let it go.

"Hi, Kiley, you look just the same," Maren says simply. "Can we come in?"

"Not like I have a choice, you're already here."

I swallow my irritation. "Not a good time, Kiley."

She waves her manicured hand in a wide arc, opening the door further and allowing us in while still talking out of her ass. "No, really, it's fine. All day I've heard a thousand stories about *Maren this* and *Maren that*. I can't *wait* to watch the miracle worker in action."

I open my mouth to say something, but Maren gets there first, pressing closer to Kiley, her voice deathly calm and so low I can barely make it out.

"It's not called being a miracle worker, Kiley, it's called paying attention. Giving a shit. *Loving*. Take your pick. You should really give it a try some time."

My ex narrows her eyes in the sharp glare of the hallway lighting, taking in Maren's full measure. Eventually, she blinks, her lips curling into a practiced Realtor smile, and gestures with her glass behind her. "Be my guest. See if you have any luck with the unholy terror."

"Christ, Kiley . . ." I start, but Maren just walks past with a quiet, "Thank you."

We follow the jagged crying to the back of the villa, and I don't bother taking in the surroundings. I just want to get my kids. Maren heads straight for the screaming, but I stop to follow Anders to his room and the bags.

"I tried to calm her down, but she's pretty bad, Dad."

"It's okay, bud. She's just overstimulated. It's happened before."

Suddenly the screaming ratchets up and I drop the bags, sprinting to the last room in the hall. I blink against pure darkness, trying to find my way. There's a freezing-cold breeze like a window is open. Is this why I could hear Lucy from outside?

"What the actual FU—"

"Baby," a low voice soothes. "Baby, it's me. It's Maren."

The screaming stops, but the crying doesn't. I blindly search for a light switch until suddenly a soft glow emanates from Maren's phone. Just her phone, but dimmed. Her fingers are dancing as she pulls up quiet piano music and then tosses the phone to the ground beside her and looks toward a trembling, tear- and sweat-soaked Lucy, who is hiccupping, but no longer screaming.

Maren doesn't reach for her, just settles in front of her on the floor, her legs crisscrossed and her phone lit. I close the window with a soft thud and dig through the bag I packed for Lucy from home. Finding her headphones, I hold them out so she can see them. Then, I squat in front of her, smoothing her sweaty hair from her face and wiping away her tears before placing the noise-canceling headphones over her ears. Her little mouth moves, as if she's still crying, but no sounds come out. She's twitchy and clammy, and I sigh, settling next to Maren on the floor.

"I'll need to change her before we go. Put some clean pajamas on her," I say.

Maren nods, not taking her eyes off Lucy.

"Maybe a bath would be better," I think out loud. "Warm her up."

Maren nods again, but this time it's jerky. She sniffs and swipes at her eye, angrily.

"Are you—"

"No," she whispers harshly. "No, I'm *not* okay. I'm the furthest thing from okay. What the actual fuck?"

My blood freezes over and the ground swings up in front of me, even though I'm sitting on the floor. My heart crushes in my chest. I knew this could happen, but I really thought Maren could handle it . . .

"I'm sorry," she's saying. "I know *you* loved her, but . . ." Maren swipes at another angry tear. "What kind of monster puts a little girl who is in distress in a pitch-dark room with the fucking window open in fucking December?"

My breath whooshes out in a rush. *Not* Lucy. She's not angry at Lucy, she's angry *for* Lucy. "Well, I told her . . ."

"I know exactly what you told her. I heard every word. She didn't even try to use logic. She's drunk! And demented."

"She's sad. And feels guilty."

"Don't try to make me understand her right now, Josiah Cole. It won't work." She holds out her hand to Lucy, who's calmed down to small hiccupping sighs, and this time Lucy crawls into her lap, curling into her, staring ahead. Maren doesn't try to stem the tears pouring down her own face as she lets her hands fall to the sides of Lucy, closing her in, but not touching her. Not yet.

I get to my feet, pressing a kiss to Maren's head. "I'm going to load us up and then start a bath."

I meet Lucy's eyes and point to my mouth. She can hear with the headphones on, but it's muffled, so eye contact helps.

"Bath, then pajamas, then home with Dad and Anders and Maren," I tell her.

She shakes her head and I'm tempted to let it go, but if she wakes up and she's wet herself or she's sticky with sweat . . .

"Bath, pajamas, then home," I repeat.

"Because I'm Maren's baby?" she says, not really asking. I'm stunned, but Maren doesn't seem to be.

"She's said it before, usually when she's tired. It's okay," she explains softly, seeming more composed and more than a little exhausted. "Yeah, baby. You're mine. Bath, pajamas, then home with us."

She stands, carrying Lucy, and I lead us to the bathroom. I start to run the bath, but Maren stops me with a hand.

"Go on and get us packed up. I can give her a bath and get her pajamas on."

I nod, feeling at once heavier and lighter than before. "I've left a pair on the vanity."

"Perfect."

And I guess, despite it all, it kind of is.

ʃʃʃ

We make it home late, both the kids and Maren sound asleep. On the other hand, I'm more alert than ever. My brain is racing with everything that's been revealed tonight. Between

Kiley's complete failure to even try to accept our daughter, to Maren's furious defense of Lucy, to Lucy saying she's Maren's "baby" . . . and when did Maren learn all those techniques? With the music and the light and not touching . . . but I guess I know when she learned it. She learned it from watching us over the last four-plus months. She paid attention and put in the work. She cared enough to learn. I know it hasn't all been smooth going, and it won't always be smooth going, but Maren stayed.

I'm overwhelmed and grateful and profoundly moved by this woman.

I gently rock Maren awake first, and then we move to carry in the kids. I pick up Anders, who is dead to the world, and therefore weighs as much as a ton of bricks, while Maren takes Lucy. Without a word, we carry them to their beds and tuck them in. Then I return to the car to get their bags and Maren walks to the kitchen. "I could use a glass of wine. Want one?"

"Sure."

When I return, closing the door behind me and locking it against the cold, Maren is sitting on my couch, her feet curled up on the seat beside her.

"No Rogers?"

She grins, soft. "He's curled up in Anders's bed."

"I bet he loves that."

"For now. Just wait until he's bigger and they're competing for space."

My chest squeezes at the mere thought of Maren and Rogers being a part of our lives long enough to watch my kids grow. Long enough for them to become *our* kids, even.

"I'm sorry I lost my cool back there," she says, after a long sip of wine.

"You have nothing to be sorry for."

"Has she always been like that?"

"Kiley?" I check. At Maren's nod, I grimace. "Not that bad, no. Had I known she would be that bad, I never would have let the kids stay with her. She's always struggled with Lucy. She was late to speaking, so there was a lot of frustrated screaming on both their parts as Lucy tried to communicate her needs. Meanwhile, Kiley only wanted her perfect newborn."

"She's still perfect."

"Well," I say with a smile, settling beside her and crossing my legs at the ankles. "She's perfectly *her*, anyway. I won't pretend I haven't lost my cool a time or two with her, but never like that. There have been a few times, though, that I've had to call my mom over just so I can go for a run and clear my head."

"That's reasonable."

"Thank you—it didn't feel that way at the time, but I'm learning to give myself a break." I exhale in a rush. "She's just . . . it kills me that Kiley won't even try to get to know her kids for who they really are. She doesn't even know Lucy likes to color, let alone that she might be a talented artist."

"Are you kidding?" Maren offers lightly. "I'm about to start selling her handcrafted lures to put aside for her college fund."

I grin, but it's so precarious, it slips just as fast. "And she hates that Anders paints his nails or wears so-called feminine colors. She's always razzing him to dress more masculine. Did you notice his hands?" Maren shakes her head, and I continue, "She made him remove the glitter polish you guys did together. It lasted less than twenty-four hours."

Maren's sigh is heavy, and I can feel the ache in it. The ache for my kids and the mom that won't ever love them the way they deserve.

"You're a really excellent father, Joe."

It's not the first time she's said it, but after tonight, when my nerves are raw after walking into what I walked into, knowing I'd allowed it to happen . . .

"I'm trying. I'm not sure I would have made it tonight, though, without you."

"I love your kids, you know that. Not the same way I love you, of course. But I love them so intensely, it kind of scares me. I've never reacted to something the way I did tonight. But I honestly feel like if she'd walked in right then, I would have clawed her fucking face off."

"Honestly," I tell her, taking my own sip and letting the wine work its way down and warm my frayed edges, "it was nice to see someone else acknowledge it for a change. I understand *why* Kiley is the way she is, but that doesn't mean I understand it, if you know what I mean. For years, I've made excuses for her because I left her so much when I was in the military, and she was so angry about that. But I can't make an excuse for tonight. I don't think I know that person anymore. The woman who answered the door, half drunk and letting her child . . ." I shake my head. "I don't know her."

"What are you going to do?"

I sigh. "I guess call my lawyer. After the new year. I already have full custody, but I don't want her to have vacations with Lucy again."

"Do you think she'll even try after this?"

"For Anders?" I shrug. "Maybe?"

"I'm sorry, Joe," she says, scooting closer and tipping her head onto my shoulder. I tuck my arm around her and kiss the top of her head.

"Me, too."

TWENTY-NINE

I'll Stand by You

Maren

IT'S REALLY TOO COLD TO BE SITTING ON THE END OF THE DOCK, watching the sunrise creep over the frozen expanse of Fost's piece of paradise, but as it has a million times before, the water called to me. I've folded a thick quilt and laid it over the bench, and my hands are wrapped around a thermos of steaming coffee. Even with that, I huddle down into the layers of my heavy winter coat and tug my knit hat further down over my ears.

New Year's has come and gone and I'm still here.

Not only that, but I don't plan to leave. I haven't had any official conversations about it, but then again, I don't need to. Fost's bait shop is complete, along with the apartment. There was a time I felt weird about selling them off. Not guilty, necessarily, but awkward about it. Like Fost gave me this gift and I gobbled it up before venturing out, pretty much aimlessly, once more.

But that was before I found the letter in his drawer. Before I decided to stay. Fost wasn't trying to keep me here, but he was trying to give me a way to stay—a way to be my own "boat daddy," if I wanted.

And I do want. So I'll sell the bait shop and the apartment, and the piece of shoreline that comes along with it, and I'll buy myself a top-of-the-line fishing boat. One with all the bells and whistles and as glittery as a frigging sunbeam. One that I can run my guide business out of.

I should have enough extra for licensing, and if Cole's Landing doesn't want to take me on, since they already have two other guides, I'll branch out on my own.

I could rent a place in town with anything left over, but I suspect *someone* might take issue with that, considering I spend every night at his place anyway.

Maybe this is moving too fast, but I don't know. It seems like Joe and I got our start in the middle and once I stopped freaking out about it being wrong, I realized it felt overwhelmingly right.

Who am I to argue? So we took the long and windy path to find each other. Does the journey negate the destination? Or does the journey prepare you for it?

I sip my cooling drink and take a deep breath. The frigid up-north air freezes my nostrils and makes me cough a little, but I can't help the smile spreading across my lips.

Feels like home to me.

🎣🎣🎣

After I made the decision to stay, things started to come together pretty quickly. With Donna and Simon's help, I found a Realtor and put the bait shop and apartment up for sale. The location and access to the flowage was a prime investment, but it was Shelby and Cam's *HomeMade* touch that really drew the numbers. Knowing the reality show stars had sprinkled their home-renovation magic over the place was the clincher.

I felt super weird about name-dropping them, and at first I avoided it altogether, but then Shelby was on the phone and in my ear yelling about family and loyalty and sisterhood and anyway, you don't mess with a woman who is nine whole days past her delivery date.

So yeah, Fost's gift was enough for *ten* top-of-the-line fishing boats, and *plenty* of cushion for me to get my business up and running. Joe thinks I should consider revamping Musky Maren, and I'm not sure he's wrong. Though I believe a new name and a new angle would be more appropriate. I would love to share my obsession with the Northwoods, fishing, and the outdoors on a new platform. I miss the educational aspect of my former life as a park ranger, after all.

So it's been in the back of my mind, as winter slips into, well, later winter. It's nearly April and while the lake is still frozen over and the ground a blanket of white and ice, the resort is in full-on summer-prep mode. Casper's decided to stay with his thriving charter business in the Keys, so the Coles formally took me on as their second guide. I worried my Musky Maren fame might be an annoyance to Johnson, but he assured me he's making the most out of his retirement after decades spent topping the financial district and is more than happy to lose customers to me.

While we wait for the ice to melt, there's been plenty of work on the villas to keep us busy, not to mention the day-to-day management of a resort and raising a family. I brought Joe and the kids with me to Nashville in February for Craig and Lorelai's wedding, and we extended that into a weeklong vacation on a quiet beach in the Keys where we did little aside from play in the water and take naps in the sand. It was the perfect low-key kind of trip to reintroduce Lucy to vacations and hopefully erase the disaster from Christmas out of her memory. Next time we're even thinking of adding an afternoon at Disney World.

Joe's not so sure, but I'm confident we can make it happen with lots of planning. I've been reading up on it, and it seems like Disney is pretty famous for accommodating autistic kids.

I officially moved out of cabin twenty a few weeks ago. I kept it eight weeks longer than I should have, but I didn't want the added pressure of "Oh gosh, now we're stuck with each other." Truthfully, Joe and I weren't actually worried about that happening. It was more for the sake of our parents, and, well, okay, my brothers. Liam said he would chill out and he did, mostly, but . . .

It makes sense to move my stuff all the way out. Not to mention all of the things I left behind in storage in Michigan when I sublet *that* apartment in my rush to flee the proposal that wasn't.

Wow, what a difference six months makes.

Which is why we are going out tonight. Alone. Just the two of us and I'm *giddy*. Sure, we occasionally get stolen moments around the resort when Joe's bartending late and his parents keep the kids, or maybe when I sneak us into the boathouse for an afternoon delight . . . but an entire evening, preplanned, dressed up, and a quiet house when we come home?

We don't know her.

Simon stops by the house to grab the kids at four, and even Lucy is waiting at the window. They've been promised hot dogs (with no cheese) and at least two rounds of Clue before cuddling up with their (still) favorite movie, *Home Alone*. Bless the Coles. Bless them all the way to heaven.

I take over the master bath and treat myself to a long soak

with scented oils, followed by completely blowing out my hair, applying full makeup, and wearing actual jewelry. I skip the heels and pearls because I'm an adult woman who makes her own choices, and those choices recognize there is half a foot of snow on the ground and my true love is a former Marine who only wades into politics when it's a debate of Lions versus Packers.

We live in a ranch, so there's no bottom-of-the-stairs moment, but Joe still looks at me like the sun shines out of my eyelashes when I come around the corner. He then proceeds to thoroughly mess up my lipstick before laying me back on the kitchen table and making me forget my name for a while.

We're late for our reservation.

I could not care less.

"I'm just gonna let them know we're here," Joe murmurs into my ear as we step into the cozy entrance of the high-end Italian restaurant he picked out. "I'm guessing we'll have to sit at the bar for a bit, do you mind?"

I'm already shaking my head. "Not at all."

I watch as he slips into the small crowd surrounding the hostess station and try not to drool at the way his golden hair curls over the edge of the fitted gray sport coat that outlines his broad shoulders and tapered waist.

I might fail, who even knows.

"Musky Maren!"

I jerk back from my musings as a too-familiar face practically jumps in front of me, blocking my view. It's Bryce.

"Mr. Callahan," I say, using the name I'd decided on when planning this out. Of course, I hadn't planned on a surprise attack at date night, but I'm comforted that I don't feel as rattled as I have in the past.

"Whoa, *Mr.?* I like the sound of that."

I ignore his leering expression and hold out my hand as if for a handshake, keeping a professional boundary between us, the way it should have been all along. "You can call me Ms. Laughlin, thanks."

His smile slips, but it hitches back just as quickly.

"What are you up to? Visiting for the weekend, or . . . is your family around?"

"I'm here with someone important, actually," I tell him, seeing no need to lie.

"With me," a smooth voice says from over Bryce's shoulder. "Nice to see you again, Bryce."

"Joe Cole? Good to see you, man. Wow, so you two . . ." Bryce's eyes dart between Joe and me, taking in the way Joe's body settles at my back. "Wait, I thought you said you were married."

I scrunch my eyebrows together, looking confused. "I don't think so. But, I have been with Joe for some time. Hm. How weird." Joe and I exchange looks and he brushes my hair off my shoulder.

"Well, you're a lucky man, Joe. Catching Musky Maren. The way every guy I know was panting after this one back in the day," he continues as if I'm not even there. My stomach lurches at the gleam in his eye.

I open my mouth to cut him off, but he's on a roll.

"Many a night I fell asleep to her videos . . . her voice in my ear, helping me fall asleep, if you know what I mean . . ." he confides in a low voice, elbowing Joe, who's stiffened next to me.

And I'm done.

"That's enough, Mr. Callahan," I say, my tone icy, despite

the surge of hot blood and adrenaline pulsing through my veins. "I can't fathom how you think it's acceptable to speak about a woman that way. I'm right in front of you. I don't even want to think about the things you say when I'm not around. You're disgusting, disrespectful, and small-minded. I've tried to be patient with you. I've tried to be polite. But it's clear you have confused common courtesy with interest on my part, which is absolutely not the case. Don't speak with me again, unless it is about professional matters."

Bryce is gaping at me, his face red and covered with a sweaty sheen. *Good*, I think. For once, let him be the one left shaken.

I turn to face Joe, whose face is split near in half with his proud grin. "I could use that drink?"

"It would be my pleasure."

I nod. "Great. Excellent." His large, warm hand slips low on my back and he propels me gently toward the gleaming bar, but at the last moment, I spin to face Bryce once more.

"All those things you and your perverted little friends dreamed up about me, they're true. But"—I reach for Joe's hand and squeeze it—"he's the only one who will ever know for sure and he's too much of a real man to talk."

Bryce swallows and nods his head, stonily, his eyes unwilling to meet mine. I half expect Joe to add something and meet his gaze with a questioning glance.

He shakes his head, his eyes glittering with humor. "I have nothing to add. After all, *I caught Musky Maren*. What more could I ask for?"

"Please," I scoff, as we walk toward the bar, leaving Bryce behind. "You're terrible at fishing. *I* obviously caught *you*."

Only Want to Be with You

Maren

Four months later

THE LODGE WAS PACKED AFTER A NOONTIME RAINSTORM WAYLAID A lot of boaters. I don't always help behind the bar, but my only booking for today isn't until four o'clock, so I decided to offer my assistance.

That was four hours, seventeen pizzas, approximately twelve thousand beers, and at least two hundred dollars in tips ago. I don't mind, though. Time passes quickly on afternoons like this. Even though the sun is streaming in through every window, the bar, dining area, and surrounding wraparound porch are teeming with half-dressed vacationers, their day-drinking turning into night-drinking. Some thoughtful humans put Lorelai's latest chart-topping album on the electronic jukebox and I'm swaying my hips and singing along as I mix up another complicated Bloody Mary.

"Where's that pup of yours, Mare?" a guest asks as I pass him the drink and chaser and he offers me a large bill in return.

I beam, glancing out the giant picture window over the bar. Rogers is a bit of a celebrity these days around the resort. He's never short of back scratchers and stick launchers. "Out front with the kids." There's a group of them, led by Anders and Lucy in matching life jackets on the shallow beach dock. Anders is demonstrating how to toss sticks off the end for Rogers to retrieve. Lucy's sitting on the edge, dangling her toes in the cool water. If I know her, she's studying the way the water and light play off the bluegills swimming beneath her. Not far from them is Donna, in a beach chair, supervising and spoiling their dinner with ice cream.

"Hard to tell who's having more fun, Anders Cole or Rogers," the man notes.

I laugh. "Both should sleep well tonight!"

A hand finds my waist and drags gently across the small of my back, sending tingles up my spine. "It's nearly four," Joe reminds me.

I nod. "I'll cash out as soon as they show. I already set up the boat this morning." It's a little unusual my group hasn't shown up yet, but not completely out of the ordinary. It makes no difference to me. It's their money, after all. I get paid either way. And to be honest, I've made more money this summer than I thought possible. If I'd known, I'd have left the park service years ago. Between guiding and the sale of Fost's place, I've replaced my nest egg and then some. Enough that I'm thinking I might try branching out to fishing tournaments next winter.

Or not. Maybe I'll just stay here and help Joe at the resort. It'd be no hardship, that's for sure.

Joe glances out the back window, taking note of his kids out of habit, before asking someone what they want and tossing a cardboard coaster on the bartop in between them. He starts pouring another draft and I glance at the door. Another group walks in, but they're dressed for Jet Skiing. Not catching musky.

Simon walks out of the kitchen, along with one of the summertime employees, Angela, and enters behind the bar. "Have you cashed out?" he asks. I shake my head, checking the door again. "I might have my first no-show. Did anyone call off because of the rain?"

Joe passes his drinks and then reaches for the tip jar, sliding it to me. "No cancels. Go ahead and count tips."

I sneak to the back corner, tilting the jar over and splitting the tips, as if Joe and I aren't headed to the same place where we basically share all our expenses anyway. He likes to keep it professional, though, and I like to carry cash, so I play along with it, pocketing my half and tucking the other half into his back pocket.

He pats his pocket and grins. "Ready?"

"For what?"

He spreads his arms wide. "For your guided tour."

I blink, confused. "Sorry?"

"I booked you for the night. Ready?"

Warmth wells up inside of me at his boyish grin and sparkling blue eyes. He's clearly very proud of himself.

"Seriously?" I half groan, half laugh. "It's you?"

"Yeah!"

I look at his dad and Angela. "You were in on this?"

"And Donna," Simon says, his smile matching his son's. "Go." He shoos us. "Have fun."

"You didn't have to schedule yourself," I tell Joe.

"Like hell—you're Musky Maren. I booked this months ago. Four hours, paid in advance."

I roll my eyes but am feeling giddy. Four whole hours. He must catch the look in my eyes because he leans in. "Don't you dare look at me like that. I have plans."

"Well, then we'd better get moving."

I was telling the truth about packing everything earlier, so we head straight for my Ranger, hand in hand. The Ranger is sparkly and ruby red and reminds me of Dorothy's shoes in *The Wizard of Oz*. I fucking love the way it glitters in the late-afternoon sunshine.

"You sure you don't want anything els—" I ask before my steps stutter on the dock and my head whips to his. "Did you pack all this stuff?"

"Yup."

"When? It was raining!"

Joe jumps in, rocking the boat slightly, before holding out his hand for me to step in.

I raise an eyebrow. "That's usually my job." He shrugs his shoulder and smirks and I step in. "Does this mean you think you're driving, too?"

His eyes widen. "Would you let me?"

"Heck no." No one drives my baby.

He laughs out loud. "Didn't think so. The coordinates are already programmed in your GPS."

I settle into the driver's seat and tilt my head, considering him suspiciously. "What is going on here?"

"Ah, ah, ah," he tells me, leaning into the passenger seat and crossing his arms over his broad chest, staring straight ahead. "You're mine for four hours. Bought and paid for," he reminds me.

I turn over the motor and my instruments light up with a soft glow. Sure enough, the coordinates pop up on the screen. I skim them with a trained eye.

"Is this an island?" I ask.

"Laughlin, I swear to god. Would you please stop trying to ruin the surprise and just drive us to the coordinates I painstakingly snuck onto your precious boat to input in the middle of a monsoon?"

I giggle at his peevish tone. "All right, all right. Yes, sir."

"That's more like it."

I back us away from the dock and, without leaving a wake, motor us through the shallow bay. Anders and Lucy are standing on the shore, waving, as we pass. Rogers barks and Anders yells something like "Good luck, Dad" but honestly the motor is too loud to know for sure.

Better that I don't know, apparently.

I follow the coordinates on the twenty-minute drive to a tiny, densely wooded island in the middle of a chain of several lakes.

"Around the back," Joe directs and I slowly motor around the opposite side of the island, where it's even more remote. There's a sandy beach there, and, after checking to make sure I won't bank my motor, I park us right on the sand. Joe nimbly jumps out over the side into the sand, walking to the front and checking that we're stable. I reach for the familiar picnic basket.

"Is this coming with us?"

"Not yet," he says, holding out his hand. "First, just you."

He helps me over the side and when I land, he doesn't let go of my hand. There's a small sandy trail that leads into the woods and he guides me toward it.

"Is this private?"

"Very," he says with a waggle of his blond brows.

"I mean," I say with a laugh, "are we allowed to be here?"

"It's mine."

I gape at him. "You own an island?!"

He keeps walking, leading me through the dense underbrush, and points out a patch of poison ivy to avoid. "I own *this*, which is barely an island. It belonged to my family when they first bought the resort. They wanted to use it for camping, but it's a pain in the ass. Too far from the resort, shore, and town to be of any real use."

"Oh. Still cool, though."

He looks over his shoulder at me, letting go of my fingers. "I think so, which is why I bought it. To be fair, my parents gave me a deal."

"When did you buy . . ." My voice trails off as the brush clears and I feel confident enough that I won't trip to look up. When I do, my questions fly out of my head and my mouth drops open in a gasp. We've made it to a small, circular clearing, a meadow, with tiny purple blooms and white clovers dotting the lush green grass. The sun shines unimpeded here, warming the ground and making it appear as though everything is glowing. Loons call, western chorus frogs chirp, the wind rustles the supple summer leaves, and Josiah Cole in the middle of it all, down on one knee in the muddy grass.

"You cannot be serious."

"How's your stomach?" he jokes with a grin. "Feeling nauseous? I have some ginger ale back in the picnic basket."

I walk toward him, feeling like I'm floating, and shake my head. "What are you doing?"

He squints, tilting his head, his hair glowing in the sunlight. "Is that a real question?"

I narrow my eyes, coming to stand in front of him so he has to look up to see me. He shields his eyes. "Is *this* a real question?" I counter.

He holds up one finger before reaching into his shirt pocket and pulling out a diamond ring, holding it up between us. "Maren Laughlin, my Jig, love of my life." He grins and I press my lips together. "Still good?" he checks, and I throw my head back with a loud, laughing groan, before I gesture for him to continue. He takes a deep, cleansing breath. "In the immortal words of Jon Bon Jovi, 'I'd live and I'd die for you, I'd steal the sun from the sky for you.' Will you let me be there for you? Forever?"

I barely hear him over the giggles erupting past my lips, doubling me over, and the tears pouring out of my eyes and down my cheeks. He bites his lip, valiantly keeping a straight face, and I fling myself into his arms, tackling him to the ground with an *oof*.

I kiss him hard, the smile still curling my mouth when I pull back. "How could I refuse Bon Jovi?"

"My ploy worked, then."

"Tell me you didn't buy an island to propose to me."

"I wanted it to be *private*. I knew that was important to you. Besides," he says, putting his finger across my lips, keeping me from talking. "Now whenever we want to be alone, we can pack some bags and camp out here."

I drop my head to his chest. "God," I tell him sincerely. "I love you so much."

"Enough to marry me, possibly in front of other people?"

"I'll marry you in front of the entire world."

He holds up the ring. "You forgot something."

It's perfect. Not too big, not too small, not too flashy, but it dazzles in the clear rays of sunshine. I hold out my hand, and he slips it easily onto my bare finger.

"Holy shit, I'm gonna marry Josiah Cole," I say.

"Holy shit, I got Musky Maren to say she'll marry me," Joe says in return before pressing up and capturing my mouth in a long, sweet, forever kind of kiss.

ᔑ ᔑ ᔑ

Eventually, we unpack the boat, which it turns out is full of camping gear and dinner, along with champagne. We eat, drink, and make love under the blinking stars, and wake up in the morning slightly hungover but with zero regrets. By the time we've packed up the island—*Joe's island*, I think, with a belly flip—and motor back across the lakes, it's midmorning. As we get closer to the resort, Joe turns to me.

"Now, I have something to tell you, and I hope it's okay, but there's one more surprise."

"Okayyy," I drag the word out. "Though you'll have a tough time topping the last one."

"I'll never top the last one as long as we both shall live."

"I like the sound of that," I tell him, dreamily. "Is it a stop in the boathouse, because . . ."

He snorts, but his eyes flare with want. "Later."

We turn the final corner to the resort and a large group of people come into view. I shoot to my feet behind the wheel the moment I spot the familiar glowing blond and shining blue-black heads of my best friends.

"No way!"

"Hey, lovebirds!" Lorelai shouts from the edge of the dock. It's early, but she already has a beach drink in hand. Shelby has her newborn daughter, Gracie, in her arms, and a sob breaks in the back of my throat. And I raise both my hands to my mouth to muffle it. I hadn't realized how much I missed them.

"Whoa, whoa, hey there, you'd better let me take over the wheel," Joe says, chuckling low. I gasp, looking down, and realize I've completely let go. He eases me up and out of the seat.

Moments later, he's steered us safely toward my dock, and I'm out before he's cut the engine. Simon breaks away from the crowd to help Joe as I jump into the arms of my best friends.

"When did you get here?"

"Last night," Shelby says.

"Are you here—"

"The rest of the week," Lorelai says. "But don't you say another word and stop that crying. Let me see that ring finger!"

I show them and they both squeal, hugging me tight.

"Maren?" A little voice calls to me just as Joe is wrapping his arm around my shoulders and accepting congratulations and back pats.

I spin to see Anders and Lucy, being held back by a tearful Donna. I immediately spread my arms, and they rush to their dad and me. "Does this mean we get to keep you?"

I sniff, swiping my eyes. "This means *I* get to keep *you*," I tell them. "I love you both so, *so* much."

"Love you, too," Anders says. Lucy holds up her arms to be lifted and I happily oblige, cuddling her close.

We spend the afternoon sitting on the shore of the lake, sipping drinks from the lodge and watching Rogers and the kids swim. Joe's never far from me, not even when he's standing knee-deep in the water, a beer in hand, as he shoots the shit with Cameron and Craig. Lorelai suns herself on one side of me, while Shelby nurses Gracie in the shade on the other.

I'm surrounded by love. Every one of my brothers calls me to offer their well wishes, but it's not until Liam calls that it all feels especially real.

"Excuse me," I whisper, getting to my feet. "I'll be right back."

"If you happen to pass the bar . . ." Lorelai says with a wink and I laugh at her easy transition into outright vacation mode.

Joe catches my eye and I mouth my big brother's name. I watch him excuse himself to join me. I put my brother on speakerphone.

"Hey, Jig," he starts. "I hear congrats are in order!"

"Yep. I caught myself a Cole."

Liam laughs and it warms me to my toes. "I knew you could do it," he says. "Joe there?"

"Right here."

"No one could be good enough for my little sister," Liam says gruffly, and I worry my lip between my teeth. "Except for you, man."

My breath slips out of me in a rush and Joe's throat works. "I'm glad you feel that way, since I expect you to stand beside me when I make her my wife."

"Wouldn't miss it. I love you both."

My voice is barely above a whisper. "Love you, too, Liam."

I end the call, shoving my phone in my back pocket, and Joe reaches for my hand. "So that's that," he says.

"I guess so," I say, tipping my head onto his shoulder. "Now all we have left to do is get married and spend the rest of our lives together."

"I'm ready," he says. "You?"

I pretend to think. "Question: Will it include more Bon Jovi karaoke?"

His deep chuckle vibrates under my cheek. "I'll add it to the vows."

"Then yes. A hundred billion times yes."

Acknowledgments

~~~~~~

SEVEN LOVE STORIES IN AND THIS PART NEVER GETS EASIER. I'M always so SO worried I'll forget someone. This book came together quite quickly, and I think it did because I know the characters well, as it is the third book in a series, but also because I know the subject matter so well. I'm a proud lake girl, and if you're reading this book, you are automatically an honorary lake girl, too. That's how it works. We midwestern lake folk are a welcoming people. So order yourself a Bloody Mary with an extra beef stick and buckle up.

First of all, thank you to my agent, Kate McKean. Seven books?! Look at us. Who knew? You did, I guess. Here's to many more! I'm so lucky to have you on my side.

Secondly, huge thanks to my editor, Vicki Lame. YA, adult, we've been through it all, and I'm so grateful I've had the chance to work with you. Thank you for loving on my characters the way you do. I'm gonna miss your editorial letters telling me, "No, wait, I think THIS couple is my favorite Erin Hahn pairing . . ."

Now for the list. Forgive me, but I don't want to miss anyone!

Many thanks to publisher Anne Marie Tallberg, assistant editor Vanessa Aguirre, jacket designer Kerri Resnick, designer Meryl Levavi, managing editor Chrisinda Lynch, production editor Ginny Perrin, copy editor Linda Sawicki, proofreader Nicole Hall, production manager Janna Dokos, marketing managers Alexis Neuville and Brant Janeway, and publicist Zoe Miller. I also want to give special recognition to Arlyn Miller-Lachmann, who did me the honor of reading an early version of this story to review the authenticity of my representation of autistic kids. Any mistakes in the representation are my own.

All my gratitude to the audiobook narrators and producers at Spotify Audio who bring my spicy stories to life. I can't bear to read my published books, but I can and do *listen* to them, and they are fantastic!

Thank you to the ladies of The Void: Cate Unruh, Meg Turton, Jess Steenlage, and Angie Swope. You've been my best cheerleaders, my favorite early readers, and the only book club I need to hear critique from. If I don't win you over, I don't want it. I'm so happy to report that so far I'm seven for seven.

Thank you to the readers, booksellers, bookstagrammers, students, and librarians who have cheered me on my way. Thank you for sharing about my books and loving on my characters!

Thanks to the Hahn, Jenkins, and Vrtis families. You're very brave to pick up one of my stories! Might I recommend you start with some of the YA titles . . .

Thank you to Abbot Elementary. Not that one! The one that has the very best staff in the entire world. I'm so lucky to have been adopted into your gracious fold. You've bought my books, kept me sane, made me laugh, and taught me so much about making school a safe haven for students.

Finally, thanks to Mike, Alice, and Jonah for letting me do my thing and write these stories. I couldn't do it without you three in my corner, and I hope you know I don't take that for granted.

About the Author

Erin Hahn

Erin Hahn is the author of the young adult novels *You'd Be Mine, More Than Maybe, Never Saw You Coming,* and *Even If It Breaks Your Heart,* as well as the adult romances *Built to Last* and *Friends Don't Fall in Love.* Romance is her vibe, grunge is her soundtrack, and fall is her signature color. She fell for her flannel-clad college sweetheart the very first day of school and has two hilarious kids who keep her humble. She lives outside Ann Arbor, Michigan, and has a cat named Gus who plays fetch and a dog named June who doesn't.